"He's alive?"

Bolan nodded. "Yeah. He'll live to stand trial. If you want."

"We'll see what's left when we're finished interrogating him," Angrekal said. The Russian commander looked from the unconscious traitor to glare at Bolan. "Something tells me you're going after his boss. What if that boss is in the sovereign state of the Russian Federation?"

The Executioner looked his ally square in the eye. "It won't be the first time I've cleaned house there. Nothing is going to keep me from General Constantin Garlov."

"Garlov," Angrekal repeated. "Oh, hell."

Don Pendleton's **Mack**

Bolan®

Explosive Demand

BLOOD
MONEY

BOOK 2

A GOLD EAGLE BOOK FROM

W★RLDWIDE®

TORONTO • NEW YORK • LONDON
AMSTERDAM • PARIS • SYDNEY • HAMBURG
STOCKHOLM • ATHENS • TOKYO • MILAN
MADRID • WARSAW • BUDAPEST • AUCKLAND

Recycling programs
for this product may
not exist in your area.

First edition October 2013

ISBN-13: 978-0-373-61564-3

Special thanks and acknowledgment to
Douglas P. Wojtowicz for his contribution to this work.

EXPLOSIVE DEMAND

Printed in U.S.A.

It is lamentable that to be a good patriot one must become the enemy of the rest of mankind.
—Voltaire

I'm a patriot. I wish to see my country grow, to prosper. Only a fool makes enemies of those who do not seek to harm him. I have only one enemy—the self-serving savages who profit from pain, suffering and death.
—Mack Bolan

CHAPTER ONE

"This is Jonni Rivera for World News Network, reporting on the incredible gang war incident that occurred in Tumaco, Colombia, last night. Authorities are still combing through the wreckage, but apparently two factions, one of them known to be the Western Bloc of the FARC, the armed revolutionary front of Colombia, engaged in a pitched-fever battle over a huge shipment of contraband, including drugs and military-style assault weapons.

"So far, more than one hundred dead have been recovered, though many of them have suffered wounds so horrible that there is no means of identifying them. This place is a war zone, with flames still burning across the area and the freighter. Money has been discovered, cash from the United States, China and a dozen other smaller Southeast Asian nations, though the authorities are stating that it is counterfeit.

"This reporter has personally found one sheet of uncut bills, charred and half turned to ash. Here you can see…"

The camera cut off, switching to static for a brief instant and then to a long shot of the dock. Firefighters were busy putting out individual blazes while corpses in body bags were being hoisted onto gurneys and rolled to waiting wagons. The camera swept a warehouse, its walls shattered by an explosion, or more correctly, a line of explosions.

"We're sorry, we seem to have had some difficulty

with our transmission," the WNN anchor said over the stock footage, which appeared to be on a loop, close-ups of details interspersed with long shots and aerial views.

Rivera had not been far from wrong saying the place looked like a war zone. Corpses were in dozens of places, while scorched stars of destruction marked where detonated bombs had scarred the dock. The freighter itself was a smoldering mess. The superstructure had taken several hits by rocket fire, and the wreckage of containers detonated on deck mixed with the corpses of riflemen who had been cut down in close combat.

AFTER A FEW more minutes of watching the news report, Nik Onn, Malaysian "entrepreneur" and nightclub owner, finally turned off the television. Erra Majid bit off the sudden reflex to complain, to say, "Hey, I was watching that." It wouldn't do for the boss's favorite whore to show an interest in anything other than being facedown in his lap and making him feel good, the undercover cop thought bitterly.

She took a sip of alcohol to wash the taste of the "entrepreneur" out of her mouth, wishing that she were back on the beat, or at least close enough to a service revolver to pump a slug into Onn's misbegotten skull. Right now, she was not just in plain clothes, she was barely clothed, wisps of gossamer draped strategically across her hips and her breasts as much to tantalize as to conceal her nudity. A good hard stare would punch through the gauzy silks barely concealing her most private, precious areas.

In a way, the negligible clothing was an even more effective armor than a Royal Malaysia Police–issued vest. Like this, she didn't look like a policewoman. She was just another Senoi, one of the indigenous tribes of Malaysia, and to many on the island, especially the dominant Malay Muslim community, a second-class citizen.

Majid knew that she was oversimplifying things regarding national racism, but she encountered this kind of garbage even within the police community. It wasn't every day, but it was still there, and she didn't care much for it. Here, posing as a little girl lost, searching for a fast track to big stardom, she blended in. Here, skinny, hungry and too brown to be anything more than a novelty attraction, she was "stuck." Fortunately here was where she wanted to be, close to Onn, a big wheel on a small truck.

The Royal Malaysia Police had needed someone who could get close to the heart of Onn's gang. For some reason, he was doing a lot of middle-ground work between the Russian mob and others. They were curious as to Onn's expansion into the brand-new world of working with foreign gangsters when simple prostitution, gambling and extortion had been his original gig. Majid was chosen because she was just pretty enough to catch the eye of the gang boss, yet convincingly not attractive enough to be splashed across a dozen magazine pages or television screens as a legitimate star, at least in the eyes of her RMP supervisors.

Majid didn't care for the fact that Onn felt that she was worthy of camera time, even if it was for cheaply made pornography, both photographs and movies, which were splashed on the internet under a new false name on top of her cover identity.

"Mila," Onn barked, taking the undercover cop from her reverie. She cringed at the thought of having to service him, especially in the wake of watching such grisly death and destruction on the television screen.

"Nicky?" Majid asked softly.

Onn pointed to his wet bar. "I'm thirsty."

Majid got up and went to prepare him his favorite drink, whispering a tiny prayer of thanks that all that he wanted was some booze, not more sexual favors. It wasn't that Onn wasn't an attractive man; he was lean, young, muscular and swarthy. If she hadn't known that he was responsible for the sexual slavery of women and youths, she might even have given him a second look in other circumstances, but the knowledge that he was someone who trafficked in human lives tainted him.

She wanted to vomit just looking at him. And yet, she had a job to do. She had to pretend to be his slave.

This was a temporary situation, and she hoped to live long enough to see Onn stripped of his power and made to kneel as a slave himself.

To do that, she did her job, biding her time. Once she had enough evidence to give to the RMP, Nik Onn would topple, and his fall would be long and hard.

She endured.

MACK BOLAN, AKA the Executioner, had made certain that when he left the Tumaco docks, he had gathered up the cell phones and personal computers of Diego Milla-gro and Alfa Molinov. The two men hadn't had a chance to knock out the memory on their devices or to remove the SIM cards or any other bit of flash memory, so he had a record of phone calls and stored numbers as well as locations.

One name kept cropping up on Molinov's phone and it was in Malaysia. Kuala Lumpur to be exact. The same city where the American Embassy was located, and where one corner of the building had been brutally oblit-erated by a wave of anti-tank and anti-bunker rockets.

Nik Onn.

Bolan had found out the man was a club owner in Kuala Lumpur. His was the kind of club where you could rent a dancer who was on a forced antibiotic program so that you wouldn't spend one night with the flesh and end up paying for years from whatever disease was in her crotch. HIV testing was mandatory.

The soldier had a lead.

Bolan's current mission had forced him to take on an army of hardmen. From the depths of the Orinoco River Basin to the coastal city of Tumaco and its sprawling docks, the Executioner had waged a war against a counterfeiting conspiracy that was more than just simple money-making. It was an economic terrorist attack aimed at Colombia, at the United States and, oddly enough, the People's Republic of China.

No, not oddly enough, Bolan corrected himself. Right now, the United States was in a world of debt to China, the unintended consequences of a decade of warfare in Iraq and Afghanistan. Financially, America and the PRC were united, making the two global superpowers' economies inexorably tied together. An attack against one would cause crippling repercussions in the other.

In Kuala Lumpur, a Chinese intelligence official had visited the U.S. Embassy carrying a briefcase with samples of counterfeit notes, yuan and dollars, the day, the exact moment, of the missile strike on the building. Dozens had been killed, hundreds injured, and the evidence of the counterfeiting in Southeast Asia had been utterly destroyed. The American intelligence officers and the PRC agent had been instantly killed in what was brushed off as a terrorist act in the world news.

The only problem with this severed lead was that

Stony Man Farm had picked up on the rumblings of the meeting and Director Hal Brognola had brought in Mack Bolan to look into the situation. However, the day that the two friends met, a similar counterfeiting operation engaged in a brutal missile strike on a joint Colombian federal and United States' Secret Service strike force in Medellín. Rather than make Malaysia his first stop, the Executioner picked up the freshest trail of blood and violence.

That had been a week ago—the battle of Tumaco the previous night.

Bolan's bruised and sore body reclined in the Gulfstream jet's seat, and even as his mind went over the information, the data gathered, the battles fought, he allowed his body to rest. He breathed deeply, let his muscles relax, felt his heartbeat slow as the private jet carried him thousands of feet above the Pacific Ocean, hurtling at more than 550 miles an hour toward Kuala Lumpur. The hum of the plane proved a subtle, needed massage as Bolan allowed his body respite, his mind balancing information and speculation.

Alfa Molinov also had another contact in Malaysia: Grev Solyenko.

Whereas Onn was a behind-the-scenes man who never got his hands bloody, Solyenko was hard-core Russian mob who'd learned his skills before washing out of the Spetsnaz, the Russian army's elite commandos, akin to the U.S. Army Rangers or Marine Force Recon. After his duty in special operations and a dishonorable discharge, Solyenko disappeared into the underworld, joining the group to which he'd been selling grenades and other munitions from the armory.

His career on the supply side up in smoke, Solyenko

had became more hands-on, setting booby traps for his mob family's competition. Multiple warrants were out for Solyenko's arrest in Moscow and a dozen other Russian cities. The trail of warrants followed through Chechnya and even as far as Vietnam and Laos before the man fell off the radar again. Interpol had been of the opinion the Russian *mafiya* had grown tired of him attracting so much attention, but in the end, that just hadn't been the case.

Like a rotten Roman Catholic priest, he was shipped out to more and more obscure parishes, but left to keep up his activities. The *mafiya* was glad to have a deadly human weapon in their repertoire. They weren't about to lose him now.

That was the Malaysia part of the operation. Bolan wanted to look closely, to make certain that he had the right handle, or to find out if Molinov was working some other overseas scam aside from the counterfeiting. Bolan doubted it.

Solyenko hadn't been revealed as being more than a doer, but the demolitions-based assassinations he pulled off were a sign of a canny, dangerous mind. The man knew how to plan, how to sneak, how to get around things like customs or to gain explosives illicitly on a local scale. Combined with someone on the ground, Solyenko would easily be in the position of local boss. Even if he wasn't in charge, the man's history with explosives and man-portable missiles colored him as suspect numero uno in the attack on the U.S. Embassy. Bolan was going to Kuala Lumpur, and if he wasn't going to sink a stake in the heart of the operation, then he'd at least avenge the lives of dozens of Americans and obliterate the infrastructure set in place by the conspirators.

Cleansing flame was coming to Malaysia.

Whether it moved on depended on how much he could get out of Onn and Solyenko.

Bolan looked across the aisle and paid close attention to Zachary Winslow. The young Secret Service agent was one of the two lone survivors of the joint task force ambush in Medellín, the other being Captain Miguel Villanueva. Winslow and Villanueva had been instrumental in helping Bolan cut through the South American portion of this conspiracy. Unfortunately, the Colombian National Police officer, Villanueva, was of such a rank and responsibility that he had been left behind in Tumaco to clean up the mess of open warfare on the docks. Winslow, however, had volunteered to go with Bolan across the Pacific.

"In for a penny, in for a pound, as the British say," Winslow had announced. "There are still people to avenge."

"That doesn't have to be your job, Zach," Bolan had countered.

Winslow shook his head. "I'm not going to go all 24/7 dark stalker of the shadows of the Earth like you are, McCormack. But I'll be damned if I'm going to see this shit through only halfway."

Mack Bolan had undertaken this mission using the alias Justice Department Special Agent Matt McCormack.

Bolan took a deep breath. "Good way to get killed."

"And going solo isn't?" Winslow asked. "I'm a big boy."

The soldier sighed and nodded. "Remember my rules, then."

"I do," Winslow said. "They kept me alive through the last dance."

"The trouble is, we're not competing for some glitter ball trophy," Bolan replied. "You get eliminated, you never take a step again."

Winslow smirked. "I'm smoking again. I'd rather catch a bullet than lung cancer."

"Fair enough," Bolan told him.

The Secret Service agent was asleep now, earplugs in, eyes shut. Winslow's slumber was undisturbed by nightmares, though Bolan knew that the brain only entered REM sleep for a brief few moments, an explosion of electrochemical that painted entire vistas, broad universes, or particularly troubling memories within the space of seconds. Winslow could sleep normally now, his body shut down for a relaxing snooze, but once it was time to awaken, his dreams would kick in, his brain using stored thoughts and images as a natural, neurological alarm clock.

How he'd awaken would be the big tell on whether Winslow would need therapy for Post Traumatic Stress Disorder, or whether he could handle his emotions in a healthier manner. That he'd returned to smoking was no real sign, as his first reunion with cigarettes had come only moments before his team had been ambushed and slaughtered.

Then again, Bolan realized, that pause was a source of guilt in itself. Had he not stopped for a shot of nicotine, he would have been with his friends and partners while they were attacked. If he couldn't have helped them to fight, then at least he would have been dead with them. The inhalation of poison could have been a panacea, a means of slow self-destruction, self-punishment for being a survivor, not one of the dead.

Bolan would keep an eye on him.

Right now, the soldier had his own health to deal with. He had cuts and bruises, aches and pains that had been treated but still needed some gentle favoring. He got up and went for a vitamin-fortified sport drink. Rehydration had been important in the more humid parts of Colombia and Venezuela, but in addition to that, right now he was in need of so much more. He grabbed a protein bar, knowing that his muscles would need the fuel, the raw material, to build themselves back up.

Bolan finished a second protein bar, filling the void of calories left by the war he'd fought the night before. He was about to catch a catnap himself when he received a message from Stony Man Farm, his Combat Commander Digital Assistant—Combat CDA—buzzing in its pocket. He plucked it out and took a look at the screen.

Striker, be advised. Royal Malaysia Police have secured files pertaining to Nik Onn behind firewall. Will attempt low profile penetration. Indications point to precious ally inside enemy ranks.

Bolan texted back.

Acknowledged.

The Executioner wasn't surprised that the RMP was interested in Onn. It was a major, modern agency with more than 100,000 sworn officers, with equipment ranging from standard sedans to the latest paramilitary light armored vehicles. The service even had its own air fleet, though it was a mere twenty aircraft.

Detectives would want a bead on a gang boss who seemed to be making big deals with Russians in-country.

The last thing that Bolan needed was to get into a cross fire between the law and a bunch of violent criminals. Be it simple surveillance or an undercover operation, the Executioner would have to tread carefully. This wouldn't be like the Venezuelan state-sponsored terrorism in Colombia.

One wrong move and Bolan could end up shooting a cop.

He went back to his seat and mentally reviewed the Farm's files.

The soldier couldn't afford to make a mistake. This was the city, not the jungle.

Though, Bolan reminded himself, the concrete jungle was as deadly, if not deadlier than even the predator-stocked rivers of South America.

CHAPTER TWO

Night settled in on Kuala Lumpur, falling like a shroud across the outskirts of the great metropolis, but where Mack Bolan, the Executioner, strode, he was surrounded by the glare of neon and headlights. He was far from the iconic Petronas Twin Towers, but he could still see the glass-and-steel spires, lit up and gleaming like spear points stabbing at the night sky.

The glare at the top of the towers illuminated the clouds wisping around their rooftops some twelve hundred feet above, turning the sky a dull, dark purple. Light pollution spewed up from the city, touching clouds and reflecting back down. There was no way for the stars to compete with the blaze of the sprawling city, nor the satellite cities and towns clustered around it. This particular neighborhood was where honest laborers and immigrants made their homes, near the tangle of towns where they plied their trades as servants, day laborers and sweatshop workers. This was no place for a tourist.

Bolan was rolling light this night. He didn't need to start a war, not here. People in the area were blowing off steam from a hard day's work. Yet predators were everywhere. Packing heavy might inspire others to take shots at him, shots that would likely end up in an innocent bystander.

The soldier's action this night was an alternate to the play he'd made in Sorreno's club. There, he'd gone in to impress, with the goal of minimizing violence, while still making the maximum of his intimidation. Now, Bolan was in chameleon mode—role camouflage they'd said about him for his covert operations back in the day. As a six-foot-three, blue-eyed man, he'd proved able to assume the daily life of a rice farmer in Asia, just as he'd blended in with Italian organized crime, or penetrated the ranks of the KGB, having learned their languages, picking up culture and mannerisms.

Even so, Bolan wasn't completely unarmed, completely naked. He had his folding Karambit fighting knife in one pocket, and he had a powerhouse of a pocket gun, a Ruger .357 Magnum LCR revolver. A polymer frame and an almost skeletonized cylinder made the small weapon as light as a feather, but that same flexing polymer frame and a cushioned rubber Hogue grip made the gun relatively gentle to fire.

Bolan preferred to have a .44 Magnum in a full-size nearly three-pound Desert Eagle, but the LCR gave incredible stopping power with a finely honed trigger mechanism. The load he had within the 5-shot cylinder was the legendary 125-grain semi-jacketed hollowpoint round. Out of the LCR's short, sub-two-inch barrel, it would only heave along at 1160 feet per second, generating just less than 400 foot-pounds of energy at muzzle distance.

It was about as fast as Bolan's preferred 9 mm load, but the semi-jacketed part of the hollowpoint round meant that the lead core would flatten much more easily than the Parabellum round, producing massive internal tissue damage on contact with human flesh.

The Karambit fighting knife was also small. No bigger than a fist-load when folded, when it was deployed, its hooked two-and-a-half-inch blade proved to be wickedly effective. One slash would pierce flesh and then open up a long, tearing furrow along its concave cutting surface. The Karambit was sharp and sturdy enough to cut through chain link or to open a two-foot, eviscerating wound along an enemy's torso.

Bolan packed light, but that didn't mean he couldn't take out an opponent with a single shot of the revolver or single stroke of the knife.

Even so, the Executioner was there strictly on recon. It was still the evening after the Tumaco battle, so few of the enemy would even realize that he was in-country. As he was, wearing a white shirt, which made his tanned skin seem that much darker, brown contact lenses hiding the cool, piercing blue of his eyes, his hair jet-black, he could fit in as a tall-person local, a resident alien, or just someone blowing through for a good time. He didn't look, act, even smell the part of a Westerner. A regular diet of Venezuelan and Colombian food had given him a slightly different scent, and he spoke English but with a Vietnamese accent, mixing in bits of the Chinese and French influences on the language to alter a listener's perception of him as an American.

He could have come in as a Russian, but Bolan lacked the necessary tattoos, or the stencils to make convincing fakes, at least for the moment. Even if he were trying to pose as a *mafiya* goon, it would be easy for the locals to be suspicious of someone coming in from South America, right where another of their operations had crashed and burned.

Bolan had looked over the specialists who had been brought into South America for the freighter's protection. He'd taken photographs of those corpses still with faces, gathered up fingerprints of those who didn't. Two of them came in from Interpol's files as being members of Russian organized crime. There would be too good of a chance for Bolan to be recognized as a pure fake, especially considering the amount of effort that Alfa Molinov put in to protecting the transfer of billions in counterfeit bills onto the freighter.

No, pretending to be Vietnamese, most likely Eurasian, was Bolan's best shield of anonymity. Kuala Lumpur was an international hub, and there was a good deal of both local native Southeast Asian residents in the population, and a more transient population. Tall and lean, his face ageless yet still rugged, he could have easily passed as a half-breed, exiled, yet still not wanting to go too far from his home. There would be a community for him in Malaysia.

Bolan sipped from a bottle of local beer, watching girls writhe and gyrate in cages to Chinese versions of international pop music. The young women, shaking and shimmying, would have been attractive, winsome, except that the soldier had seen what had led these ladies to this kind of life. Where others could only see sexuality and low morals, Bolan could see desperation and self-loathing. This wasn't a goal in a woman's life: grinding one's hips to chintzy synthesizer music and being pawed at by drunken, cigarette-stinking cretins.

This was a trap. A dead-end existence. The dancers in the club were just steps removed from being led to the street and leashed to a corner to be traded and rented out as nothing more than human livestock. There would be rooms in the back of this club where these girls would be manhandled, violated.

And if they knew what was good for them, the man-

agement of this club would say, they would smear some
makeup over the bruises, suck up any sore joints and
pulled muscles, and head right back out. If they didn't
earn their keep, if they didn't put out for the clientele,
they either walked the streets with far less protection, or
were relegated to an existence that would end with their
bodies in a garbage bin.

Bolan knew he didn't have the resources at the moment to attempt to rescue these girls. If he was going to
bust this club wide-open, he'd leave them without even
the meager support that Onn's predatory staff could provide them. Homeless, they'd be easy pickings for the next
human parasite to come along.

Right now, Bolan's priority was to gather information
against a cabal of counterfeiters. And one thing that ensured the success of any mission was to have a single,
focused goal. Deviation, especially while working undercover, was a sure means of making certain that you
ended up out in the open and exposed as a target.

Security in the club was pretty good, though they
didn't frisk anyone. Their eyes were sharp, alert, but they
knew better than to try to keep some of the club-goers
from coming in with weapons. The club was located in a
rough area, and security was at the door to instill a sense
of order. The real troubleshooters were somewhere in the
shadows, probably watching through security cameras.
Bolan picked out decorative mirror domes that could easily hide such electronic surveillance, but he also noticed
that there were catwalks above the latticework of lights.

The blaze of the lights could easily hide a couple of
gunmen, but looking up there would only attract attention to the soldier. He did, however, lower his observations thanks to a small hand mirror that he used to sweep

the ceiling. He did that for short intervals, and always when he wasn't in a position where the reflective surface of the mirror would flash into the lens of a spotlight, betraying his subtle surveillance.

It was two hours into the probe, and he knew that Winslow would be anxious for Bolan to return to their base so that they could plan their next step in Kuala Lumpur. Moving too quickly in the club, however, was not on Bolan's agenda. He needed to pick his maneuvers carefully. So far, he'd seen two men, and from their silhouettes, he could make out that they were packing some form of bullpup assault rifle, either Steyr AUGs built under license for the Malaysian Reserves, or the newer Berapi LP06 rifles.

That was serious firepower for close quarters, which only demonstrated that Onn had a lot of concern about what he was involved in. A bullpup assault rifle brought all the power of a full-length rifle in the compact length of a submachine gun. Security wanted the maximum firepower in the minimum package, which was even more than simply getting a sawed-off 12-gauge shotgun. The guards were fairly comfortable with the compact rifles, meaning that they either had been pulling security duty for a while, or they were heavy-hitter security brought in especially to watch over the Malay club owner and his premises.

Bolan took out his Combat CDA and ran an application that picked up on wireless electronics around him. The program had been designed by his friend, technology wizard Hermann "Gadgets" Schwarz. Utilizing the antenna built into the Combat CDA, the application could pick up on radios, cell phones, even wireless communication between cameras and central hubs all around it. It took just a tap of the button, and then Bolan could pocket the device as it mapped the area for its sources of signals. Rather than map things out in relation to the device, the application placed signal sources via GPS so as not to anchor the user to one particular spot.

Still, Bolan could only endure so much of the chintzy stripper music. By the time the third hour came around, he was back on the street. Fortunately he'd gotten enough information on the place, enough to make the headache and ringing ears worth the effort.

Bolan wanted to head back toward the safehouse. He had a route that would take enough turns and detours that he could ascertain the presence of a tail. Onn and Solyenko probably weren't expecting him to be in Kuala Lumpur so soon after the violence in Tumaco, or if they were, they were expecting him to come in much more overtly, as indicated by the two gunners up on the catwalk and a sprinkling of heavily armed guards at doorways leading to offices, bed quarters or day-to-day operational areas of the club.

He stepped through the door of the club and paused. Some undefined feeling kept him from wandering too far. He didn't know what it was, but he was going to stick around to find out. Bolan decided to move someplace to get a better vantage point, so he melted into an alley and the shadows within.

GREV SOLYENKO PACED. He hadn't touched his drink, but he was on edge in a way that Nik Onn had rarely seen him. It was like being in the same cage as a restless lion, right down to the rumbles of unissued roars bubbling beneath the Russian's craggy surface. His eyes were dark orbs of glass that flitted to and fro, like the camera lenses on a high-technology assault helicopter, seeking targets.

Solyenko was a big man, six and a half feet in height, and his shoulders were wide, broad with the promise of a strength that could uproot a tree stump. That barrel chest narrowed into a slender waist and long, lean legs, the rest of the leonine power of Solyenko apparent in his thick neck and rippling, long arms. The only thing missing in the lion analogy was that he was close-shaved, his skull buzz cut to a fine fuzz of short hair.

Solyenko's square jaw jutted as he paused, looking at the tumbler sitting on Onn's desk. He then looked toward Mila, Onn's favorite girl of the moment. "Why is she hanging around this office?"

Onn glanced sideways toward Mila. "To relieve some stress."

Solyenko wrinkled his blunt pug nose. "Really? When a one-man army just finished his rampage against our people in South America?"

"I've done everything that I can to lock this town down," Onn replied. "You've got a lot of pressure building up…why not let some go with her?"

Solyenko glared first at Mila, then toward the Malay. "No, thanks. I don't want whatever plague you pass on to her."

Onn gagged on his drink as he heard the slur against him. "You're out of line, Grev."

Solyenko rolled his eyes. "So what?"

"You act like he's going to be here any minute now," Onn replied. "He's on the other side of the Pacific, goddamn it!"

"Yeah. Thank God there're no magical flying machines that can zip through the sky at over five hundred miles an hour!" Solyenko snapped back.

Onn shook his head. "You're paranoid. Even if he was the man who single-handedly took down the freighter and all the gunmen on the scene, he'd be hurting. People get beat up when they engage in a battle."

"We in the *organasatya* used to believe that," Solyenko told him. "But you are talking about a man who has resources. If he doesn't pop by any minute now…"

"How is he going to know that this club is going to be his next spot to hit?" Onn asked.

Solyenko grimaced and then lunged toward the desk, picking up the Malay's cell phone. He turned it on, scrolled along the screen, then showed it to Onn.

Once the screen faced him, Onn read the name, "Molinov, Alfa."

Solyenko let the phone drop onto the desk blotter, the plucked his own phone out. A few taps and once more Molinov's name showed up on the screen for Onn to read.

"Satisfied?" Solyenko asked.

"But we only communicated the particulars of the operation through burners," Onn stated.

"I didn't pull up a goddamned telephone number. I pulled up your notes," Solyenko snarled. "Stuff that you shouldn't have direct contact for, but it's where you put the numbers for your burner calls. The same would go for Molinov. He'd have contact with our random burners in his personal computer notes."

Onn looked down at his phone, frowning.

Idly, he flicked his finger on the screen, scrolling to Goomabong, who was waiting with the rest of the club's enhanced security just outside the office door.

"That doesn't mean I can't blow off steam," Onn told the Russian. "You deal with stress by being a crass, grouchy son of a bitch. I take care of it by getting it on with some slut."

Solyenko glanced toward Mila. He spotted a grim, disgusted expression on her slender face, but that disappeared, buried beneath a sheen of nervous discipline. Solyenko didn't trust her, but if she showed little love for Onn, then that was one thing in her favor. Unfortunately a girl who was kept in line by fear and sexual assault was someone who could be grabbed, brought outside and turned into an informant.

Solyenko wanted to say something about that, but so far the Malay was resistant to most attempts at common-sense operational security. The Russian would have loved nothing more than to take Mila and break her neck, flushing her down the nearest storm drain. With no small irony, his own means of relieving stress were similar to what Onn had suggested, but that all came with a payoff of a cooling lump of flesh taking all of that sexual frustration. Solyenko usually caught attention for some of his larger escapades for the *mafiya,* but his real liability for local operations was that he was wired as a predator. To him, sex and violence were inescapably intertwined.

For him to empty himself of rage and lust, it had to come at the end of his partner's existence. Nothing quite flipped that switch, pulled that trigger, like watching eyes bulge, tongue swell, lips turn purple as her windpipe crushed beneath the pressure of his thumbs.

Solyenko grabbed the tumbler of liquor and threw the drink down his throat. He needed not to think about taking Mila and slaughtering her. That would only put him more on edge. But even now, he wondered what her succulent brown skin tasted like, what her hair would smell like, what her cooling flesh would feel like.... "Give me another."

Onn poured another round for the Russian. There was a flicker of recognition in the Malay's eyes. Solyenko's glance at Mila had revealed just a little too much—that hunger for destruction coupled with death. Onn nodded. "I could get someone else for you."

Mila looked between the pair, her expression blank, seemingly confused, but there was a tension now in the girl. Had the simple country-folk, second-class aboriginal sensed Solyenko's predatory nature just by jungle cunning? Or was there more than just an untrained intellect working behind her big, brown, soulful eyes?

Solyenko's upper lip twitched and he finally plopped into a leather chair, letting it cradle him while he sipped at the liquor. It wouldn't matter. If he did release all that pent-up energy onto her, he wouldn't be hungry enough to do what had to be done when the Soldier arrived. He needed to hang on to that edge, that irritation, that urge to crush, mutilate and destroy. It was the same fire that had made him such an efficient assassin for the *mafiya*.

Mila would live, for now. Solyenko let the booze burn in his stomach.

Killing her would only deprive the ex-Spetsnaz killer of the edge he required to take on one of the world's most dangerous men. But once the Soldier, a man that Molinov had called Matt McCormack, was dead, planted in the ground or blown into ashes through the stratosphere, the little brown whore, Mila, was going to be an awfully tasty dessert.

CHAPTER THREE

Erra Majid, aka Mila, could smell the blood in the water now. Grev Solyenko was more than just a common gun thug from Moscow. He was a monster, a terrible predator that looked at human beings as nothing more than a means to an end, objects to be used and discarded, and often, for Solyenko, the discarding was the most satisfying of all. Solyenko looked directly at her, sized her up, and the wheels in his head turned. She could feel the malice, the malevolence bleeding off him like toxic smoke from a burning waste dump.

Even if he wasn't seeing her as nothing more than a security risk, he was sizing her up. She noticed how he'd licked his lips, tasting her in the air. Right now, she wanted to vomit. She knew his type, and she knew the kinds of horrors she could expect at his hands. The way that Onn seemed to be nodding in approval of those leers also told Majid that if she didn't get the hell out of there, she was a dead woman, a sacrificial offering so that the Russian would be happy, humming along. Majid tried to calm herself, settle her nerves. She could feel the waves of panic.

In the club, Majid was outnumbered. She looked toward the window, but knew it was reinforced, a multilevel sandwich of glass, polymer and wire framework. Onn had had it installed to keep his enemies from shooting at him. The last pane had been replaced because chips had been knocked from it by a salvo of heavy bullets. Majid didn't know what had shot the window, but everyone who had been working on the damaged pane was surprised at the level of damage the bullets had inflicted, nearly penetrating all the way to reach the club owner.

Those rounds had been issued by Solyenko, testing out Onn's club, checking the base of operations he had intended to set up. They muttered among themselves, the Malay gangster and the Russian gun thug, a conspiratorial tone that went back and forth as they had looked over the office, seeking signs of weakness.

And every time Solyenko observed Majid, as "Mila" in Onn's lap, that assessment of weakness, security risk, flashed in his eyes, a glimpse of murderous intent showing just beneath the surface. Danger threatened, and like a frightened animal, Majid was filled with the urge to kick free. That panic knifed through her, and she knew that if she gave in, she would be doomed.

Her exit would have to be calm, swift, but slick.

"Baby…you're gonna have to get me some more cold beers," Onn told her. "I don't have the stomach to down any more liquor."

"But, Nicky," she asked, "don't you want to be clear for…when that scary bastard shows up?"

Onn glared at her as if she'd questioned his sexuality. "That's why I'm going to beer. Now shut the hell up and go get me my beer. You okay, Solyenko?"

The Russian glowered at her. "You're letting her walk around?"

Onn's exasperation spread now to his foreign partner. "What's she going to do? Find the Soldier's direct telephone number and hunt him down? She doesn't even have a cell."

Solyenko glanced at Onn, then back toward Majid. "Then can I at least send Goomabong with her?"

Majid felt ice water splash within her veins. Goomabong was ethnically Thai, though he was a Malaysian citizen, and he was a solid six-and-a-half feet, the vast majority of it muscle covered with a layer of fat that kept her from guessing whether he was three hundred or three-hundred-and-fifty pounds. Despite the fact that he was as big as a truck, the man was aware and quick of mind. Trying to sneak under his notice would be as close to a magic act as she could ever attempt, but if she was going to get out of this, she'd have to try.

The best she could hope for would be for one of Goomabong's soccer-ball-size fists to crush her skull and snap her neck with a single punch. He was capable of that. It would be a swift mercy, but if she died, there would be no way for her superiors to know exactly what Onn was up to. The plus side would be, if she was killed by a single punch from the giant bodyguard, she wouldn't suffer at the mutilating hands of Solyenko.

"Keep a close eye on her," Solyenko told the huge Thai as he opened the door for her. "If she makes a move you don't like, bring her back to me."

Majid swallowed as she stepped into the hall ahead of the Asian giant. Goomabong had been given the order not to kill her outright with his massive strength. Instead, she was to be kept alive.

Just what Majid feared the most.

Goomabong walked her to the kitchen. She was screwed if she tried to run, she was doomed if she stayed and waited, biding her time until Solyenko finally con-

vinced Onn of her untrustworthy nature. She no longer
wanted to move, wanted to delay, to stay inert and let the
world flow around her, pass her over, forget about her,
but Onn had given her orders. Delay would only anger
the man, focus his attention on her, doom her.

The bustle of the club was enormous. Music shook
the air, rattled Majid's teeth, made her eyes throb with
constant pressure; the same unbearable sonic force that
could be ignored by the mind-numbed, the drunk and
the drugged.

They quickly turned off, finding the hallway to the
kitchen, Goomabong not losing sight of her thanks to
his height. It was as if he were looking down on the
crowd, a towering figure who could follow her with focused black eyes as grim and implacable as the lenses
of sniper scopes. Majid continued to walk, slithering between bodies before they could part in front of the Thai
titan. She could only hope to get to a doorway and escape through the kitchen before he could hurl his massive bulk toward her.

The doors opened.

"Go left," Goomabong growled.

The crowd had parted for the big man, and there he
was, right behind her. Majid obeyed, heading closer to
the refrigerator where the club kept its bottles of chilled
beverages. She didn't want to be boxed in by Goomabong, but as they turned down the little inlet between
cooler and freezer doors, she looked back and saw
Goomabong, his shoulders so wide he was a living wall
at the end of the short corridor. Majid looked at herself.
"I need a basket."

Goomabong had to have scooped one up on the way.

He thrust his hand forward, and Majid reached out to catch it.

"Don't waste any time in there," Goomabong ordered gruffly. "Nik's thirsty, and I'd like something, too."

"Anything special?" Majid asked. She opened the door.

"The same beer as you're getting for Nik." Goomabong's voice boomed around the door.

Majid grabbed bottles, putting them in the basket. She looked at what she'd gathered and wondered what she could do. The bottles had twist-off lids, which might help a little. She could build pressure inside the beer, carbonation turning the beverage into a foaming stream that would blast right into the big Thai's eyes. He'd be blinded, maybe for a moment.

That would have to be enough. She gave the bottle she intended for him a good, long shake.

"Hurry up in there!" Goomabong bellowed.

"You want it so fast, you crawl back in here if you can!" Majid said.

"Just hurry! No funny business," Goomabong snarled.

Majid was out, holding the bottle for the big Thai. "Here!"

Goomabong plucked the bottle from her grasp, standing back a little to allow her out of the corridor. He put the bottle up to his lips, leveraging one thumb beneath the cap and pushing it off with the strength of his massive hands. Even as the cap popped loose, foam vomited out, splattering his chest. He looked down at the sudden spurt going all over his shirt before his face was in line with the open mouth. Beer splashed into his eyes, and he winced, staggering back from the surprise.

For all his height, weight, muscle, the effects of being

splashed in the eyes was the same. No amount of discipline could fight off the effects of pure reflex. The human body sought to protect the relatively fragile eyes at all times, and the first bit of contact snapped lids shut.

It was that brief instant that gave Majid her opening. She slithered behind him, rushing toward a service entrance in the kitchen. Goomabong cursed and roared, his blunt, domelike head snapping to and fro as he wiped beer foam from his eyes. It took another instant for him to spot her, but Majid was at the back door, pushing against it. The humidity of the night broke through the cracked door, rushing in to greet her as she shoved through.

Two steps out she realized that all she had on were gauzy panties and a wisp of a bra, nothing that would have been of notice within the club, and maybe not even in the street, but the alley floor was rough and full of garbage and broken objects. One bad step and she'd slice the soles of her feet apart. Even so, Majid had committed to this escape. She took a running stride, a short leap, and grabbed at the top of a fence to pull herself up.

The service door hadn't closed before Goomabong struck it, crashing it open hard, and barreling out into the open.

Majid was balanced atop the fence, looking back, her eyes wide with horror as Goomabong glared at her, one lip curled into a sneer.

He was coming after her, and suddenly the chain link didn't look as if it would be enough to slow him.

Steely fingers suddenly wound around her wrist, snatching her off balance.

Erra Majid tumbled toward the tall, dark shadow in the alley.

MACK BOLAN WASN'T certain what detained him, what made him decide to look around the street, through the alleys, for a weakness in the headquarters that Nik Onn had made for himself in this slummy, red-light district of Kuala Lumpur, but it might have been a number of factors. One, he was still stirred with concern over the young women who worked the club, who had been trapped by addiction or destitution to where their only hope of a longer, continued life was allowing themselves to be pawed over, manhandled by the kind of trash who regularly flowed through these gutters. Two, he knew that there was an undercover operative inside the club.

The Royal Malaysian Police hadn't allowed that information to be available, only an intensive search for Onn's files had produced the slightest blip on the radar of the cybernetics crew at Stony Man Farm, the soldier's number-one source for electronic information. Algorithms had sifted through incredible loads of data, and the only thing not buried behind a wall of paranoid computer security had been an inkling of an investigation and undercover operation.

Those two bits of information had consumed Bolan just enough for him to want to hang out a few more minutes. It was a long shot, but Bolan knew enough about Onn's non-club duties, and about the cruelty of Grev Solyenko to realize that someone who was stuck undercover might want a chance to break free, especially in the gap of peace before a coming storm: the blazing fury of the Executioner and his blitz. The presence of firepower and extra guards proved that the club boss was aware that trouble was on its way.

Those idle thoughts, however, were given vindication as, on the other side of a chain-link fence, a nearly naked young woman exploded into the alley. She was small, a shade more than five feet, with dark skin and flowing black hair. The woman was fit, muscles moving easily under velvety skin, though she'd seen better days as she was painfully thin.

What attracted Bolan's attention the most, even past her near nudity, dressed only in black panties and bra, was the look of fear on her face, a mask of terror that would have been unthinking except for a grimly set jaw. The woman was focused as she rushed toward the fence. Bolan had been standing in the shadows, maintaining a low profile, but her sudden appearance made him edge toward the limit of the darkness.

Instants after she grabbed the fence, crawling until she was atop the six-footer, the service door slammed open again. Bolan didn't know who the man was, but he was a living slab of muscle that crashed the door off its hinges with the force of a rampaging rhinoceros. The giant's sudden appearance caused the woman to stop, look back. Bolan could sense the sudden weakness in her limbs, a loss of hope as what looked like three-hundred-fifty pounds of muscle crashed out into the alley, his face soaked, flecks of foam around his mouth as if he were suffering from rabies.

Bolan reached out, grabbed the woman's wrist and pulled her. Off balance, she toppled from her perch, but the soldier caught her in his arms, tucking her to his chest. He glanced back to evaluate the newcomer, and realized that the big man wasn't in the mood to slow down. He was coming through the chain-link fence.

Bolan whirled and took off, charging toward a causeway he'd spotted earlier. The woman, slender and trembling, curled tightly against him as they slipped through into the gap between buildings. Metal jangled violently, and the sounds of pipes, the frame of the fence likely, banged off the floor of the alley. That human beast had torn through the fencing, though it had been so rusted, it might have come apart with any good hit from an NFL linebacker. The man who was on this woman's trail wasn't superhuman, but the Executioner wasn't going to engage in combat.

The woman was in trouble, and she needed to be taken somewhere safe. That meant a studied retreat.

Bolan was in the open on a street, market stalls stretching left and right as far as he could see. There was a clear view of the alley through the causeway, but that was suddenly eclipsed by the enormous shadow of his charge's pursuit. Bolan pivoted and worked his way through the throng. As far as he could tell, that man would have a hard time scurrying through the causeway, and all Bolan would have to do was to find another one and slip into it.

The crowd took notice of the new arrival and his nearly naked charge, and they began to part for him. Some were stepping forward, however, nosy curiosity making them wonder why the big brown man was out in the open with some dancing whore from one of the clubs. Bolan sidestepped a man who tried to get into his way, and he vaulted over a small barrier of crates, only three feet tall, and disappeared behind the row of stalls. He spotted a gap up ahead and was hoping that he'd lost the giant when a scream arose.

Tables crashed and a shock wave of terror rippled through the crowd behind Bolan.

And sure enough, where the monster of a man appeared, the attention of many suddenly snapped in the direction of Bolan on the run. He couldn't blame them, it was simply human nature. What did surprise the soldier was that this huge thug was quick on the uptake, following the turning heads to focus right on him.

"Goomabong," the woman sputtered.

Now the soldier had a name to go with the giant. Bolan turned and burst into the causeway. Once more in darkness, and away from the press of bodies, he had enough room to gain some distance. Goomabong, however, made a racket behind him. Bolan could tell that the big man was on a rampage, and he would follow the soldier and the woman to the ends of the Earth if necessary.

Bolan entered another alley and had more room to maneuver. He set the woman on her feet, grabbing a large garbage bin and putting all of his strength into dragging it across the causeway exit.

"My name's McCormack," Bolan introduced himself, taking the woman's hand.

"Majid," she responded. It sounded like a last name, which seemed appropriate for how he'd introduced himself. Bolan filed that away and pointed back in the direction that they'd come, at least in terms of their advance along the market street. It would buy them a few moments, and Majid took the cue and the two of them ran. Her legs were much shorter than Bolan's, but she kicked along as fast as she could. He wondered how her feet would be at the end of this. He at least had the protection of shoes, but there was nothing except a wisp of fabric covering her breasts and loins to protect her soft brown skin.

Majid pointed out a new cutaway in the alley and Bolan followed her lithe form into the shadows. Even as he disappeared into the dark, he heard the thunder of the garbage bin rocked by an impact, rolling and crashing into a wall on the far side of the alley.

"Mila! You bitch!"

Goomabong's voice was an inhuman roar. Bolan considered pulling his pocket .357 Magnum gun, but there didn't seem to be any profit in going that route. The sudden outbreak of a gunfight in the snarl of alleys near Onn's club, especially with the rapid flight of Majid, would only put the gang boss on higher alert. He looked up ahead at the woman who snaked herself out of the causeway, in the rear of some stalls. Workers glared at her as she cast her gaze around.

Bolan was out in the open with her, the lights allowing stall staff to work at night, showing off Majid for the first time. She had scooped up a spare apron and had thrown it on over her neck, tying it off. It brought her some semblance of modesty, and she was still looking around when Bolan's eyes locked on something on the floor. He bent for the two objects, pulling money from his pocket.

A cook started to complain as Bolan picked up the sandals on the floor, but the Malay notes were more than enough to cover the finest of shoes and a dress, let alone flip-flops and a threadbare apron. The cook took the money, smiled and waved them out of his kitchen, saying in Chinese that they didn't belong there. Bolan bowed his head, took Majid by the hand, and the two of them slithered out onto another market street.

"This way," Majid said, pointing toward an alley entrance across the street and through the crowd. "You duck down."

Bolan stooped and followed her, blending in a little

more easily with the local crowd, rather than his six-foot-three height making him stand out like a sore thumb.

The cook who had taken the money started speaking again, loud enough for Bolan to recognize his voice. Machinery crashed, and Goomabong officially announced his appearance out in the open again. The soldier and Majid were now in the shadows, though, and the darkness could probably hide them. Even so, Majid continued to lead Bolan until they were behind a wooden slat fence surrounding the back of a kitchen. He couldn't hear any sound of pursuit. Just to be sure, he stayed still, only occasionally taking a quick glance around a corner with his pocket mirror.

"Do you speak English?" Bolan asked.

"Yes," Majid answered.

"Who's Mila?"

Majid pursed her lips. "My name, undercover."

"Officer Majid, then?" Bolan ventured.

"Who are you, McCormack?" Majid countered.

Bolan pulled out his ID wallet, flashing his credentials.

"Your eyes aren't blue," Majid countered again, but that was solved as Bolan took out his contact lenses.

A few blinks, and he was glad to be rid of the disguise. The soldier stood straight, held up the pocket mirror and scanned again, this time over the top of the wood fence.

Goomabong was gone, at least for now. Bolan would still keep his eyes peeled for the big giant.

"How'd you know—?"

"I have good sources." Bolan cut her off. "Let's head to my safehouse."

"I can't. I have to report in," Majid told him. "Onn

and Solyenko…the men I was spying on…they've assembled a small army, and they're awaiting the arrival of someone called the Soldier."

"Well, I've arrived," Bolan stated.

Majid looked over her shoulder, then back at him. "Who are you, and why are they so scared of you?"

"Because they sent an assassination crew after me in South America, and those men failed," Bolan told her. "They're dead now."

"I wish to hell I could understand why they had business in Colombia," Majid said. "Did you really do all that at the docks by yourself?"

Bolan poked out his mirror once more. "The Colombians did a lot of that work themselves trying to get at me."

Majid bit her lower lip. "Your badge says that you are a part of the American Justice Department. The last time I checked, the Justice Department didn't have one man obliterate a small army of thugs."

Bolan shrugged.

"But the man that these two call the Soldier, he's a killing machine. So, what do you want here?" Majid pressed.

Bolan locked his gaze with hers. "A little over a week ago, the man working with Onn, Solyenko, masterminded an assault on the American Embassy, killing two dozen people."

"You're an assassin?" Majid asked.

"It's a little different than that," Bolan told her. "How are those sandals holding up for you?"

Majid looked down. "I've been running pretty well in them."

"So you speak some English, eh?" Bolan asked.

"I've learned enough in my time," Majid responded. "You said you have a place to go?"

"A safehouse," Bolan told her. "Come on."

Once more, he took her hand and they entered the streets, moving toward his headquarters.

CHAPTER FOUR

Zachary Winslow looked up as the door unlocked. He pulled out his SIG Sauer P229, clasping the handle with both hands, aiming at the doorway. When he heard Bolan's voice, he relaxed and lowered the muzzle to the floor.

"Winslow, it's us," Bolan said.

"Us," the Secret Service agent answered. He looked and saw a young Malaysian woman wearing an apron and flip-flops enter beside the tall American. "Another lost soul?"

"Another?" Erra Majid asked.

Bolan smiled. "We picked up a couple of stragglers on our journeys in South America. Don't worry, we left them behind."

"Where did you find her?" Winslow asked. He put the gun back into its holster.

"The club. She was the UC there," Bolan said.

Majid nodded. "My name's Erra Majid. I decided it was time to get out. People were becoming a little too short-tempered."

"They're already expecting us?" Winslow asked. He stood, squinted, and realized that there wasn't much else that the woman wore underneath her apron. "You must have had to get moving in a hurry."

"I was Onn's lap kitten," Majid answered. She sat on the sofa, laid her head back and moaned at the comfort the cushions provided to her. "He sent me for some beer and I ran. Just in time. He looked as if he was going to serve me to the Russian as a buffet. Mostly because they heard *he* was coming."

Winslow didn't have to look in the direction that she'd jerked her thumb. The man he'd come to know as Matt McCormack had proved himself to be a force of nature right in front of Winslow's eyes. He'd been there for not one but two raids on jungle hideouts. And then, in the midst of a Venezuelan support base for the counterfeiters, Bolan had rallied Colombian rebels with enough vigor to lead them to blunt a DGIM military intelligence force attack to cover their involvement in the conspiracy. Against tanks and helicopters, his inspiration and leadership had turned the tide from slaughter to stalemate.

That the Malaysian portion of this operation, having already sent a half dozen trained killers to deal with "the Soldier" and protect billions in counterfeit bills, was frightened of his arrival in Kuala Lumpur was no surprise.

The thing was, Bolan and Winslow had already destroyed the machinery responsible for creating the money as well as several huge shipping containers full of them. What more could be on hand? Sure, Bolan was here to put down the animals who had engaged in wholesale slaughter at the embassy, but other than that, what else?

This was mop-up as far as Winslow could tell. And yet, "McCormack" had spent hours running reconnaissance against an enemy's nightclub. Even now, he was heading to his computer, plugging in his Combat CDA and uploading information the device had recorded.

"What's going on?" Winslow asked him.

Bolan looked up from the linked devices. "I'm trying to figure out why there's still so much security at Onn's club."

Winslow looked at the map of the place and suddenly he could see a series of signal sources laid over the blueprints. He frowned as he looked it over. "Wireless hot spots for video cameras. Motion sensors, as well, according to the legend on your screen. Who developed this software?"

"A friend of mine."

"With all of their heightened security, they must have known that you had a device in there," Winslow observed.

Bolan nodded and then opened his event log on the Combat CDA. He scrolled. "They tried about thirty times to hack into the device. Tried to clone it, but the security software was too good."

"Thirty times," Winslow muttered. "It must have been on a schedule. They'd run through the effort to clone the phones and personal computers in the club. That kind of information would be worthwhile."

"Yeah," Majid said. "They'd found a couple of under-cover operatives with that kind of technology. The only way I was able to spy on them was going in…"

"Almost naked?" Winslow asked.

She nodded, reluctance showing in her features.

Winslow extended a hand to her. "Zachary Winslow."

"Are you part of his organization?" Majid asked.

"No. I'm Secret Service, but I've deputized myself to his team," Winslow responded.

Bolan took closer looks at the signal sources. Even now, the information he'd gathered was uploaded to the Farm.

Winslow watched his face, the screen's glow highlighting his features. Where he'd seemed fairly young before, as his brow furrowed, as he frowned, Winslow could sense a greater age in the man, as if he'd been fighting this war for an eternity before arriving at this little safehouse in Malaysia.

"McCormack?" Winslow asked.

"I'm still thinking. There's something odd here," Bolan said. "I'm hoping that my people can separate these signals a little better."

"Why?" Winslow quizzed.

"There might be more beneath this club," Bolan stated.

"'Beneath the club,'" Majid repeated.

"That ring a bell?" Bolan asked her.

"Well, I was never far from Onn, except when he went downstairs," Majid said. "And he'd go down with Solyenko and Goomabong."

"Goomabong?" Winslow asked.

"Six and a half feet tall. Six feet wide. All muscle," Bolan explained. "He chased us."

"One guy?" Winslow queried.

Bolan nodded.

"Why didn't you take him out?" Winslow asked.

"The last thing I need is to let Goomabong's bosses know that someone good enough to take him down is in the city. If I eliminate him, sure, he's one less threat, but then they start calling in more support. And unlike the Tumaco docks or the Venezuelan forest, there are just too many innocent bystanders around," Bolan explained.

"All right," Winslow replied. "It's just that I've seen you take on tanks."

"At the proper time," Bolan replied.

Winslow nodded, accepting the man's response. If

there was one thing that McCormack wasn't, the agent knew, it was a coward. He'd gone nose to nose with impossible odds. If he decided to avoid a conflict, then he had a good reason. Fear was nothing in this equation.

Bolan stood, looking down on the monitor.

"Whatever is in the basement is putting out a lot of signal for its size," Bolan announced. "But the strange thing is that it is virtually noiseless outside."

Winslow looked confused now. "So what does that mean?"

"It means that there's a tight-beam communications link inside the club itself," Bolan said. "Unless we're literally staring straight at it, it's invisible."

"Communications isn't a major problem, is it?" Majid asked. "Unless…"

"They had links all the way across the Pacific," Bolan added. "The whole plan of counterfeit bills may have only been one small part of a bigger puzzle."

"Because once it was learned that there was counterfeit cash on the market, the nations affected would compensate with more security measures," Winslow said. "We learned that at the end of the cold war when the Soviets made one last push to bankrupt the United States via artificial inflation."

Bolan nodded.

Majid frowned. "So there is a computer network in the basement of Onn's club that can affect the virtual money world. The solid bills, in concert with electronic cash, would combine to make cash stocks plummet."

Bolan tapped his nose with his index finger.

"That is a nightmare waiting to happen," Winslow stated.

"That's why I have to get back in there, but this time,

I'm going to have to go in ready," Bolan said. "This may just be a relay station, but they have more than enough technology and security to hold off a SWAT team."

"I could help out," Majid offered.

"This man *is* a one-man SWAT team, at the very least," Winslow told her.

Bolan looked at Winslow. "But she knows the home ground. I'm not going to drag her in there…"

"Nor me?" Winslow asked.

"You've proved yourself," Bolan said. "Though, you are acting strange, Zak."

Winslow took a deep breath. "I've invested a lot of time into this. I just don't want to be cast aside and ignored."

"You won't," Bolan promised him.

"Thank you."

"Now, let's get to work," Bolan told Majid. "The more time we use here, the more likely they'll double or triple the defenses of the club."

"Work. Now you're speaking my language," Winslow said.

"Good. Check the place for some hydrogen peroxide," Bolan told him.

"Erra, right?" Bolan asked.

The woman nodded.

"I need you to write down the places that no one but Solyenko, Onn and Goomabong were allowed to enter. Also, give me some idea who they've been talking to for the past week or two."

"The most notable ones were the Thais, who Solyenko went to meet personally," Majid answered.

"Goomabong must have been doing the translating. Did they leave the city?" Bolan asked.

"No," Majid answered.

Bolan nodded. "Good. I'll have more questions."

Winslow saw a light behind McCormack's eyes. A plan of penetration was boiling to the surface of his brain. There was magic in the air now. The Secret Service agent was excited, because a master strategist was at work.

SOLYENKO SHOULD HAVE been primed to explode, but there was a cold, deadly calm over the man. Onn couldn't blame him for showing rage, but this quiet unnerved him. There was only a grim glare aimed at the Malay, an unspoken accusation. That glare was also directed toward the massive Thai, Goomabong, and his fury was such that it gave even Goomabong pause, despite the Thai weighing almost a hundred pounds more. Solyenko was Spetsnaz, and in the world of the Russian *mafiya,* that entailed an unholy truth that he was built and optimized for murder.

If he wanted to release that anger on anyone else, there would be few things that could stop him. Onn had made a deal with an atomic bomb, and its timer was ticking down so fast to zero that he had no opportunity to reach a safe distance.

"It's my fault," Solyenko said finally. "I should have dealt with the security risk when I first saw it."

"I let her sucker me, boss." Goomabong spoke up.

"It doesn't really matter. Don't worry about it," Solyenko stated.

Goomabong looked a little confused, tossed a glance toward Onn, then turned back toward the Russian.

"We were lucky that you at least maintained operational security with the little witch around," Solyenko said. "She doesn't know what we're really doing, and that's going to be an ace in the hole."

"Really?" Onn asked.

"I've been straight with you from the start," Solyenko replied.

Onn frowned. "You're not just trying to lure me into a false sense of security, are you?"

Solyenko shook his head. "Listen, blowing my top isn't going to give me any benefit. Yes, I'm upset. I'd need a heart made of stone to not let this anger me. But losing my temper isn't going to solve anything. On the other hand, I'm ready and primed. I've got fuel in the tank for when the Soldier comes after us."

"I hope so," Onn said.

Solyenko managed a smile. "I'll only be upset if she saw anything past my quarantine procedures."

"She didn't," Onn answered.

"Then they won't get to what's important," Solyenko told him. "Sure, the club gets shaken up, but what you and I are betting our money on isn't going to be touched."

"Are you sure?" Onn asked.

Solyenko shook his head. "I don't know. But this much we're certain of. McCormack or the Soldier or whatever he really calls himself is now in Kuala Lumpur."

"McCormack's stone-cold dangerous, if he is who we think he is," Goomabong noted. "Why didn't he just turn on me if he's so deadly?"

Solyenko sized up Goomabong. "People would remember a clash between a giant like you and a skilled murderer like he is. Plus, you were chasing him through throngs of people in the night markets. There's one thing that will stay the Soldier's hand, and that's the presence of innocent bystanders."

"So he avoided a fight because of what might spill over into this neighborhood's crowds?" Goomabong asked.

Solyenko nodded. "The man is a professional. He's precise and disciplined. He doesn't waste energy on unimportant targets, and he probably has the morality to not involve noncombatants in his operations. He might even have been hanging around inside the club last night."

"It's only been eighteen hours since Tumaco," Onn observed.

"That's probably why he felt bold enough to walk through our doors, look around and gather as much intel on the club as he could," Solyenko stated. The Russian frowned. "Nothing showed up on our security, did it?"

Goomabong opened his laptop. Aside from being Solyenko's primary translator while dealing with the Southeast Asian crime gangs, the big Thai was also in charge of security. The big man tapped a few keys.

"We had one device resist repeated attempts to clone its encryption and allow us access," Goomabong said.

"Probably something more powerful than even a smartphone," Solyenko mused. "Run through security footage during the time when those clone attempts failed. Check for someone with a tablet or some other kind of personal computer."

"Makes sense," the Thai answered. Goomabong nodded, feeling more confident now. "I also got a good enough glimpse that I could probably identify the man with Mila."

"We can't go by hair or eye color," Onn said. "There

are all kinds of dyes and contact lenses that can alter that."

"But you can't alter height and build, especially not on a hot summer night," Goomabong countered.

Solyenko smiled. He seemed pleased now, as if the two men were performing up to expectations.

"I'll help you review that footage," Onn said. "Maybe we can get an early warning before he shows up again."

"He won't be coming in soft clothing next time," Solyenko countered. "He'll enter the club, and then he's going to find out what is off-limits. Where we have security at its heaviest."

"I'll call in more people," the Malay said to the Russian.

Solyenko shrugged. "We tried that in Tumaco. Look what happened."

"Then what?" Onn asked.

Solyenko rubbed his chin. "Well, he's obviously working with Mila. The fact that he swooped her up means that he must have either known she was an operative, or at least suspected that there was someone working undercover in our operation."

Onn could see that flash of irritation again, before Solyenko's craggy face smothered the emotion.

"I'm sorry," he told Solyenko.

The Russian smiled. "We all make mistakes. Learn from this and never let it happen again."

Onn stood from his seat behind the desk. This kind of reaction was alien to him, but then, he was more used to dealing with pirates, regular gangsters who saw any affront to their explicit orders as an act of war against them personally. A level of diplomacy was needed not to step on eggshells, not to end up with a bullet in the face.

However, he had to remember that Solyenko, even with being dishonorably discharged from the Spetsnaz, was still a professional, a man who lived a life of discipline and aloofness. The Russian had been discharged for the sole purpose that he'd made one small mistake and was discovered. Since then, Solyenko had been avoiding mistakes, leaving the area before the attention of the law could turn toward him.

That included his more violent, predatory sexual pursuits.

Murder and sex intermingled might have been his release, but he kept even that under control.

Solyenko's current mood was one of concern; his mind was alert, not casting wildly around for blame in actions that had already occurred. He wouldn't be a threat to the Malay, at least for now. Once the menace of the Soldier was gone, however, there was an excellent chance that he'd end up in a gutter, at least if Onn didn't do something to redeem himself in the eyes of the ruthless Russian.

A shared glance with Goomabong told the Malay that the titanic Thai was going to be on board with that kind of appeasement, as well. Both of them were going to be on their best behavior, which was something that Solyenko was perhaps counting on. Fear of failure, knowing that the ultimate sentence was a brutal, slow death, would keep Onn and Goomabong in line for the immediate future. The Malay, however, didn't want to bet his life on unconditional mercy. He had to watch his ass, and as he was doing that, there was going to be no room for him to get creative and try to put down the Russian.

One wrong step, even with the muzzle of his pistol pressed to the back of Solyenko's skull, and Onn was dead.

If he went after the Russian, he'd be killed before he could get a shot off.

If he failed the Russian, He'd be executed and disposed of like trash.

If he tried to run, bail on this whole disaster, he'd be hunted to the far corners of the Earth and slaughtered.

All he could do was behave, and hope that once Solyenko was done with him, he'd have forgotten such a minor affront, or the end of Onn's life would come in one swift instant.

ERRA MAJID LOOKED like an entirely new person with the peroxide lightening her hair to an ash-blond, the length of her tresses trimmed to only a few inches, and large-framed glasses on her face. Bolan had given Winslow and the woman some cash, and the two of them had picked up clothing that would replace the cargo shorts that had been cinched to half their normal waistband and a T-shirt that hung too long on her, requiring the administration of scissors to keep it from being a dress on her tiny frame.

Winslow had been operating out of a duffel bag full of BDU pants and T-shirts, as well as combat boots that still had mud from Venezuela caked into their treads. The two of them bought clothing; Majid providing some fashion criticism for him, Winslow confirming that the smaller Royal Malaysian Police officer could wear anything and look fine in it. He started to have some doubts as to whether people would believe him as being her man, but Majid pointed out that Winslow was not only ruggedly good-looking, but that once he was dressed in the right clothes, he'd look like someone who could afford a dozen women to escort him.

Winslow didn't know about the role of pimp, but a purple silk shirt and a white sport jacket with blue pinstriping helped him stand out. Matching cream-colored slacks and finely cured crocodile-skin moccasins, no socks, completed a look that vaguely reminded the American Secret Service agent of one of his favorite television crime dramas from his youth. Winslow was tempted to ask if McCormack had a shiny, stainless-steel .45 in his arsenal, but Winslow and Majid were simply to go to the club as a distraction.

Security, now that Majid had run for the hills, was going to be tighter. Carrying a gun into the club would be akin to painting a target on his back and shouting ethnic slurs at the top of his lungs. No, Winslow was armed; he'd taped a couple of razors under his waistband at the small of his back, and had a pocketknife that he could open with the swipe of a thumb.

Slim edge, pardon the pun, Winslow thought at the weight in his pocket. At least he'd be the nicest dressed corpse in Malaysia if things went wrong.

"Nervous?" Majid asked, but it was an unnecessary question. Little tics of nerves were apparent. He couldn't keep his energy under taps. He'd gnawed the skin on the side of one thumb down to the quick. He'd left a trail of cigarettes behind him, smoking like a chimney. His jaw was clenched tightly enough that he'd developed a constant ringing in one ear.

"Nope," Winslow lied.

"Me neither," Majid returned, smiling, at least on the lower half of her face. Her eyes, in contrast to her bright teeth and the upturned corners of her mouth, were intense, constantly moving, constantly sweeping and scanning for danger.

"Good," Winslow answered. "We're calm, cool and collected. Ready for anything the Russian mob and the Malaysian underworld can throw at us."

"We're not supposed to get into a fight," Majid reminded him.

Winslow nodded. "But if one comes to us, we'd better be ready."

Majid held out her hand, and he took it. She was small, her fingers long and slim, and her grasp would have felt delicate had it not been for the strength her life had provided for her. Hidden inside her slender, small frame was a reserve of strength, a toughness bred by the forge of youth in a rough Senoi town skirting a "proper" Malaysian city, and then later the trials of becoming a policewoman in the RMP. Along the way, her young face had picked up a line or two, remnants of scars, betraying that she'd literally run face-first into trouble in the past.

Winslow made a mental note to ask her about all of that when this was over.

Provided they both made it out alive.

Right now, however, they were in front of Nik Onn's nightclub. Winslow reached into his pocket, turned on his smartphone and hoped that Matt McCormack and his people had loaded it with just the right stuff to attract attention, but not end the night in a hail of deadly bullets.

Winslow raised an elbow. Majid hooked her arm through his.

He leaned down, kissed her.

"For luck," she whispered in response.

Winslow nodded, one last thought racing through his mind. *And now, into the lion's den.*

CHAPTER FIVE

As Majid and Winslow entered the club arm in arm, Bolan was in a sewer tunnel just off the club. He walked along, stooped over, following Kuala Lumpur public works' files and blueprints to a spot that would take him within inches of the subterranean entrance of the club. It was dark in the tunnel, save for the glow of his Combat CDA's screen displaying the GPS-enhanced sewer map, and the red cone emitted through the filter over his pocket flashlight. Red light was harder for the human eye to pick up in relation to surrounding darkness, thanks to its shorter wavelength on the electromagnetic spectrum.

This would keep Bolan from betraying his presence to anyone on the street above should he pass by any grating or cracks in the road. Fortunately, even out here, in the darker, seedier part of Kuala Lumpur, the sewers were kept in good working order, especially since it was in proximity to several nightclubs, each of them filled with criminals who were willing to spend their ill-gotten gains in a place that had a working toilet and clean water. Bolan could also see state-of-the-art trunk lines for power and phone usage.

Bolan ran his Combat CDA along the data cable, electronics built into the pocket device picking up some good signals, some of them even operating on similar channels to the one that had led him into the bowels of the city. He returned the device to its map function, and he continued along, feeling the data line with his finger-tips, displaying no surprise when it turned into the wall where he intended to go.

The soldier took out one of his knives, a search-and-rescue design that was only nominally a knife because it had a steel shank protruding from a tang wrapped in micarta scales, and it had some cutting function. The point of this blade was a broad, flat chisel, sharp enough to cause mortal injury in a human, but strong and rein-forced enough that it could be driven into the mortar be-tween bricks or between a door and its jamb. The entire length of the "knife" could then be used as a crowbar, uprooting bricks, snapping dead-bolt locks, knocking the pins from hinges.

Bolan stabbed a crease between two cinder blocks, the mortar between crumbling under the force of his thrust. It took a couple of strokes before he got the chisel point between the tightly packed blocks. With all of his strength, the brace of his boot against one block and the added leverage of a long, slender steel pipe fitted over the search-and-rescue blade's handle, the block cracked, then edged out of the wall. A second thrust went in be-tween the next block. More leverage, more of Bolan's long, lean, powerful muscles and the unyielding spine of the thick pry-bar knife, and a second block was gone.

No light spilled from within the basement, and Bolan leaned into the hole, scanning through the opening with his filtered flashlight. There was a space between the sewer wall and the concrete of the basement itself. Bolan threw himself into his work, maneuvering more of the blocks free from the wall, and now he was in the gap, wide enough possibly for even the gigantic Thai Gooma-bong to stand and walk through comfortably. Bolan followed the pipe containing the telecommunications lines and found the next weak point in the basement.

This time, in the face of a solid slab of concrete, likely reinforced, the soldier wouldn't have bricks to knock out. That was why he'd brought low-velocity detonation cord. The puttylike line would explode with enough force and energy to cut through concrete, provided that it was pressed firmly against the surface, but without the kind of overpressure of a more conventional block of composition plastic explosive. The safe distance from the det cord was minimal, and when it went off, it wouldn't be loud.

The club might feel a rumble, but considering the thumping bass of the music that the patrons danced to, it wouldn't be noticeable. Indeed, it was because of the noise in the club that Bolan would have the opportunity to cut through the basement wall with the det cord.

Bolan swiftly set to work to weave his web, laying lines out so that he could make an entrance wide enough for himself, and deep enough, as well. He had brought enough to cut through two feet of solid, rebar-reinforced concrete, but he had to be correct on the first try. Subsequent booms couldn't be excused by music, and those within the club, concerned with its security, would know that something was amiss.

Bolan backed off his breeching charge, equalized the pressure inside his eardrums, then hit the detonator.

It was a long, extended crack, not the usual throaty boom of a conventional blast, but the sound of rocks tumbling from the wall greeted Bolan's ears, informing him of at least partial success. He returned to the hole and began scooping chunks of concrete to the floor. Exposed nubs of steel poked from the edges of the portal that he'd blown, the det cord's force having sheared through the inch-thick strands of metal webbing designed to hold the weight of buildings or millions of pounds of commuters and vehicles on a bridge. The sharp, cutting energy of the detonation had been applied perfectly, and there was a darkened basement beyond the wall.

Bolan turned off his flashlight, made certain his gear was secure, then slithered through the opening.

Above, the ceiling vibrated with the stomping of dancing feet and raving music, muffled by distance and at least one basement level above. This was a subbasement, where utility pipes had room to sprawl before winding their way up to the club, the rooms, the offices, water, electricity, data and telephone landlines streaming through this tangle of pipes. Bolan navigated the level, having to stoop below the ceiling, which was just a little too low for even the average height of a local Malaysian islander.

The soldier stooped, adapted, overcame. It took little time for him to find an exit to the club in this nest of modern technology. There was no breeze in the sewer tunnels, very little smell, and even if there was a wind, Bolan had staggered his entrances so that nothing would blow straight in. He stuck an attachment onto the Combat CDA, a fiber-optic camera on an arm slender enough to slide under the utility room door. He poked it out beneath the crack, scanning up and down a dimly lit hallway. The corridor was empty, but Bolan couldn't be certain how long his window of solitude would last. He withdrew his Karambit knife, opened the utility door slightly, and slid out into the hall.

The last time Bolan had visited the club he was dressed in jeans and a crisp, white, short-sleeved shirt, his cold blue eyes disguised by contact lenses, their shape masked by a pair of glasses. Now he was a shadowy figure from head to toe, his naked skin smeared with grease paint, hands, face and neck blacked out. His torso and limbs were clad in a formfitting blacksuit. Over the suit, hanging on his shoulders and wrapped around his waist, was a harness bearing two holsters.

This time, the Executioner was ready for conflict. He had his traditional stealth pistol, the custom-machined Beretta 93R. Equipped with a blunt sound suppressor of Mack Bolan's own design, the sleek machine pistol could hammer out its deadly 9 mm Parabellum rounds either one shot at a time or spit out three at more than 1100 rounds per minute cyclic rate. Either way, the Beretta would make only a scant sound, the pop of escaping gases no louder than a polite cough, yet still recognizable as a gunshot to someone close enough.

He had carried the Beretta throughout his War Everlasting, and the reliability of the high-capacity 9 mm pistol had carried him through those battles. It was an extension of his hand, a part of his body, and when one was lost, Bolan acquired a new one, or had one cobbled together, like a firearms Frankenstein. It rode in its usual spot, his shoulder holster, under his left armpit, a few inches from his heart, like some dear friend, in balance with its counterpart, the mighty Israeli-made .44 Magnum Desert Eagle.

Where the Beretta was soft-spoken, yet quick in delivering its message, the .44 Magnum autoloader was loud, brash, sending its message loud and clear, often fresh from the holster, worn low on the hip in a modern equivalent of a classic cowboy quick-draw rig. To call the Magnum "brash" was no indication of the content of its .44-caliber missives. It spoke with authority, and its single word—*stop*—was nearly universally heeded by man, and often by machine. These two handguns cooperated, giving him the fighting power and the range to handle almost any crisis while working with a minimum of space and equipment.

Bolan left the handguns where they were. A gunshot, no matter how good the suppressor technology, was still a gunshot. Right now, he had his Karambit knife in one hand, a pocket mirror in the other, extending the little reflective square out at corners and intersections to avoid stumbling into a guard on duty, checking his six at other times to make sure no one was sneaking up on him.

He took his time exploring the corridors and the rooms leading off them. He kept his Combat CDA in "peek" mode with the flexible-necked, fiber-optic camera peering within. Fortunately, the little head also possessed a night-vision screen with an infrared illuminator so that he could tell what was inside without much difficulty.

So far, he'd found a day room or recreation center, with tables, chairs and at least two large-screen televisions and a shelf full of gaming consoles and systems. It looked like any one of dozens Bolan had seen in operational theaters such as Iran or Afghanistan. Another room was an armory, with rifles stacked in racks, as well as cases for ammunition and other such things. These rifles were the same bullpups that Bolan had observed in the hands of the gunmen who'd stalked the rafters above the dance floor.

Bolan also located three separate barracks rooms. The men inside were asleep, but not all of the beds were being used. Unfortunately, due to the angle of the lens, the distortion of faces against pillows, and the lack of

color in the night-vision camera, there was little way to
tell the nationality of the men in the bunks.

That was all right. Bolan could wait a little for identification of the muscle, though he had his educated
guesses, especially considering Majid's reference to
Solyenko and Goomabong meeting with the Thais, and
the people sent to Tumaco after him.

There was another doorway that led into a spiral stairwell. This was the top, which meant that there was something more below. Bolan frowned. To have dug this deep
in a vital city such as Kuala Lumpur, the crews had to
have torn the nightclub apart, or had started work on it
years ago, meaning that Nik Onn was the Johnny-come-
lately. This quite easily could have been a long-standing,
preexisting cold war installation. Bolan opened the door
into the stairwell, trading the Combat CDA for his red-
filtered light, but only turning it on after he'd shut the
door behind him. He leaned over a rail and saw that there
were four flights below him.

This was definitely cold war vintage. Bolan found one
sign still on the wall: a traditional radiation symbol em-
blazoned in red on a yellow panel background. He didn't
have to read the Sanskrit writing to know the international pictograph for a bomb shelter. He descended and,
sure enough, there were no doors leading off the stairs.
The level that he'd just left had been more recently installed, or rather, updated to accommodate Solyenko's
soldiers. He reached the flight just above the bottom,
then crouched, noting that the door was open. He could
hear the blare of fans, multiple fans, and knew what that
sound meant.

Back at Stony Man Farm, when the main computer
banks had first been installed, Bolan had been amazed

at the amount of support hardware needed for the main
data banks and processors. One set of fans had been set
up specifically to suck up and filter out dust in the air
that would have caused a malfunction in the electronics. Other fans had been installed to cool the processors
and circuits.

The din was enormous in the room, and from his vantage point, he could see that there were two guards present who were wearing headphones, probably to cancel
out the roar of the machinery.

"So much for inert gas-cooled electronics," Bolan
mused. He looked up the stairs, then back down at the
doorway. The guards, in addition to their Steyr AUG
bullpup rifles and hearing protection, were wearing body
armor. They were Asian, but neither Malay nor Thai,
meaning that they had been brought in from some other
country. Bolan remembered past missions to Vietnam.
These guards were lean, determined Vietnamese, and
they were larger, taller, than the average Asian.

Bolan studied the pair from his vantage point, his
mind hard at work trying to figure out exactly what
these two men were. He wondered if there were additional guards down here, as well, and did some quick
math in regard to who and what he had seen in the barracks, and what he knew was security up above in the
club. There were ten men unaccounted for, two of them
obviously the pair standing in the vent room. Eight more
in addition to them?

Most likely.

Maybe even more.

Bolan returned his knife and his other gear to their
slots in his battle harness. The time for absolute stealth
was over. He took out the suppressed Beretta, confident

that the roar of the fans would further muffle the sound of gunshots. The Executioner had spent enough time skulking around the periphery. These conspirators had gone two days without his pressure on them.

"Turn on the phone, Zach," Bolan whispered into his throat mike.

"Affirmative," Winslow replied.

The Executioner waited for a few moments. The smartphone that Winslow had been equipped with was loaded with all manner of powerful viruses targeted at cloning programs and devices. Working at the speed of thought, the custom-assembled, highly focused programs assaulted the defenses of the operation. While it might not have attacked anything of note, it still would raise a ruckus upstairs, getting people more interested in that. He flicked on his Combat CDA again, checking the wireless sensors now, having "stealthed" its profile so as not to be tagged by the data-hijacking software Solyenko and Onn were using.

There was plenty of signal traffic now, and alert messages were flying.

It was time to move. Bolan vaulted the stairway rail and landed in a crouch in front of the doorway to the vent room. One of the guards jerked in response to the sudden movement outside. He was packing an assault rifle, but it was slung. The appearance of the big American, however, spurred him to go for the rifle. That sudden movement caught the attention of the other guard.

Bolan punched the first man with a single tri-burst from the Beretta 93R, the sound-suppressed slugs leaping across the space between him and his target. Midweight Parabellum rounds struck the man in the upper chest, the first two rounds striking body armor. Bolan had allowed recoil to push the muzzle up, the third bullet drilling the guard in the throat. The hollowpoint round struck the guard in his windpipe, crushing it instantly. That would have been more than enough for a slow demise, but the 127-grain round flattened into a jagged-petaled blossom of death that continued to spiral through his neck.

The round finally came to a definitive stop, ramming the guard's neck vertebrae, shoving one hard against the other, compressing the cartilage between the two bones. In the ensuing scissoring of bones, the man's spinal column was snapped, severed. Suffocation was supplanted by instant paralysis, and the man tumbled to the ground, his half-gathered rifle tumbling from dead fingers and clattering on the concrete floor.

The second man knew better than to hang out in the open. As soon as he saw the bullets strike his partner, the sentry leaped out of view from the doorway. That would give him precious moments to get out his rifle, but Bolan decided to press the attack, surging to the doorjamb. He swung around the door, spotting the gunner just as he pulled the butt of his Steyr tight to his hip. The Executioner opened up, putting another burst into the rifleman's face—each 9 mm round within a tight triangle that shattered the guard's facial bones easily before tumbling into the brain behind. The trio of slugs, tearing through central nervous system tissue, killed the man quickly, so fast that he didn't even have the reflexive impulse to trigger the rifle in a death spasm.

Flopping backward to the floor, the Vietnamese thug lay in a quickly spreading pool of crimson.

Bolan took a moment to check the pulse of the man

he'd hit in the throat, then quickly replenished the Beretta's partially spent magazine. Things were going well enough now, but the Executioner had gone through enough operations to realize that things could go completely to hell in the space of moments.

Bolan looked toward the guards' rifles. So far, he'd been lucky, but if he ran into trouble...

He decided to pick up some extra firepower and quickly secured himself one of the rifles and a couple of spare magazines. He then went to work, dragging first one dead guard then the other out of sight of the doorway. There was nothing he'd be able to do about the puddle of blood. He secured the door to the stairwell. There was no window, so no one would be able to tell there was a splatter of gore on the tiles, and if anyone tried the handle, Bolan had set the lock. It would slow him on a fast escape, but at least it would slow anyone trying to swoop in from behind.

There was another doorway leading farther into the building and down. As far as he could see, that way was heading toward more stairs. Bolan would close that door, too, once he passed through. Before he did, he set a small, cigarette-pack-size object on one side of the door and turned the selector to the Proximity setting. He had packed a few of the Selectable Lightweight Attack Munitions with him. He'd considered grenades, but the SLAMs were lighter and handier. They would provide some backup and delay if security came swarming down from above. Bolan had a tiny identification transponder on his person that the SLAM would recognize and allow him to pass, even allowing him to defuse it if necessary.

First, however, he fitted the hearing protectors over

his head, and threw on the shooting glasses he'd taken from one of the Vietnamese sentries. Couple that with the load-bearing vest and he'd pass for at least a momentary blush as one of the guards. Hopefully that one moment of mental processing would give the camouflage expert the instant he needed to get the drop on any foes.

He didn't secure the vest, simply let it drape over his shoulders and down his chest. He wanted to be able to get out quickly, and to be able to access the suppressed Beretta if necessary. He let the Steyr AUG hang off his shoulder on its sling, then took the body posture of a man stepping off duty for a momentary break.

Bolan walked out onto the stairs and took a few steps down. His vantage point gave him a good view of an entire farm of old sixties-style computer banks, classic reel-to-reel machines that were backed up by racks of more modern processors. Even as he scanned the equipment, he also realized that there were well more than a dozen men down there, each of them going over the machinery.

Computer technicians.

He couldn't see if any of those men were armed, but twelve to one odds were still dangerous, even to a man with an assault rifle. Bolan's evaluation was quick, his senses attuned and trained to take in data swiftly, to size up potential dangers in the space of seconds before an enemy could respond to his presence.

However, against fourteen pairs of eyes, Bolan's quickness at observation was against long odds, and one of the men recognized, or rather, failed to recognize the Executioner as one of their own.

And Bolan's understanding of Vietnamese didn't need to be sharp to pick up what the man said.

"Who the hell are you?"

Eyes locked on Bolan, as did a pair of AUG assault rifles.

The two automatic weapons opened up.

CHAPTER SIX

Even as the curious technician recognized Mack Bolan was not one of them, the Executioner was already switching from the layout of the area as to its purpose to scanning his surroundings and evaluating fields of fire and avenues that would provide cover, or at least concealment. In the periphery of his vision, he picked up on the two armed guards with their 5.56 mm Steyr AUG bullpup rifles. Bolan did a quick estimate of his drop to the ground. He had twelve feet from railing to floor, something he could easily do, especially since he knew how to land with minimal chance of injury to himself.

With a solid grip on the rail, he launched himself over the rail, gravity taking hold of him in an instant. The pull of Mother Earth dragged Bolan out of the twin streams of full-auto 5.56 mm rounds, which, even at 3200 feet per second, had been fired just an instant too slow to catch up with the lone warrior. The concrete floor came up to greet Bolan, and he landed on the balls of his feet, flexed his knees and somersaulted forward. The two sentries fired, trying to track his darting form, but their rifle fire was blocked by a reel-to-reel machine's bulk.

Bolan had picked his escape route, and the lightweight rounds might have torn apart Kevlar vests and human tissue, but they were still not much when it came to punching through the bulk of solid-state, old-school electronics. One reel-to-reel cabinet was the equivalent of a full inch of steel armor, minimum. A volley of 5.56 mm bullets could cut clean through a standard sedan one shot at a time.

Potentially, the cabinet could be cut through if the two Vietnamese gunmen emptied whole magazines into the machine. Bolan, however, didn't intend to sit still for that long. He looped the armored vest from over the top of his head, and then lobbed it forward, where his path would have gone if he'd kept going forward.

Sure enough, the two guards compensated. Tracking where he could be going, they opened up on the fluttering bulk of the tossed vest. The 5.56 mm projectiles punched through the "bulletproof" vest they were designed to defeat at out to 500 meters. All the penetration in the world, however, wasn't much use when a person was shooting at the wrong target.

Bolan backtracked, bringing his "borrowed" bullpup rifle to bear. There was no selector switch on the AUG, as it regulated its rate of fire by how the trigger was pulled. A half pull set the rifle off on single-shot. Bolan, however, mashed the trigger back all the way, the 20-inch barrel spitting out bullets at 700 rounds per minute. He had the two Vietnamese targeted, gauging their position by the sounds of their guns, and as he emerged around the corner, they were in the low-power scope atop the weapon.

Despite holding down the trigger for a full-auto salvo, Bolan kept his bursts economical and concise. He whipped the muzzle across the guards, the one man on the left catching four rounds through his upper chest, the 5.56 mm projectiles striking ribs, flipping out of control and spiraling through lung tissue before coming to a violent halt at the back of the sentry's rib cage and shoulder blades. The second sentry took three rounds in a line between his shoulder and face. One round ruined the joint to the point that it would be irreparable. The second bullet sliced through muscle, severing it. Finally the third slug splintered the man's lower jaw before spiraling upward through the roof of his mouth. The man was dead in an instant.

Two armed guards were down, but now the soldier had to wonder just how much fight was in the technicians. He also had gauged that there were at least four more trained gunmen in the area to work security for this mainframe farm. Bolan dumped the partially spent magazine and fed the weapon another one to make certain he wouldn't run out in midfight with those four missing soldiers. Even as he did so, he heard the stomp of feet behind him. Bolan turned and saw a technician armed with an almost comically long screwdriver with a flat point.

It would have been funny, but Bolan had seen the effects of a flat-head in human flesh. The blunt edges and sharp corners intended to make the most contact inside a screw slot meant that it was even more dangerous than a combat knife. It would cause much more tearing damage, especially with about 150 pounds of charging opponent behind it. The Executioner pivoted and brought up the frame of his rifle to deflect the point. He stood into the charge, and having swept the stabbing arm away, Bolan's bulk went chest to chest with his assailant. With one leg back to brace him, the soldier bounced the computer tech off him and back to the floor.

Angry eyes looked up at the soldier, and Bolan knew that there was a level of hatred in that gaze that went beyond simple offense at his intrusion. Bolan was loath to turn the rifle around to shoot an under-armed man, so he took two long strides and brought the steel-reinforced toe of his boot up to the man's jaw. The tech's head shot backward, blood, spittle and teeth flying from the full-force kick. He would be out of the fight for more than a few minutes. If he got up after that impact...

Two more bodies in motion caught the soldier's attention. Bolan spun, bringing up the stock of his rifle. The pair of techs was hoping to blindside the Executioner, but his analytical mind was able to operate independently of his battle-tuned reflexes. The rifle's buttplate met one of the men in the center of his face, bones crunching under the violent collision. The technician tumbled, staggered by the force of the blow, but the other man swung a fist into the soldier's ribs. The blow knocked the wind from Bolan's lungs, and he could see the rubber-coated steel handles of a pair of pliers, the second handle braced over the man's knuckles.

The improvised brass knuckles struck hard, and Bolan staggered backward one step. His side ached, a burning pain that informed him that there was at least a hairline fracture from that punch. Bolan saw the technician go for a second strike, but the soldier sidestepped that swing, lashing out with the heel of his palm. The *shuto* strike glanced over the computer guy's chin and up into his nose. There was an ugly crunch, blood exploding down Bolan's wrist. He formed his fingers into claws and pulled his hand back, raking the man's eyes.

Pain brought the technician's hands to his ravaged face, giving the Executioner a moment to clasp both hands behind the back of the guy's head and yank him face-first into Bolan's rising knee. A second crunch and the tech flopped bonelessly to the floor.

These men, Eastern European by their appearance, had been chosen not only for their skill with the machinery in this basement, but for their tenacity. Small and wiry, they had the close-sheared heads and neck tattoos of soccer hooligans, maybe even part of the quickly growing neo-Nazi scene in Russia. Either way, they were scarcely harmless, as four more men were rushing toward him.

Bolan was about to put aside his qualms about opening fire on them when he caught a flash of movement. He hit the floor just as a rifle cut loose on full-auto. The drop to the floor sent a spear of pain up through the soldier's side, and he released the bullpup rifle. Instinct wouldn't let the soldier stay still. He was under fire. With a kick, he rolled behind the base of another computer cabinet, slivers of concrete kicking up as rifle fire slammed into the ground. Once behind something solid, he brought out the Desert Eagle, thumbing off the slide-mounted safety in one clean movement. At the same time, he came up to one knee.

One of the technicians pursued him around the side of the cabinet. The guy had thought ahead and was holding a fire extinguisher like a club. Bolan fired a .44 Magnum slug, the heavy bullet punching through the attacker's lower jaw and tunneling up into his brain. His scalp burst open like a trap door and the extinguisher toppled from his lifeless hands.

Bolan took the opportunity to kick the canister farther into the open, tracking it with his mighty Magnum pistol. Another shot, and the red extinguisher burst under the sledgehammer effect of the Desert Eagle's round. Ice-cold clouds of CO_2 jetted from the ruptured side of the container, providing the Executioner with concealment and derailing the charge of the computer techs lagging behind their leader. The wispy white smoke vomiting from the side of the extinguisher would buy Bolan some precious moments as he listened keenly, trying to discern the location of the Vietnamese riflemen.

Once the Executioner had a general location for the men, he swept around the cabinet, the front sight of the powerful handgun tracking. As soon as he locked on to a silhouette of a man, Bolan pulled the trigger. Through the chemical fog, he couldn't be certain that he hit his target, but the muzzle-flash of the big pistol would call attention to him. Bolan couldn't afford to stay still, so he put another cabinet between himself and the enemy.

A technician stumbled out of the CO_2 smoke, blinking chilled tears from his eyes. Even as he did so, Bolan grabbed him by the shoulder with one hand, and whipped him face-first into the heavy-duty plastic covering a reel-to-reel panel. The plastic cracked, but the Russian's cheek split, blood spraying across the window. Staggered, the technician was easy pickings for Bolan to put down with a blow from the butt of his Desert Eagle in the crook of the man's neck. Rifle fire slashed between the cabinets, sentries looking for their opponent in the mist.

An Eastern European–accented voice let out a shriek of pain as 5.56 mm tumblers punched into him, one of the gunners mistaking the other man for Bolan. The real Executioner, however, focused on the killer's muzzle-flash, adjusted his aim and slammed two .44 Magnum slugs downrange. The Vietnamese guard shuddered under the twin impacts, then collapsed to the floor in a lifeless heap of cooling flesh. The other rifleman spun, ripping off a burst from his AUG until the weapon clicked empty. Bolan wasn't about to allow his foe to reload, not with the kind of firepower he was packing. Emerging from cover once more, the Executioner fired the Desert Eagle, bullets tearing the face off this guard. The bloody mess was visible now that the CO_2 smoke was clearing. Unfortunately, with the fog dissipating, that meant that others could see Bolan once more. The riflemen were down, but two gunners leaped on Bolan simultaneously. The Executioner held on to the Desert Eagle with a death grip in one hand, but speared a thumb into the eye socket of one of the attackers.

Someone started to utter the Russian phrase for "Son of a bitch!" but was cut off in a squeal as Bolan burst his eyeball with relentless force. One opponent paused in battle; the Executioner was able to turn his attention to the other attacker who was busy wrapping his arms around Bolan's head and neck. With leverage, the soldier knew his neck would be snapped in moments. He pulled the trigger on the Desert Eagle, blasting two huge tunnels through the attacker's abdomen.

Coughed-up blood fountained down over Bolan's neck and chest, but the soldier's head was free. He pushed the gut-shot wrestler off and away, punching a third .44 Magnum slug into him, smashing the man's brain to jelly to end his suffering in this world.

The fourth of the group running toward him made his move, throwing his arms around Bolan's forearm, dragging him off balance. The other, one socket running blood down his cheek, snarled in vengeful fury. Bolan let the weight of the one man pull him toward the floor, pivoting so that he'd drop all of his weight on the man who'd trapped his arm. There was a grunt; an explosion of breath was knocked from the wrestler.

One-Eye lunged in on what he assumed was a helpless Bolan, but the big American braced himself against his fallen foe and brought up his boot, stomping his heel into the Russian's pelvis. Bolan could feel the snap of bone from that brutal kick, even through the sole of his footwear. The man paused, clutching his mashed genitals and losing strength in his legs rapidly. The soldier followed up with a second kick, this one striking him squarely on the chin, turning the man's lower jaw into a guillotine, crushing his windpipe.

The man that Bolan had fallen on was struggling to get free, but the soldier wrenched his arm from the man, twisting violently. He brought his elbow down viciously into the throat of the pinned technician. These men had demonstrated a willingness to go lethal against him, so now wasn't the time to show mercy. Bolan rammed his elbow again on the crushed larynx. The man wasn't going to be getting up soon.

Bolan had his Desert Eagle free, but he'd blown off several rounds. He dumped the spent magazine and fed in a fresh one. He sat up, surging to his feet, and that sudden rise had barely saved him from a Russian who'd snatched up a dead guard's rifle. The dying tech on the floor was snuffed out swiftly by a salvo of high-velocity bullets stitching the floor.

The soldier sidestepped, snap-aimed and fired. The ambitious tech's rifle was no shield against a .44 Magnum precision-placed bullet that cored his skull. The Executioner only peripherally paid attention to the falling corpse, just to make certain he wouldn't spring up again from a merely glancing blow. His attention, however, was cast out like a net, looking for more enemies in these rows of tape drives and processor cores. Someone had finally hit the alarm, which meant that the locked door wasn't going to provide much of a delay.

No one else seemed to be charging at him, but Bolan had to watch his step. Two more gunmen were likely down here, and though the rest of the technicians seemed to have lost the will to attack, Bolan didn't doubt that they would try to put up a fight. So far, he had a few moments.

The soldier worked his way through the machinery, staying low, out of sight and always having the cover of a computer cabinet. He'd managed to recover another of the assault rifles and returned the Desert Eagle to its holster. He also pulled out his Combat CDA and checked the device. This far down, in a radiation-proofed bunker, the device wouldn't likely be able to contact the outside world unless its software could find a signal to piggyback. The software in the compact combat computer searched, performing dozens of checks per second, looking for an outside conduit.

Sure enough, this facility had a line to the outside world, one or more of the cables from the tangle of pipes several levels above providing an outlet. The trunk line also had to have had some wireless potential, because the Combat CDA was serving its purpose. The hackers back at Stony Man Farm were now able to access the mainframe setup.

Above, Bolan heard the thunder of a door being blown off its hinges. It was the cavalry, and from the sounds of things, they were loaded for bear. They weren't coming, however, expecting the half pound of LX-14 high explosives, or the copper explosively formed penetrator cup that it turned into: a searing lance of armor piercing death. The SLAM munitions detonated as gunmen rushed the stairs, and despite Kevlar and trauma plates, they were helpless in the deadly spear of liquid metal that was intended to slash through 40 mm of tank armor at a range of eight meters. At a range of two feet, the two gunmen in the path of the booby trap had their legs sliced off by the superheated copper.

The sudden shock of amputation followed by the over-pressure of a half pound of high explosives granted the two an instantaneous death. Those not touched by the tendril of molten metal, however, were bowled over, ear-drums and sinus cavities ruptured from being in such close quarters to the blast.

The SLAM had brought the enemy to a skidding halt, but Bolan couldn't tell how many of them had fallen. It had evened the odds, however. He didn't have to worry about assault from that front for a minute or so.

What he did have to worry about now was the loca-tion of the two remaining riflemen here in the computer area. Bolan allowed himself to be visible for an instant, and a savvy Vietnamese rifleman spotted him, aimed and triggered his bullpup rifle. Bolan dived for the floor as rounds punched through the air where he'd stood a moment before. He whipped his AUG around and fired a short burst, enough to discourage continued pressure from the gunner.

The Executioner reached new cover and peered around it, scanning for the rifleman who'd taken the opportunity to attack him. What he found was the second of the pair attempting to flank Bolan, padding along the wall, hoping that his friend's distraction would conceal his movement. The two men saw each other, but Bolan was on the draw, pulling the trigger and peppering the Vietnamese guard with a salvo of high-velocity bullets that pinned him to the wall. The dying guard slipped to the ground, blood from through-and-through wounds smearing the concrete behind him.

"Bastard!" the other guard swore, watching his friend die. Even as Bolan translated the curse, he whirled toward the sound of the cry. The Executioner shot the gunner, 5.56 mm tumblers cartwheeling through the flesh and bone of his torso, churning internal organs to a pulpy froth.

Bolan wouldn't have an opportunity to rest on his laurels. The sounds of battle below had emboldened the reinforcements at the top of the steps, and they had made certain that no more mines blocked their path. Gunmen rushed to the stairs, one standing point at the top of the railing to provide cover fire.

The soldier turned on them and punched a single bullet into the face of the overwatch gunner. Blood exploded from where his features had once been, and he bounced off the wall behind him, the corpse slithering down the stairs aided by gravity. The other three hardmen on the stairs paused and swung toward the muzzle-flash of Bolan's rifle.

Back behind cover, the Executioner listened to bullets slam into the computer cabinets. He couldn't help but wonder what the impact would be on the processing that these machines were performing. At least two of the reel-to-reels were smoldering, giving off smoke from where the electronics had been wrecked by incoming fire.

The trio on the stairs was firing in disciplined bursts, each providing cover for the other to pause and reload.

The Executioner detected movement and cursed himself for being distracted from one front as the other technicians gathered up their courage to make one more run at him. Five men were in motion, two of them going for the dropped rifles, the other three charging straight at the soldier in an effort to overwhelm him and buy their allies some time. The Executioner spotted knives and clubs in their hands, so these three survivors weren't going to be easy to handle in hand-to-hand.

Bolan fired off a short burst into the leader of the group, the salvo of rounds smashing him in the chest and plowing him backward. The other two men darted aside, avoiding the falling form. They were now coming at him from two separate angles. Bolan didn't worry about that as he charged the man attacking him from the right, reversing the rifle and bringing its stock to meet the club-wielding attacker's face. Bones cracked from the strike, and Bolan threw his entire weight behind the impact, knocking his adversary off his feet. The other tried to nail the Executioner, but the tip of his knife flicked only empty air, Bolan's change of direction and position taking him outside the blade man's reach.

One of the Russians had the fallen guard's AUG in his hands, and Bolan pivoted his rifle around, shooting him with a 6-round burst. Bullets punched into the newly armed gunman, removing him from the fight before he even had a chance to pull the trigger. Bolan swung around, continuing to back away from the killer with the knife, firing from the hip and filling that Russian's stomach full of 5.56 mm NATO lead.

Blade Man folded over, his guts shredded, his spine crushed by a lone slug, and he collapsed into a dying mess on the ground. The shooters on the stairs spotted the Executioner's movement, and now there were two more among their ranks.

A rain of gunfire sizzled around Bolan as he rushed

to cover, dumping the empty mag on his bullpup rifle. He reached for another, but he'd either used them all up or they had come dislodged from where he'd simply stuffed them into his belt.

The whys of the magazines' disappearance were unimportant. No ammunition meant that the AUG was now a liability, and he let it go, his left hand snaking around into the shoulder holster for the Beretta machine pistol. Bolan drew the 93R and snap-aimed, selector switch thumbed to 3-round-burst mode, the highest gunman on the stairs. Parabellum rounds zipped through the sound-suppressed weapon and caught the enemy gunman in the chest and side of his head. The 9 mm rounds that struck body armor were wasted shots, but the third round of the burst glanced along the back of the man's neck, violently ricocheting off neck bones, through the skin and into the wall. It might not have been a fatal injury, but that last bullet folded the man away like fresh laundry, collapsing him onto one of his fellows.

The guard at the bottom of the steps vaulted the rail to get out of the way of the human avalanche, but in doing so, he presented more of his body as a target. Bolan's next burst slammed into the inside of his left thigh, tearing through muscle, one bullet stopped cold in the heavy structure of the femur. There was no high-pressure arterial spray, so this gunman had been lucky enough to avoid having his femoral artery severed, but a 9 mm slug in bone was still enough to flop him on the ground when he landed from his vault. The broken thigh bone knifed agony through the gunman, causing him to collapse and discard his rifle, clutching his ruined leg.

The second man on the steps shoved hard, getting out from beneath his stunned comrade, but even as he did so, Bolan withdrew the Desert Eagle again. He was fighting against thugs in body armor, and the Beretta had been loaded for stealth, not Kevlar and trauma plates. Bolan fired, punching a .44 Magnum slug into the center mass of the sentry. Shock and dismay showed on the man's face as the heavyweight, pointed-tip bullet sliced through ballistic armor, shattered his breastbone and sliced his aorta before lodging in vertebrae.

The man was dead on his feet, coughing up blood, even as he swooned and raked the ceiling with half a magazine of 5.56 mm bullets from his rifle.

"Fire in the hole!" Bolan heard someone shout in Vietnamese.

The enemy was turning to hand grenades now, and the Executioner grimaced at this development.

A canister cartwheeled through the air toward the soldier, packed with more than enough high explosives to flatten him.

CHAPTER SEVEN

Zachary Winslow didn't know what was going on, but McCormack had to have been busy on the lower level as security went from casual observation to full alert. He pulled out his phone and took a look at the screen. Things appeared to be going crazy. The viruses installed on the device had infected whatever technology was hijacking cell phone and personal computer memory cards, exactly as Bolan had wanted it to.

Winslow felt good enough with his contribution, but there was still the concern on Erra Majid's face. She was looking at the young women dancing in the cages, their half-zombified gyrations having transformed into nervous sidestepping.

"What's wrong?" Winslow asked her.

"The guards are taking to the floor now, pushing people out of the club," Majid noted. "They're even kicking men out of the champagne rooms."

"That's not good, is it?" Winslow asked.

"This place is locking down," Majid told him.

Winslow grimaced. He glanced upward through the lights, spotting one of the riflemen walking the rafters, studying the flow of people around him. The crowd grumbled, griped, gave a hint of resistance, but complied. Titties, blow and booze were important to many of these men, but it wasn't worth a gunshot wound. The women here were of the same opinion.

"Move!" A voice broke into Winslow's musings. The undercover Secret Service agent turned, looking at the thug who'd interrupted his thoughts. He was a squat, swarthy man, and he held a 5-shot revolver, which in relation to his hand looked like a full-size service pistol.

"I just got here," Winslow complained.

The muzzle jammed into his ribs. "Move now! Club closed!"

Majid's big brown eyes locked on Winslow's. She was worried for her friends. Winslow's jaw set and locked, but he turned away from the man. "All right. All…"

With a sudden surge, Winslow spun and brought his elbow up into the man's throat, pushing his body close and past the gun in his hand. The move was quick, deadly, efficient—something that Winslow discovered he was becoming despite his role as a law-enforcement agent for Homeland Security. A week and a half ago he wouldn't have thought about going on an operation without a rifle, body armor, a helmet and a team of other guys similarly equipped. Since then, he'd battled Colombian rebels in the jungle, assaulted a Venezuelan military installation and engaged a thug in close-quarters combat in a criminal-run club in Malaysia.

Even as his elbow sent the club security guard into a state of stunned paralysis, Erra Majid, undercover cop for the Royal Malaysian Police, lunged and seized the pistol in the man's hand.

Good. Now at least she was armed. They were still in the thick of things enough that Winslow could hope that no one in the rafters could see them. Bodies were all around them, and Majid quickly tucked the compact revolver under her half jacket, her breasts producing enough of a swell that no one would see the butt of it poking from her high-waisted, hip-hugging skirt, or beneath the body of the outer garment.

Winslow looked at the young woman's figure, noting that the drape of the jacket barely concealed the grip of the revolver.

"You'll need something soon," Majid said.

"Yong!" a voice called down from the rafters. Majid's features tightened.

"He's looking for the guy we just put down," Majid quickly translated. The two of them had joined the flow of people walking toward the exits. "Why did we drop him?"

"I didn't like being pushed around," Winslow admitted. He didn't have the brain to think of anything else. Pure honesty was his one recourse. He plucked his folding knife from his pocket. "Things are getting weird."

"McCormack's obviously tripped an alarm. Either that, or the infected phone in your pocket," Majid commented.

Winslow pursed his lips. "If that's the case, what do you think we should do?"

"Two options. We sneak out and go squirreling into the sewers, no guns...except this little thing," Majid offered.

"We could hit up McCormack's car. He might have brought something extra," Winslow added.

Majid nodded. "We could stay here, in the club, and maybe get some of these kids to safety."

Winslow frowned.

"You said that McCormack was a force of nature back at Tumaco," Majid added.

Winslow nodded at that statement.

"These girls aren't," Majid said.

Winslow's mouth turned into a flat, bloodless line. "Five bullets in that thing."

Majid swallowed. "I'm not SWAT trained."

"I've done a couple of raids. We're not dressed for that kind of thing now…"

He held out his hand.

"What?" Majid asked.

"The revolver," Winslow requested.

She withdrew it, keeping it low profile, and pressed it into his hand. Then Winslow turned, pushing against the tide of people. Majid stuck with him. They were going back to where they'd left Yong and the man in the rafters calling for him. Majid knew it was a foolish idea, a bold, insane plot that might as well be akin to dancing in front of a firing squad and taunting the riflemen. But it might work. It might get them something more.

Majid was concerned for the women who were on the stage, secluded in cages suspended above booth tables. She'd spent six months among them. She'd made friends with a couple, seen many more suffer, a few actually die due to malicious treatment. She had made up her mind to do something for their sake. Back when they were planning this, even as her hair was bleached from black to a copper-tinted blond, she'd made inquiries about breaking the enslaved, prostituted dancers free from Onn's chains.

McCormack had looked at her, said he'd see what he could do, but he couldn't make promises. He couldn't split himself in two—fight the gun thugs in the club *and* penetrate the top-secret computer center buried far beneath the club at the same time. To attempt one would endanger efforts at the other, and the computers of the conspiracy threatened the global economy, if his suppositions were correct.

She'd seen the pain of that decision in his face.

Winslow had, too.

Bolan hadn't had to turn Winslow and Majid into well-dressed club-goers. He could have brought the phone, turned it on and injected viruses into the system while he'd entered the basement. He could have left the two cops alone.

The Executioner couldn't split himself in two, but that didn't mean that he couldn't have a special weapons-trained Fed accompany an undercover RMP police-woman into the den of ill repute, just in case there was an opportunity to act.

"This is suicide," Winslow muttered as he stepped under the catwalk. The lights above had been killed, more conventional lamps brightening the normally dimmed club, allowing people to see where they were going so as to evacuate the building. With those lamps on, Winslow could see the rifleman on the catwalk above. He slowed and looked at Majid.

"Call out that you see Yong right now," he told her.

Majid spoke up, her voice ringing loud and clear over the noises of the thinning crowd.

The rifleman heard her. He leaned out over the railing, peering down into the crowd. Winslow was right beneath him. He pulled the revolver, a little Smith & Wesson Airweight Chiefs Special. He cycled the trigger, smooth and without a hitch. The hammer dropped on a live primer, and the gun kicked, barking, exploding a .38-caliber slug right up and into the face of the distracted rifleman.

The crack of the revolver threw the club into stunned silence. Club-goers froze. Security men looked toward the gunshot. Gravity tugged the dead rifleman off the catwalk, pulling him to the dance floor with a crash, Winslow only barely stepping out of the way of the tumbling body. The impact of the corpse reinforced the signal that Winslow's borrowed revolver had put out. Something was very wrong here.

Security on the floor might have had a chance to react, but a sudden wave of screams and scrambling bodies surged against them, a tidal force that swept them away from Winslow and Majid. He lobbed the revolver to her and then bent to pick up the dead man's rifle. It was one of those olive-green weapons that he'd seen in half a dozen movies—an exotic weapon with the pistol grip in front of the magazine. As far as he could tell, there was no safety or selector switch on the rifle.

The only thing Winslow could hope for was that it was primed to fire. He shouldered the weapon, glad for the low-power optic mounted on top of the receiver. He could see another rifleman looking down at his comrades being jostled by the panicked crowd. The guard turned back toward Winslow and Majid and saw the rifle in the Secret Service agent's hands.

Winslow saw the crosshairs of the rifle focused on him.

The rifle bucked against Winslow's shoulder as he pulled the trigger hard. He'd cut loose on full-auto, and if he hadn't had both hands on the weapon, leaned his weight into the stock, the Steyr would have jumped all over the place. As it was, he'd ripped the sentry in the rafters to shreds with a 10-round burst. With the blast of automatic rifle fire, the screams rose to shrieks. Panic was now a wild animal, the crowd surrendering itself into a stampede. Somewhere in that chaos were the security personnel, trying to fight their way past the throng.

One of them got tired of wrestling, pushing, and he opened up with his .38, blasting into the air three times. People dived to the floor in a wild panic. Now gunfire was coming from everywhere, and the civilians in the club weren't used to such wild, crazy violence.

The security man had cleared the area around him, but also isolated himself from the bodies shielding him from reprisal. Majid rushed closer to him, the Airweight Chiefs pistol locked in her fist. Once she was within arm's reach of him, she punched out, jabbing him in the sternum with the muzzle of the borrowed revolver, firing twice. The snubby's report was swallowed by the yielding stomach muscles of the security guard.

The extra-superheated gunpowder and the accompanying force along its acceleration added to the dreadful devastation of two 158-grain soft-nosed slugs tearing through the guard's sheet of diaphragm muscle. Suddenly with no more ability to inhale or exhale, the Malaysian muscleman toppled backward, forgetting his pistol and seizing his unresponsive chest.

He gaped like a fish out of water. He was doomed, dying, but Majid ignored him, grabbing up his fallen weapon.

Winslow briefly wondered at the coldness of her reaction to the doomed guard, but then, she'd been a dancer here. She'd been at the mercy of these slimy thugs, and there was definitely a sense of familiar malice about her as she sneered at the fallen, suffocating man. Whatever her reasons for not showing mercy, it had come from the guard's own cruelty, and he had been paid, in small measure, before his death.

"Erra!" Winslow shouted. The woman turned toward

him, and he motioned toward the fallen body of the second rifleman. "Something bigger! With more ammo!"

Majid slowly retreated from the front of the crowd, then spun and grabbed up the rifle, dropping the partially spent revolvers. She frisked the dead man for more ammunition, plucking two spare magazines from the inside pocket of his suit jacket. One of these was jammed into her skirt's waistband, and she grimaced at the uncomfortable fit.

"McCormack!" Winslow called over his throat mike. "McCormack!"

Nothing. Static. Wherever the big man was, he was behind plenty of concrete, maybe even lead shielding. There would be limited channels out, most likely through a hard line. Communications through that were going to be out of the question.

More club security appeared, and this time the gunners were packing more than revolvers, but thankfully not rifles. Winslow took a more measured approach to the trigger this time and capped off one round into the leader, who carried a machine pistol in his hand. The 5.56 mm bullet struck the gunman in the chest and cored through him. Even on semiauto, the full-length barrel of the AUG provided the rounds with more than sufficient power to bring down a target with a single shot.

Majid entered the fray with her rifle, punching two slugs into another guard before he could react to the death of the first man. That double-tap flattened the guy, throwing him into a gunner rushing up on his heels. This was a case where tailgating proved fatal, because while the impact of a lifeless body didn't bowl the new guard over, it stood him still for a moment, long enough for Winslow to punch a 5.56 mm round through the side of his skull, ejecting the contents of his brain pan onto the wall next to him.

The nightclub had become a full-fledged war zone. Those not already in full flight accelerated to a full run now. Handguns cracked among that crowd, and Winslow felt a sudden surge of regret, but so far, he couldn't see any of the fleeing club-goers fall over, injured. Most of the bullets seemed to be searing into the ceiling, not human flesh.

"Erra, get those cages open!" Winslow snapped.

She glared at him for a moment, ire rising from being ordered around in such a harsh tone, but she realized that someone had to free the dancers.

Majid moved to the first cage and looked for a latch. She grimaced as she realized that she'd need a set of keys. Rather than fuss with that, she stood back, kept the muzzle pointed away from the imprisoned woman, and pulled the trigger. The lock mechanism on the cage door blew apart as the bullet deflected off it. At nearly three times the speed of sound, the bullet disintegrated on contact with the hard steel so that only lead dust and jacket splinters filled the air.

Winslow heard her talk to the dancer within, the black-haired young woman nodding at the newcomer with bleached hair. There was a brief flash of recognition, and then the dancer was off, searching the fallen men's pockets for keys.

Winslow pushed toward the back offices, AUG shouldered and searching for targets. He had both eyes open, one unobstructed by the low-powered crosshairs, allowing himself full peripheral vision, the other using those crosshairs as a gauge for where the rifle was pointed. This was one thing he'd learned while training for SWAT operations for Homeland Security—one eye shut meant that you could be blindsided and killed. The scope was a tool, not your only view of the world. Using it and it alone was the very definition of tunnel vision.

His eyes-open approach allowed him to spot movement—two thugs with more rifles like his. They came out of an office, scowls on their faces. There was a situation in the club, and the white man and the woman with the bleached hair had to have been a part of it.

With one smooth swivel, Winslow shot the first of the two men, pulling the trigger three times and chopping the guy's heart and lungs to pieces. The other gunman threw himself against the wall and fired his own gun, but in his panic, he hadn't aimed. Winslow winced, flinched, but didn't pull the trigger until he had the AUG stabilized and gripped tightly in both hands.

In the close quarters of the hallway, the thunder of the rifle fire was a solid impact, smacking him in the face, slapping his ears. He remembered why he liked goggles, a helmet, hearing protection while shooting these powerful weapons indoors. Even so, he had spent a lot of time with these unmuffled guns of late. This wasn't as abusive as it had been at first. Certainly, he was likely going to have hearing loss later in life, but for now, he was alive, and the second of the gunmen was dead, spilled onto the floor.

Behind him, on the dance floor, the bark of Majid's rifle resounded. He paused, backtracked, keeping one eye down the hall, the other glancing toward the RMP lady cop. She had flipped over a table. Bodies littered the tiers above, and from the looks of things, the frightened, trampling crowd had done most of the damage, not the gunfire of the two lawmen.

Even so, Winslow didn't want to be the accidental cause of a bystander's death any more than he wanted an errant bullet to kill someone. He spotted a head pop out around the corner and sidestepped back onto the club's floor just an instant before a storm of submachine gun bullets ripped through the air he'd occupied only moments before. Winslow popped back and fired, holding down the trigger and spraying the wall in front of the gunman. There was the clatter of something crashing to the floor, and he saw an arm flopped out through the doorway, subgun fallen just out of reach of lifeless fingers.

No gunfire chased him. At least not yet.

"Erra?" Winslow called out.

"I'm fine!" Majid answered.

Winslow nodded.

"Be careful," she added before he stepped into the hallway.

He didn't answer. So far, things had been going relatively smoothly for them, but he also realized that he was on a roll that could come to a violent stop at any moment. One misstep, and he was dead. Winslow had been operating on one mental and physical level so far, so any change might jinx him, or change his momentum, trip him up.

Even as he moved along the corridor, his eyes wideopen, scanning for any and every movement, he thought about how he'd suddenly just altered his own pace. He was about to pick up his pace once more when gunfire lanced past his shoulder. He whirled and saw Majid in the hall behind him, kneeling now and continuing to fire. He glanced back and saw that the doorway he'd hammered, the one where a dead arm lay in a pool of coagulating blood, had a new corpse in it, slumped over.

"Told you to be careful," Majid said, catching up to him.

"Yeah, and that threw me off," Winslow returned. He bent and scooped up one of the fallen machine pistols. He dumped out the partially empty magazine and felt around for a spare on the dead man who'd dropped it. Majid took the other one. She let the rifle hang on its sling. She looked more comfortable with a Heckler & Koch MP5 than she did with the rifle. That made sense, according to what Winslow had read on the flight to Malaysia. The MP5 was actually local issue.

"Through there is where Onn has his shop," Majid told him.

Winslow nodded. He pushed a fresh magazine into the butt of the AUG. He thought about running the rifle through the door, but he had to admit, he'd have liked full-auto even better. He fought the instinct to go hog-wild with the MP5 and stayed with the rifle.

The two of them staged on either side of the door. Majid looked so small, almost comical in comparison to the firepower she was handling. Winslow wondered how ridiculous he looked.

"Kick it. I'll go low, you go high?" Majid asked.

Winslow gave her a thumbs-up. It was a good plan. He brought up his foot, then stomped on the door hard. Whatever the door was made of was good and strong. He felt something pop inside his ankle, heat flowing from the joint up his shin. He let his foot drop to the floor, and found that putting his weight on it was like standing on a dead tree stump. There wasn't any feeling in it.

"Damn," he murmured.

Majid grimaced. "Sorry."

Winslow nodded to her. "Shoot the lock off."

Majid pressed the muzzle close to, but not on the doorknob's plate. With a stroke of the trigger, the machine pistol roared, burping out a salvo of bullets, fragments peppering Winslow's face, even though he raised a hand to shield himself.

"Nothing," Majid grumbled.

Winslow looked up and saw shadows in the doorway at the other end of the hall. "We've got company coming, and nowhere to run."

Majid snarled. "Then we fight."

The pair brought up their guns to greet the oncoming hardmen.

CHAPTER EIGHT

The Executioner caught a glimpse of the grenade arcing through the air, and he was in motion, letting out a bellow in anticipation of it landing. He'd recognized the design of the grenade thanks to its canister shape. Onn and Solyenko's security was determined to expel him from the computer room, but they weren't so dead set on it that they were willing to smash millions of dollars in equipment to do it.

The stun grenade landed, and thanks to the bellow, Bolan had equalized the pressure inside and outside his head, sparing him the worst of the concussive blast. No shrapnel was behind it, nothing that would damage a server tower or a tape drive machine. Even so, Bolan's ears were left ringing in the wake of this blast, and dust and smoke shot around the room like windblown snow. He had to blink rapidly to clear the grit from his eyes, and even as he did so, he noticed that the enemy was scrambling down the steps on the side of the room. Two men lunged at Bolan from his right.

Bolan met the first of the pair with a raised foot speared toward the Russian tech's chin with all of his weight behind it. Jawbone shattered, bursting under the combined force of momentum and the Executioner's sidekick. Whatever was left of the jaw provided enough of a solid surface to keep his head from advancing while his body kept charging. Neck bones stretched out, spinal cord popped, and the kick did everything to decapitate the would-be killer but sever the tendons, ligaments and muscle connecting the skull to the rest of his body.

The guillotine force of the kick didn't dislodge Bolan, who used the head to kick off and pivot, bringing the muzzle of his Desert Eagle up and into the sternum of the second attacker. As soon as muzzle touched torso, the Magnum pistol roared, blowing a massive, gory cavern through the Russian. He collapsed to his knees, long-bladed knife clattering from lifeless fingers.

Bolan had given away his position, but in the space of a few moments, he'd taken care of the immediate threat. He spotted one of Solyenko's hired thugs out of the corner of his eye and dodged back behind a server cabinet, bullets pinging off the metal shell. The guards coming after him were much more professional and focused than the technicians who were scrambling after him. As such, while one was shooting, keeping Bolan pinned, he noticed that others were in motion.

Bolan turned and brought his Desert Eagle around to meet one of the gunmen as he tried to flank the Executioner. The soldier fired, killing the Vietnamese sentry with a bullet to the face, smashing his features with an impact that put a sledgehammer to shame. Bolan rushed and brought his knees up, hurling himself into the still-standing corpse and riding the body backward to the floor. Ribs snapped under the soldier's landing, but his brief ride had forced another guard to hold his fire, recognizing the form of his ally.

On the floor, Bolan somersaulted forward, rolling himself into that gunman's knees and bowling him over. The Vietnamese thug slammed against a cabinet and bounced, spinning away from his impact against computer equipment. Bolan pushed to his feet behind the dazed guard, grabbing the neck of his armored vest and steering him out into the open. A rifle sputtered a short burst and Bolan's living shield shuddered under the salvo of rounds. There was a pained groan, and his feet were still moving of their own accord, the body armor having protected him from the short blast of autofire. Even so, Bolan aimed him at the shooter and launched him forward with a kick.

The Desert Eagle rose again, blazing away. Bolan hit the staggered Vietnamese hardman in the back of the neck, punching a fist-size chunk of spine out through his throat. Bolan's second shot snapped into the guy who'd accidentally hit the armored guard, a tungsten-cored, armor-piercing slug striking the V where his clavicle met in the center.

Two more corpses littered the floor, and the Executioner turned his attention toward footfalls that worked their way through the fading ringing in his ears. Bolan wove between two cabinets, reloading the Desert Eagle as he did so. He tucked it back into its holster and brought out the Beretta 93R, flipping down the folding forward grip. Time to face full-auto with burst-fire. If anything, the compact Beretta would maneuver just a shade more quickly than the enemies' rifles. He swung around and spotted another of the security guards trying to tail Bolan's current route.

The Executioner hammered out a trio of Parabellum rounds, stitching them across the man's left thigh. The 9 mm slugs knocked the footing out from beneath his target, and the gunner bounced his head off one cabinet before trying to catch himself. Nothing worked to stop his wipeout, and he performed a perfect face-plant on the cold stone floor.

Bolan lunged closer to him, kicking the man in the back of the head hard enough to shoot his helmet right off. The soldier spared a moment to destroy his brain with a contact-range pull of the trigger, then grabbed at the corpse's rifle.

He looked through the translucent plastic magazine in the Steyr, and, satisfied that he had at least half a full payload, cut back on his trail. Even as the Executioner disappeared in the maze of machinery, he heard the bark of rifles chasing him, bullets whining and clanging off metal.

There was no telling right now how many of the enemy remained alive, but he at least was going to face them again with equal firepower. Bolan snatched a full magazine as he passed one of the corpses, securing it in his pocket.

He felt as if he'd been in this basement for weeks, and he was no closer to figuring out the task for which all this hardware had been purposed. Luckily, right now, he had Stony Man Farm and his Combat CDA working on that mystery. All he had to do, right now, was survive, but the men down here were doing their best to harry him. A spray of lead punctuated that warning to himself, and he grimaced at being caught napping. Luckily, he threw himself to the ground as a follow-up burst chased him. The Steyr, being low-profile, was easy to shoot from down low, and he blew out the kneecaps of the enemy guard who'd tried to cut him in two.

Legs destroyed, the man dropped to the floor, floundering between retaining his weapon and seeing to his shattered limbs. That was all the opportunity that Bolan needed to end the man's suffering, shooting him through the top of his head, crushing his brains instantly with the extreme hydrostatic shock of a supersonic bullet. With a deft roll and a kick, Bolan was back on his feet. Even as he rose, however, another Vietnamese came around a cabinet, the two men colliding hard. Bolan didn't have the speed and momentum, the guard didn't have Bolan's mass and strength, so the collision staggered both men, rocking them a step back from each other. Bolan reached out and snagged the guard's collar with one hand.

The Vietnamese hardman felt Bolan's fingers close around his vest top, and reacted instantly, throwing his weight backward, snaring the big American's extended wrist with a free hand. The Executioner staggered off balance, but was still nimble enough to turn, twisting so his shoulder, not his head, roughly struck the corner of a server tower. It was a sharp, piercing pain, but it was absorbed by taut muscle, not thin scalp and skull. What would have stunned Bolan turned into an inconvenience as he kicked forward into his nimble opponent.

Bolan tackled his foe, pushing him back harder, driving him up against a tape-to-tape reel cabinet with more than sufficient force to upend the piece of equipment. At the same time, he let go of his enemy, the guard's grip gone, as well, after being sandwiched between the bulk of the Executioner and the near immovable object behind him. Man and machine crashed to the ground with a clatter of metal and a grunt of agony. Bolan backed away from the fallen pair, his retreat coming just in time to keep him ahead of a sputtering stream of automatic fire seeking his flesh.

The guard on the cabinet was still stunned, but incoming fire was keeping the soldier from sticking around long enough to take out the guy. However, he did hear only one source of gunfire.

Bolan scrambled, heading back toward the office area where the rough-and-ready technicians had been holed up. Those men had been whittled down greatly, and now that the soldier had showed them the fatal error of their assumption that they outnumbered and could outfight him, they were staying well out of sight.

The security team had backed off, as well. The gunners didn't want to get into a game of cat and mouse, especially with a man who had proved himself a tiger among rodents. Bolan had left them at an impasse, especially since they were unwilling to make a move against him from a distance, which would involve using grenades. They'd done great wrecking jobs already on a couple of reel-to-reel cabinets and server towers.

Bolan wasn't sure if this information processing center was just a small part of something larger, or if there were more computer stations like this around the globe, putting together massive amounts of processing power to assail the world's economy. Whichever the case, he had a few moments to figure out his tactics before the enemy forces decided how to proceed.

The first thing he did was to set up a SLAM mine against the side of one cabinet. Given the explosive force and the ability to project a lance of blazing hot copper like a laser made of liquid metal out to eight meters, the SLAM would not only take out plenty of processing power and memory stored down here in one blast, it would also draw a line in the computer farm that would be lethal to pass.

Bolan had set the charge for Identify Friend or Foe,

keyed in to the tag he'd installed in his harness, and motion detection. Once again he could pass in front of the SLAM, but anyone else would be blindsided by a blast meant to cripple an enemy main battle tank. He consulted his Combat CDA, looking at the screen. Unfortunately the device seemed to be suffering fits, having been overloaded. He tried to bring up his communication link to Stony Man Farm, but the touch screen was unresponsive.

He grimaced. Apparently the little combat-hardened microcomputer *did* have limits. He glanced around at the processor towers and realized that trying to insinuate itself into all of that operating capacity had to have blanked it out "mentally." He simply hoped that there was something on the other end of the data transmission. On a hunch, he moved to where the personal workstations had been.

Bolan powered on a screen and saw that it was live but password-protected. He grimaced, then began to search for a USB or FireWire port. While the CDA might have been jammed, he did have small thumb drives with their own software, designed to crack open passwords like a sledgehammer burst walnuts. He found an input, retrieved the appropriate flash drive and plugged it in.

He consulted his watch. So far, he'd been down here for seven minutes. That didn't bode well. This had been a protracted, messy fight that had grown from a simple infiltration to a full-fledged war. Unfortunately the bottleneck layout of the bomb shelter had limited his approach to full-assault mode. Beneath this much concrete, and likely all of this shielding, there would be no means for getting a message out of this basement unless there was a hard line. The workstation popped open, and Bolan went to work scanning through the graphical user interface—GUI—to find an outside internet connection. Alert messages popped up in small windows, the system complaining that it was under assault.

"Yes, I know you're being hacked," Bolan muttered, killing the windows as they popped up. "I'm the one hacking you."

Bolan glanced out the door. This area was larger and more elaborate than a cubicle, but still Spartan and spare. There were plastic windows shielding him from the sight and drone of cooling fans and humming drives, windows that extended to the ceiling. The walls also seemed sound-baffled. He'd left the door open, hoping that would be enough space for sound to enter, to alert him to a renewed assault by the hired guns.

After some digging in menus, Bolan finally found a hidden internet browser. He clicked on it and grimaced as he saw a new window pop up with the message "You are not allowed internet access without clearance."

Bolan felt his cheeks tingle with apprehension. Undoubtedly the ability to interface with the outside world would compromise all the security that had been set up. This was buried deep within an old bomb shelter for a reason—to limit its profile in relation to dozens of electronic intelligence-gathering agencies around the globe. This conspiracy was working toward a goal of international financial mayhem. One leak, one hint of trouble, and the whole world would be down on top of this bunch.

Another window popped up in response to that window: "Fuck off, here's my clearance." This was in Cyrillic font. He had a basic understanding.

Bolan smiled as suddenly the firewall disappeared and there was movement on the screen. Instantly he was taken to this particular tech's home page. It was all in Russian, but over the years Bolan had made a point of learning the basics. He was able to navigate. Within a few more moments, he had a chat window open to the Farm and was typing a message for Aaron Kurtzman, Stony Man's cybernetics chief.

Not much time. Blind on the ground here.

Kurtzman responded instantly.

We're picking up a lot of traffic upstairs.

What kind?

Comms from the security force. The club is being evacuated. There's gunfire, too.

Bolan grimaced. He had been certain that Winslow and Majid would be able to engage in some sort of liberation of the dancers up above. The trouble was that he was now unable to come to their aid. He typed another question.

Monitoring Winslow and Majid?

They're still healthy. Except for a few exchanges of gunfire, things have quieted down.

Tell them to hurry up and get the women out of there. I'm drawing the bulk of the force off them.

Will do.

Bolan wasn't sure how Kurtzman was going to do that, but he immediately typed in another query.

What's the progress on figuring out what's here in this basement?

Proceeding.

Got an overview?

Kurtzman sent back a synopsis of his findings so far.

The towers are busy cloning and infiltrating banks all over North America, Europe and the former Soviet Socialist Republics. This processing power has been used to blend into those systems so smoothly, no bank would realize that anything had been altered.

Bolan frowned.

Can you stop it?

Knock down some of the servers, and it'll crash in on itself anyway.

Bolan's smile returned, then he typed another question.

CDA's frozen from trying to hack this. Any way of clearing it out?

Hard shut down. Turn it off. We're already in this system, so we don't need to piggyback on its software.

Striker out.

Bolan turned to the towers, then pulled out the remote for his SLAM. He selected the charge and thumbed the trigger. A powerful thump filled the air, and almost instantly a row of cabinets slammed to the floor like dominoes, smoke billowing from where the copper penetrator, designed for annihilating armored vehicles, had sliced through them. The detonation itself toppled several more, sudden trauma doing little for the operations those machines were completing. Jarred and battered, the computer system itself started going on full alert. Bolan glanced back at the GUI on the workstation monitor.

Alerts were flashing everywhere. Massive trauma had been caused to the system, Bolan's mine doing far more with one brutish act of destruction than the most finely conceived hacking program. He looked back outside and noticed that fires had broken out. Insulation was melting; sparks were flying from damaged wires. Things were going to get bad around here.

The Executioner reached into his harness and fished out a small Nomex face guard for himself. The finely woven fibers allowed air to flow readily, but a carbon layer sandwiched between the flame-resistant polymers would filter out smoke and other noxious gases. It wasn't going to be a long-term solution, and if the oxygen supply down here was going to be used up, he'd need a tank and breathing mask, not a little synthetic flap once things got worse. For now, however, at least he wouldn't be sucking in any airborne poisons.

The soldier looked through his harness and found he had two cigarette-pack-size SLAM munitions. He hadn't come down with grenades, just the low-velocity breaching charge and these little programmable mines.

Given their ability to project death and flame for a straight line twenty-six feet in length, they could make improvised artillery. Bolan simply had to make certain that he didn't set the charges off while he was right on top of them. There was still a good half pound of high explosives within that could produce a bone-smashing concussion. Those who hadn't been in line with the lance of molten copper still died from internal injuries caused by the high explosives' overpressure and concussive force.

He scanned outside the cubicle, looking at the top of the steps. The burning electronics were irritating his eyes, and he noticed that the enemy had shut down the fans. They were trying to smoke him out with the very conflagration that he'd begun. Bolan smirked, giving those soldiers some grudging respect.

The soldier pulled a pair of folding goggles from his web harness and placed them over his eyes to protect his tear ducts from the burning chemicals. He was prepared and ready to wait things out. He still needed a means of overwhelming the guards perched just in the stairwell. He scanned the office desks of the workstations, found packing tape, and saw that there were roller chairs. The desks themselves were little more than folding tables. Immediately, he grabbed the tape and upended the tables.

This had to be quick. The SLAMs attached to the back of one roller chair easily. He put both on, hoping that the curved back would provide at least a good, flat platform for both rounds to go off. They'd spit out their deadly beams of superheated copper at sternum height. Good.

He placed three of the tables on the seat of the chair, and looked around for one more piece of his puzzle.

A closet contained a push mop.

That was what was going to make this work!

There was movement at the top of the steps.

Bolan leaned out with the AUG and held down the trigger, hammering out the full 30-round magazine with relentless abandon. One figure came tumbling down the stairs, gurgling before he landed with a sickening crunch. Bolan pushed toward the stairs, reloading before he did so. The chair rolled along, tables somewhat unstable but staying on the seat as he tugged it behind.

There was movement again, and Bolan cut loose, this time with more precision bursts. In the smoke and haze of the computer room, the enemy wasn't able to see him, thanks to an improvised flash hider he'd constructed from packing tape and a rolled-up, vinyl mouse pad. The full-length AUG barrel and the efficient 5.56 mm ammo wouldn't put out a monstrous fireball as had the other compact weapons he'd been using over the past week and a half.

There was a scream of pain above, and the guards' gunfire abated. Bolan pushed closer to the steps. He swiftly went to the first man, the corpse at the bottom of the steps, frisking through his gear. He found the distraction grenades they'd used to blind and deafen him. Bolan had been prepared enough for that only to receive a little ringing and disorientation. He plucked the pin on one of the grenades and fast-balled it through the door at the top of the stairs.

If he didn't keep up the pressure, the enemy would be on him in an instant. The flashbang grenade detonated, and there were groans of stunned dismay from above. The disorientation would buy him some time.

Bolan set up the first table at the bottom, forming a ramp up the stairs. He braced a second at the top. As he secured the second piece of this ramp, he took a second flashbang and hurled it through the door again. This time he chased the flashbang with a medium-length burst that sputtered and splashed the ceiling. There were grunts now as someone caught a ricocheting fragment of bullet.

Bolan moved up and had the third table in place, this time the end of the table resting at the top step. He hoped that for a moment, no one would notice the folding table. He was back down the stairs in an instant, and pushing the SLAM-laden chair up. He'd also packed the last of his breaching charges onto the seat, using the push mop to guide the whole thing. The low-velocity detonation cord wouldn't be that much of an addition to the deadly little mines, but any bit of firepower would do the job.

With a final shove, Bolan rolled the explosive chair over the top. There was a grunt of confusion in the thick smoke.

The Executioner thumbed the detonator and the chair vaporized in spectacular fashion. Most of the blast was steered and focused forward, thanks to the design of the munitions. Still, there was enough that Bolan could feel the concussive force wash over him, even as he braced himself on the steps. The tables clattered down the stairs, one edge banging off Bolan's thigh as he couldn't get out of the way in time. It hurt, but nowhere near as much as the focused force of two SLAMs detonating in unison as an improvised Claymore.

The Executioner charged to the top of the steps, transitioning to his fully charged Desert Eagle. If there was any fight left in the security force, Bolan was going to meet it head-on.

CHAPTER NINE

The Executioner entered the ventilation room and encountered only death and destruction. Body parts were mingled with apparently untouched bodies flopped on the ground. He swiftly scanned for movement on the floor, the Desert Eagle tracking along with his wary eyes. The bottom of the stairwell that had led to the bomb shelter was scorched, inflamed, glowing metal still showing that it was hot enough to melt skin on contact and burn through boots. Outside the room, beyond, there were more dead and injured.

They had been smashed asunder by the chair-mounted killer mines that Bolan had used against them.

A hired Vietnamese guard staggered into the open, packing what looked to be a machine pistol. Bolan punched a single .44 Magnum slug through his chest. The tungsten-cored round sliced through the thug's body armor as if it were made of tissue. The gunner toppled backward, the fat Magnum slug spiraling like a drill through bone and muscle alike. Cored, the gunman collapsed in a heap.

Feet were beating retreat up the stairs, but one of the rifle-armed sentries took a misstep. His booted foot landed on a dripped puddle of molten copper and he screamed in agony. The rubber sole puffed out a blast of smoke and he collapsed against the steps, bent over and clutching his smoldering foot.

Bolan realized that it had been one of the two lances of liquid copper, not having cooled yet, and possessing more than sufficient heat to vaporize rubber and melt metal. The injured guard looked pleadingly at Bolan, his face twisted in agony. The Executioner closed in on the stairs, kicked his rifle away and looked down at the man.

"Disarm," Bolan ordered him in Vietnamese. He glanced back and saw that the entire area around the bottom of the steps was strewn with charred body parts and seemingly whole bodies, untouched by shrapnel. It was likely overpressure that had caused the most internal injuries. Some might have been playing possum, or had been knocked unconscious, but as long as no one else sat up and tried to fight, the soldier had no call to open fire.

The Vietnamese guard tossed his handgun and his knife over the rail to clatter to the floor.

Bolan removed his goggles, knelt and sliced off the man's boot. As the leather and sock fell away, he could see livid, charred flesh. The man was in tears. Bolan didn't have much in the way of medical supplies, but he was able to give the man a shot of morphine, which would at least numb the limb. He took the point of his knife and pried out a hardened sliver of copper, and it dropped, steaming, to the stone step below.

Bolan glared at the man. "I don't have anything to rinse the wound out. But you won't be hurting."

The Vietnamese guard nodded.

"You have a chance to live. Take it. Pick your bosses better next time," Bolan told him.

"I shall," the injured man replied.

With that, Bolan punched the man on the jaw to render him unconscious, gathered up his gear and started up the steps.

He bypassed the entrance he'd come through and keyed his throat mike.

"Winslow, Majid, I'm coming up to the club," Bolan announced. "Can you read me?"

"Yes," Majid answered. "The shooting is over."

"All clear," Winslow said. "Boss types took off while we were trading shots with the locals."

Bolan emerged from the stairwell into a corridor. There were a couple of bullet-riddled bodies on the floor of the hallway, smashed apart by rifle fire. He skirted them, noted that they had no firearms with them. Winslow stood in the doorway of what appeared to be an office a little farther on.

The Secret Service agent gave him a nod. "What's up, masked man?"

Bolan looked back. "Not much. Just keep an eye out on the doorway I came from. If armed men come out looking for a fight, cut them down. If you see guards with empty hands, let them go."

Winslow nodded. "We're not going to be sticking around for long, are we?"

"Depends on what Majid has discovered," Bolan said. "I presume she's tearing through the office?"

"Affirmative, McCormack," Winslow returned. "She looks pissed."

Bolan frowned. "Well, she'd been undercover trying to bust these guys. No sign of any of the big three?"

"They all rabbited," Winslow told him. "We saw the door at the back of the office. Private way out. Barred shut from the other side."

Bolan looked in. Majid was busy going through paperwork and notebooks, looking through a mess. There were other women inside with her. They were scantily clad, but they still wore far more than what the RMP cop had been in when he'd discovered her.

She looked up at him, brushing bleached locks from her face. "Things went that bad downstairs?"

Bolan pulled off his filter mask. "No new bullet holes. And any opposition is knocked out."

Majid nodded. "Then you were more of a success than we."

Bolan pointed toward the women. "Freed the dancers."

Majid looked over at the two young women sitting in the office. They were wide-eyed. Confused. Things had swept down upon them like a storm. "Small victory."

"Victory nonetheless," Bolan said firmly. "Give yourself a rest."

Majid squeezed her eyebrows together. "Once the police get here, they're going to do even more to tear this joint apart. We won't catch up to that scum and his Russian and Thai thug friends."

"We will," Bolan told her. "Trust me. I won't let them get away."

Majid looked up at him.

"They will be brought down," Bolan added. He extended a hand to her. "Come with me."

She took his hand.

Winslow tilted his head.

"You're still invited on this," Bolan said to him.

Winslow nodded. "Good. I'd hate to be replaced at this point in the game."

"Let's move before the cops get here," Bolan ordered.

The dancers, dazed and confused, looked at the trio.

"What about them?" Majid asked.

"We leave them here. Hopefully the police will take

care of them," Bolan said. "Though, you might know better than we do."

"They'll be fine," Majid answered.

GREV SOLYENKO LOOKED over his shoulder as the massive Goomabong drove like he walked—with absolutely no concern for anything stupid enough to wander into his path. Nik Onn was sitting ramrod-straight, his face an inscrutable mask as the SUV barreled along.

"I don't like running," Goomabong muttered as he clipped a pedestrian, sending her crashing to the ground.

Solyenko looked at the Malaysian crime boss sitting in the backseat. The man had gone quiet. Too quiet.

"Hopefully, whatever firepower we had downstairs was enough," Solyenko said to him.

Onn didn't move more than his eyeballs, regarding Solyenko with the same disdain he'd show for a dog defecating on his breakfast table. There was a twitch of the Malaysian's lip, but he remained quiet.

"We're going to be fine," Solyenko added.

Onn shook his head. "You miserable cur. Did you hear the sounds coming over the intercom? Or the gunfight blowing up all over my dance floor?"

"Your dance floor," Solyenko repeated.

The Malay returned to brooding silence.

Goomabong looked at Solyenko. "We're going to have to go back to my buddies."

"He's already on edge enough," Solyenko returned, nodding toward Onn. "We go to the retreat."

"With all the other people McCormack is in town to annihilate," Onn muttered, glaring at Solyenko.

"We don't know if that was McCormack," Solyenko snapped.

"No. It was just one man, with an entire security force opening fire on him. Oh, and explosions," Onn growled. "You've read this playbook. I've read this playbook. We've heard the rumors, especially the past couple days, of the Soldier being on our case."

Solyenko glared back. "All right. Maybe I'm not the most convincing at trying to put a good spin on things, but what are we going to do?"

"We're going to figure out how not to end up screwed again. You're leading us right to your boys, the mercs you assembled to nail the American Embassy, right?" Onn asked.

Solyenko looked at Goomabong.

"He's going after them, sooner, if not later," Onn concluded. "We need to get someplace as far from them as possible. He'll rain hell down on those poor bastards, and I don't want to catch a piece of that."

Solyenko frowned. The Malay was making sense. McCormack, or the Soldier, or whatever the hell he was, had followed the same relentless formula every time. He was an agent of vengeance. Some said that he brought justice to those who had engaged in murder, who slaughtered the helpless, the innocent, but Solyenko had little belief in anything resembling innocence in the world. Everything lived as the result of the death of another creature or being.

Solyenko simply made his life from the death and devastation of those targeted by people with the highest payroll. He felt no guilt for living that way. It was a business that he was good at.

"So we're going to leave my people twisting in the wind?" Solyenko asked.

"Call them. Tell them to leave. Standing and fighting

is pure suicide. We've seen that again and again," Onn told him. "As of now, I'm not going to plant my feet on the ground and get killed."

Solyenko looked toward Goomabong quizzically. The Thai shrugged.

"Then we hook up with the Thais, and we run like hell."

"Sounds good to me," Goomabong answered.

"I'm not even sure I want to travel with you two," Onn said. "We head to our fallback, and split up. Does that make sense? Or do I sound paranoid?"

Solyenko shook his head. "No. It's good tactics."

"Fine," Onn whispered with a sigh of relief. "It's not that I don't like you guys…and, Grev, you were right about Mila. I'm sorry we didn't get rid of her sooner."

"And I'm sorry I let her get the drop on me," Goomabong added. "I didn't think she'd be able to surprise me like that. After all…"

"It happened," Solyenko said. "We got the hell out, and we are alive. We've already got what the bosses wanted."

Onn's forehead wrinkled in confusion. "What the hell do you mean?"

"I don't want to say anything more, just in case," Solyenko added.

Onn stifled a grimace of disdain. Just in case of what? he thought. If McCormack came for him, then Onn was dead either way.

Unless Solyenko had something more, something deeper in his agenda than the Malaysian knew about. He studied the Russian and the Thai hulk.

Goomabong had been part of Onn's organization for years, long before Solyenko had darkened his door-

step with the offer of a brand-new club with all the very
best in technology and security. However, of late, it
seemed that the Thai muscleman had grown far closer
to Solyenko than to his original employer. Onn constantly asked Goomabong for updates, insights into the
Russian's affairs, a closer, more trusted ear for Solyenko
to whom secrets might slip, things might shake loose.
But there had been few reports, and those had been of
dubious value.

Had Goomabong "gone native"? Or had Solyenko's
money simply tasted better than Onn's?

Either way, they were going to part ways, and from
the sounds of things, the Russian intended to leave the
Malay boss dangling in the wind. Bait?

Or just leaving a loose end for Solyenko to sacrifice?

Onn gritted his teeth, pulling back into himself. He'd
already known that these bastards wanted to serve him
up like a cheap buffet, maybe even as rat poison to the
man who was on their trail. Onn would ask Goomabong
about Solyenko's big mystery, and then, in turn, Onn
would receive a pile of bullshit that he was to pass off
as chocolate pudding.

I'm going down.

Onn's mood, already dark, became an impenetrable,
obsidian black.

But, Grev, you bastard, I'm taking you with me.

MACK BOLAN HADN'T become one of the most successful
warriors in the world without being thorough and willing to study everything in the cause of hunting down
and locating his prey. There was nothing he wasn't willing to look through, including the trash. Majid had been
thorough in her rifling through the desk and drawers,

working as fast as she could in the time given. Winslow had tried to get some looks in while also doing guard duty at Onn's door.

Still, Bolan went over the paperwork. The three of them didn't have much time to dawdle, simply due to the fact that the police would have been alerted to the gunfire and sudden flooding of people into the streets. He'd poured over the desk, taking in as much as he could at a glance. This would be one instance where he'd have to count more on the electronic intelligence gathered by Stony Man Farm.

He grimaced as he heard Winslow over the radio.

"Time's up. Military trucks are setting up a perimeter."

"Come back to the hallway," Bolan ordered. "We're taking the sewers out."

"Hope they don't figure out that we had that as a route," Winslow commented.

Bolan fixed Majid with a gaze. "Tell the girls that things are going to be all right for them now."

"They've figured that out together," Majid told him.

Bolan glanced at the desk.

"I'm still trying to figure out where Onn could have run to," Majid answered the unspoken question.

"We need to get moving," Bolan said.

"I know," Majid replied.

She seemed loath to turn away from the desk, but she knew that they were cutting things close.

Winslow was in the hallway, and the three people descended the stairs, Bolan pausing long enough to jam the door closed with a butcher's knife he'd taken from the kitchen. It wouldn't be the best barrier, but at least it would buy them a minute, maybe two, while the Royal

Malaysian Police or their military counterparts secured the floors. Rushing along in smaller teams, after a battle like this, might get someone shot to death.

Bolan led Majid and Winslow through the basement to the utility room he'd entered through. Majid easily snaked through the entrance; Winslow had a little more difficulty due to his larger size, his broader shoulders and thicker musculature. Bolan, however, made it through the breech easily, having had much more experience slithering into tight spaces. They had a few yards to get to the next hole, and Bolan peered through first, though there was no indication of illumination, either regular or infrared, in the sewer.

Flashlights would have been blazing in the sewer if they had anticipated someone sneaking out under a perimeter. Still, this was only a momentary respite. There was still far to go beneath the streets, as Bolan had parked a good distance away.

Majid and Winslow fell in behind him and remained quiet. Everyone was split between watching where they stepped in the claustrophobic underground tunnel, and thinking of how to not lose the trail. Somewhere out there, Onn, Solyenko and Goomabong were in the wind.

Were they going to regroup and strike back? Or were they running for their lives, disappearing into the shadows, necessitating a continuing hunt?

Majid was the one who knew Onn the best, and Bolan could see her deep in thought as she sat in the back of their ride. The day before, Goomabong had sent them running, and now, this day, the tables had been turned. The three of them were not the masterminds behind this campaign of economic terror. Sure, Solyenko had sent a response team to deal with Bolan's interference in Colombia, but there was still the leadership to track down.

Bolan nodded at Winslow, who had taken the wheel, while he took out his Combat CDA to text with Stony Man Farm. Away from the basement overload, the little microprocessor should work.

Principals took flight. Any clues to their destination?

Negative.

Success—the message got through.

Bolan sighed. He couldn't blame the Farm for missing one vehicle in as crowded a city as Kuala Lumpur, especially since there was nothing in orbit over the city for this raid, at least nothing that was able to be repurposed for this probe. He also knew that with all of the data that had come from the computer "farm" in the basement of the nightclub, there would simply be too much for them to go through to quickly locate the missing local bosses. He typed the question on his mind.

What's in the system?

Bolan realized it was likely the Farm's mission controller, Barbara Price, communicating directly with him while he was in the field. The computer wizards at the Farm were undoubtedly busy collating data and searching for the conspirators' ultimate plan.

They've left the security in half of the world's banks filled with holes. All manner of chaos can sweep in through

the sieves these guys created. They've also been cloning the banking networks.

Cloning. As in cloning a cell phone?

The mission controller's response was swift.

Yes. They have everything they need to simply make a
dozen major international banks all theirs.

Price was obviously up to date on what the Farm's
cyber crew had discovered. It had been minutes, but already Kurtzman and his brilliant staff had unearthed
where the tendrils of the cybernetic infection had
reached.

Price immediately sent a list, distilled from the hard
data, of the institutions that had been surreptitiously
usurped. Bolan frowned as he thought of the implica-
tions, then texted his question.

Did the destruction of their system do anything?

Nothing to the huge gaps in security they made for
themselves. But they now no longer have a direct line
to any updates.

How long would it take for those security gaps to be
closed?

Price's response took a moment. She'd likely checked
with Kurtzman.

We're looking at a week.

What damage can be done between now and then?

Total economic meltdown. Those banks are specifically linked to the debts that both the United States and China have extant.

Bolan let the CDA rest on his thigh for a moment. It wasn't often that he grew nauseated from the plans of an opponent. However, with two of the world's superpowers currently teetering on the edge of bankruptcy, this push would set the two nations against each other. Debts would come due in such a financial crash, and those debts would be backed by two worldwide armies, each desperate to find some way of stabilizing their economies.

Needless to say, despite not having the kinds of funds necessary to run a war, a deficit ironically forced by an administrative decision to just print money to cover an ill-run war, the U.S. and China would engage in a battle against each other. Whether it would be blatant military force, or another madness-strewed cold war as in the '60s, the '70s and the '80s, where terrorists and brushfire conflicts claimed lives, the results would be the same.

Two nations would go broke, or break each other with the biggest hammers that they could find.

Bolan picked up his CDA and texted Price.

No wonder no eyes in the sky.

Price's answer was slightly reassuring.

The team's working on filling in the gaps, getting a head start before the enemy realizes their command of these banks has slipped.

Can you bounce back the contents of Onn's and Solyenko's phones?

Transmitting.

Less than a minute later Price texted Bolan.

Trying to fight your way up the food chain.

Going to need transportation. Depending on where these guys are running off to.

Kuala Lumpur is a major economic hub. Why wouldn't the bosses stay there?

Because it'd be ground zero at the meltdown. They'd want to be where they could make the most of their machinations.

In other words, where there were banks that they didn't send into tailspins. All right, we can work with something on those grounds.

Hopefully.

We've got Jack coming into Kuala Lumpur International Airport. He's bringing along the Gulfstream.

"Jack" was Jack Grimaldi, Stony Man Farm's ace pilot. Bolan smiled.

He freed up.

Briefly. We packed the jet deep, just in case your entourage grows.

Thank you. What's Jack's ETA?

Noon tomorrow. He'll make a drop, but has to leave to pick up Phoenix.

Bolan did the math, then texted his sign-off.

Talk to you then.

Call me if you need anything.

Bolan took his CDA and began looking through the numbers and locations in the phones that had been cloned. When Winslow had opened his virus-laden device in the club, as soon as it was attacked, it struck back, spearing into any and all of the phones in the vicinity. Of primary interest were those of the three in charge, as pointed out by Erra Majid.

Now, the soldier had free time to concentrate on what might not have been left down on paper, or more precisely, in the memory cards of his enemies' phones.

Hopefully, he'd get something to work with.

CHAPTER TEN

Onn had been dropped off at his getaway, a home away from the club. There, he had at least a dozen well-armed guards as well as a staff of servants to see to his every need. Before the coming of Solyenko, he was certain that he didn't need an entire platoon, armed to the teeth, alert and ready to engage in sudden, savage violence at the drop of a hat.

Now, however, he realized that twelve gunmen wouldn't be enough. Not in the face of the force of nature that had torn through his club. He'd heard the storm of automatic fire, the explosions, wafting up through the stairwell when he'd evacuated the club. He'd smelled the porklike stench of burning human flesh and melting synthetic fibers mixed in with flaming wiring and burning ozone.

Somehow the Soldier had passed through his club without being noticed, climbed down the stairs and engaged in open warfare, bringing along enough high explosive to rock the very building and send billowing clouds of smoke up through the air shafts.

Solyenko was gone, ten minutes now, and his security team on-site around the small yet nicely sprawled mansion grounds were looking at him, wondering why Onn, the cool cat who had the hottest joint in Kuala Lumpur, now smelled of smoke and looked terrified.

"We've got trouble on the way," Onn said. "Big trouble."

"The Soldier hit you," Makka, Onn's head of security, surmised. Makka had been involved in some of the preliminary planning, but if there was one man that Onn could trust, it was he. Short and wide, he was a human pit bull, skin bronzed from the blazing sun across a dozen Southeast Asian battlefields. He had his share of scar tissue, especially along his scalp.

If there was one man that the Malay club boss felt could handle either Solyenko or Goomabong, it was Makka. There was more fight inside him than in a dozen men. Even so, against a monster like the Soldier, the mercenary might well have been an irate purse-size dog.

"What is our plan?" Makka asked.

"I want to run," Onn said, defeat filling him. "But he'll chase me, because the law knows where I live. I'm a citizen here, unlike Solyenko."

Makka's lips pulled tight. "So he'll blow in here, and once he's done, he leaves this place as a graveyard."

Onn nodded.

The rest of his security detail looked frightened. For their employer and the brawny little fireplug who led them to both seem so defeatist, the situation suddenly seemed dreadful. There was confusion among them, but Makka tilted his head.

"Are you going to fight him?" Makka asked.

"I want everyone out of here," Onn decided. "I'm not going to be chased around the globe, not by some one-man army."

Makka took a deep breath, then looked at the rest of his troops. "Dismissed. Clear out."

"How fast…" one of the other guards began to ask.

"Drop everything and leave!" Makka snarled. "I'm looking out for you, damn it, now run!"

"You're staying?" Onn asked.

Makka nodded. "If you're going down, I might as well stay for this ride."

Onn blinked, trying to understand what was going on.

"I've heard about the Soldier. We could put up a fight, but the odds always seem to favor him. He's a walking war machine, and he'll steamroll over any defenses we put up," Makka said. "But if we play our cards right—"

"And what card would that be?" Onn interrupted.

Makka raised a finger to his friend. The rest of the guards were already moving. They had set down their weapons where they'd stood. "We'll also have to dismiss the rest of the staff right now."

"I'll get on it," Onn replied.

"The Soldier wants something more. You just sat on the real estate. You're not his main target," Makka said. "And if you give him the information he needs, we could yet live."

"Not free," Onn returned.

"Living is living, in a jail or outside," Makka replied.

Onn nodded. "True."

Makka reached into his belt and pulled out his pistol, dumping the magazine, clearing the chamber, then dropping it. Onn looked at the tiny handgun in his hand and followed suit.

There was no need to antagonize McCormack or the Soldier or whatever he was. The man was on his way, and every instance in the recent past had showed that he'd been more than a match for Venezuelan armored cavalry and small armies of hired, well-armed gunmen.

Maybe just talking and surrendering would be the best survival option.

As the gangster headed to his house, he looked through his phone numbers, trying to figure out where Solyenko would be going. Onn's lips curled in concentration. Makka stood close to the gate that separated the estate from the road outside. The bodyguard was a good man, despite having been through some rough patches and working for someone who was, Onn admitted, nothing more than a whore-monger at best, a human slaver at his worst. The Malaysian gangster wondered how he could have earned so much loyalty, but he fought that down.

He wanted to live, not to sabotage his continued existence. If Onn didn't figure out where his comrades had scattered to, there was going to be hell to pay, and that hell existed in the shape of a man, a tall, dark-haired warrior who could disappear in any crowd or slither through the shadows and penetrate the most fortified of underground lairs protected by twenty guards.

McCormack had showed himself to be a threat like nothing that the Russian gangster and his allies had ever seen. Onn was a fairly intelligent man, otherwise he wouldn't have gotten where he was, at least in terms of owning a hot club that, in ages past, had been placed over an old fallout shelter. It had simply been his luck that he was sitting on the target...

Onn felt his cheeks tingle. He opened his phone. "Makka, get inside."

"Why?" the bodyguard asked.

"I've been sitting on the target long enough to know what it feels like. Get inside and out of the line of fire!"

The bodyguard had to have picked up the urgency,

the cold knowledge that made Onn feel as if he had been suffering the beginnings of a stroke. Of course Solyenko and Goomabong would drop the Malay off at his very own home!

They wanted to hang out Onn as bait, and with that, they knew that McCormack would focus on the one target whose home address was already known to the local authorities. It didn't take a genius to realize that the whole of his estate was a trap, one that those traitorous bastards would have mapped out already.

Onn grimaced. He needed something to contact the one-man army who had been his tormentor. He looked at the phone. If only there was some kind of direct line to…

Onn hit the speed dial again.

He was calling Solyenko, but he didn't expect the Russian bastard to answer. If anything, the *mafiya* goon would realize that his cell phone had been hacked, the same way that the club's setup had cracked the defenses of their own customers.

"Listen, I don't know if you guys can hear me while I've got that damned ringing on a dead line, but this is Nik Onn," he said into the phone. "Please, listen to me. Even better, talk back to me and let me know that you're listening."

A voice as cold and grim as a graveyard spoke up. "I am."

Onn's feelings were torn, a wave of relief and horror washing through him at the same time. There was a frightening aspect to how quickly the other man answered, and he sounded more than human, foreboding and intimidating. But still, he'd reached the only human in the world that could help him, guarantee his survival. His and Makka's.

Makka was so loyal; Onn owed it to the bodyguard to see that he made it through this nightmare.

"Listen, we were going to surrender to you," Onn said. "My head guard dismissed all the rest of my men. People are getting out of here, out of the way."

"'Were going to surrender'?" that Reaper's voice asked, words scraping against a whetstone as if they were scythes, ready to slash the gangster's tenuous grasp on this mortal coil. "What changed your mind?"

"We didn't change our mind," Onn said. He looked up and saw that Makka had entered the office. He had a gun with him. "But, we're not going anywhere. And if you show up here, you'll likely end up being shot at."

"Solyenko's set up a trap," the man on the other end surmised. "And you're calling to warn me."

"Please, I'll go to jail. I won't put up a fight," Onn pleaded.

"I believe you," Bolan told him.

"Where can we meet you?" the gangster asked.

"Just stay where you are," Bolan replied. "Your man just went inside, and he's got a sidearm. That should be enough to protect you while I do my work outside."

"Out...you're here?" Onn sputtered.

"Over and out" came the response.

The Malaysian gangster looked wide-eyed at his protector, sweat glistening on his skin.

They had wanted to warn the devil that he was in for an ambush, but he was already present.

MACK BOLAN KNEW that he didn't have much time to waste in tracking down Solyenko and Goomabong, but if anything, there was one man he could easily locate, and that was Nik Onn. Even as he was marking off the route to the club owner's home, his trained eyes saw a dozen places where a skilled former special operations soldier would set up an ambush, even with the most loosely trained of allies.

Given Goomabong's speed and apparent danger, it wouldn't be hard to imagine the Thai giant being more than capable to assist the Russian, nor would it be out of bounds to consider that Goomabong had allies equally as hard and brutal as he was. Bolan also realized that allies could easily be contacted surreptitiously, even with the man you intended to betray in the seat behind you.

Both of them knew that if he was on the hunt for them, then there was one place that Bolan would show up, no questions asked.

That was on Onn's doorstep.

Any shred of preparation was now going to be put into play, as fast as possible. Even now, Bolan could observe that trucks and cars of men were gathering. While nothing moved in direct line of the estate, Bolan could tell that the traffic was not normal for this neighborhood, a feeling Erra Majid confirmed to him. Another hint as to their threatening nature was that they were moving with a minimum of light and noise, despite the vehicles seemingly being packed to the gills.

Solyenko and Goomabong were setting up a staging area, and when they made their attack, things would explode.

Down the way, Winslow was filling in the gaps of Bolan's observations, their communication devices forming a triangle that allowed Bolan, Majid and Winslow to spread out and get maximum coverage of what was going on.

The information coming in to the Executioner was

far from heartening, but that was why he gathered such information in the first place. There was one way to get ahead of a stronger, more heavily armed opponent, and that was to know more than he did. Assisting in this was Stony Man Farm.

Kurtzman and his cybernetics crew were watching the place now, utilizing traffic cameras and local radio listening posts set up by the RMP and its links to international law enforcement. Even now, Bolan could see the assembly of forces in real time. It wasn't the same as watching over infrared satellite from orbit, but this was the best that could be hoped for in terms of last-minute setups. The soldier drank deep at this well of knowledge, applying what he knew of Spetsnaz assault and ambush tactics to what he was seeing unfold.

Already, he had seen Solyenko's plot, especially how he had the groups spread. It was going to be a two-pronged assault, with smaller third and fourth squads placed to provide cover fire. The fire teams on the borders of Onn's estate were six apiece. That was the standard RPG team setup—two on security, two loaders and two rocketeers. These teams would be the ones who would open up the festivities. The gates and walls were well within the range of their rocket launchers, and they would be able to sail warheads into the gate openings to allow amassed troops to rush in.

Once they "opened the door," they would begin using the RPGs as indirect weapons—a trick the elite soldiers of the Spetsnaz had found could be a force multiplier as well as a range extender. Solyenko was a man who knew the benefits of even improvised artillery on an enemy. Bolan knew that he needed to take out these rocket launchers before he could deal with the assault teams.

The two attack groups were larger. Twenty apiece, meaning that Solyenko still had the same old tactic: throw more enemies at the Executioner. It hadn't worked in the past, but what else was he going to do?

"Winslow, Majid," he said softly into his throat mike. He pointed out the locations of the rocket teams to the two of them. With the optics on the Steyr AUG assault rifles they'd gotten from Onn's nightclub, they would be able to stage a successful ambush.

"Shoot down the security men first, the rocket teams won't have the range with their personal arms, and they'll be loath to waste RPG shells against you," Bolan told them.

Majid spoke up first. "We do this at the same time?"

"What's the concern?" Bolan asked her.

"You want us to take down these two groups in unison, right?" Winslow returned.

"And as fast as possible," Bolan added. "We have the hands-free communications."

"What will you be doing while we're sniping for you?" Majid asked.

"Getting into the thick of it," Bolan responded. "But, if those RPG teams aren't put down immediately, we won't be able to get to Onn and his man, and I won't have much of a chance of survival with warheads raining down on me."

"You want Onn alive?" Majid asked.

Bolan took a deep breath. "He will face justice."

"I get to arrest him," Majid stated bluntly.

"There was never a doubt in my mind," Bolan told her.

"In the meantime, we take down Solyenko, who orchestrated the hit on the U.S. Embassy here in Kuala Lumpur..." Winslow began.

"And who likely outlined the assassination of your friends in Medellín," Bolan finished. "No. Solyenko is going to receive all the attention he deserves."

"While the man who put girls into sexual slavery gets away with minimum punishment," Majid returned.

Bolan sighed. "You can handle that thug however you wish, Erra. I promised him a respite from whatever I'd usually do to someone, but I have a code of ethics about not killing someone who has already surrendered."

There was a moment of uncomfortable silence on the other end. Majid had just been presented with a moral dilemma. Should she just give in to whatever anger she felt, no matter how righteous it may be, or should she prove herself the better person morally? Killing an unarmed man who surrendered was something that was abhorrent to most people who felt themselves to be good human beings.

Vengeance was one thing, self-defense another, but cold-blooded murder was cold-blooded murder.

"Remember. Security gunners first, then the rocket teams," Bolan told them.

With that, the soldier left his vehicle. He'd thought about using one of the club crew's AUG rifles, but right now, the Executioner foresaw a great deal of close-quarters combat, and while the bullpup combat carbines were easy to move in confined spaces, the breech of the weapon made it difficult to make use of cover. It would kick out on only one side, and switching shoulders to utilize more than half of those corners would mean a face full of hot, skin-slashing brass. No, this time he would supplement his gear with something just as handy, yet still capable of defeating body armor at out to 200 yards.

That meant using a Heckler & Koch MP7. Externally, it looked not much different from some of the Executioner's older favorites, the Uzi or the MAC-10, a T-shaped weapon with a pistol grip in the middle. The MP7, however, was an upgraded design. Where the others were simply made of stamped steel, the German design incorporated polymer and stainless steel to provide rust resistance and lighter weight. There was an integral fold-down lever and a collapsing buttstock that could upgrade the compact machine pistol from holstered handgun to stable shooting platform in an instant. There was a Picatinny rail on top to mount an optic, as well as iron sights, which could flip between standard handgun style to more precise M16-style peeps.

The biggest change in the MP7 from its predecessors was its cartridge. The gun was chambered for 4.6 mm, essentially an abbreviated version of the M4 and M16's 5.56 mm rifle cartridge.

In addition to the precision personal defense weapon that Bolan had armed himself with, he'd also decided to bring along a bandolier of fragmentation grenades. While the SLAMs had been good at controlling, repelling and ultimately shattering the security forces in the converted fallout shelter beneath Onn's club, Bolan needed something that could be used much more quickly. The M-67s weren't precision munitions, but when it came time to go nose to nose with dozens of armed opponents, on an estate where innocent bystanders had all cleared out, the fraggers were going to do all the work Bolan needed, with little worry about harming noncombatants.

He also was glad that he could keep Majid and Winslow occupied outside the perimeter wall, dealing with the RPG teams, so that they wouldn't inadvertently get caught in the cross fire or be struck by errant grenade shrapnel.

Breaking into a jog, he noted that the sun was just starting to tint the night sky with a predawn gray. Bolan wasn't surprised at Solyenko sending his men in just before dawn, but he wondered just how much the Russian *mafiya* goon's forces were aware of Onn's current defenses. The Malaysian gangster's bodyguard crew had left the estate, as well as servants, the night shift especially. The way the enemy was headed in, it was going to be an all-out war. The troops were riding their pickup trucks toward the gates, and Bolan could spot the improvised "technicals" that Solyenko's men had assembled.

Technicals were pickups with tripods and medium-to-heavy machine guns mounted to turn them into improvised combat vehicles. These were a far a cry from the purpose-built armor that the soldier and Winslow had encountered in Venezuela, but Solyenko was on the offensive. Any return fire would be put down by the sheer volume of 7.62 mm and 12.7 mm machine gun bullets put into the air. The only things that Bolan could count on was the fact that even at range, or behind the sheet metal of a pickup's cab, the gunmen in Solyenko's employ were helpless against the high-penetration MP7 rounds, and that he, on foot, wearing his combat black-suit, would be as close to invisible as humanly possible.

The first of the RPG shells had flown. One in the distance crackled first, the closer gate suddenly disappearing in the flash and thunder of the detonation of nearly four pounds of high-efficiency explosives in two warheads. On the heels of the blast, the first of the convoy of trucks accelerated, smashing aside the remnants of the shattered gate. The machine gun mounted in the bed of the vehicle thumped, bellowing out half-inch bullets toward any and all targets likely within the mansion.

Solyenko and his men would only find two targets inside. Onn had made the playing field as ideal for Bolan as humanly possible.

Blood was about to flow, and the Executioner had his deadly tools honed to their sharpest.

CHAPTER ELEVEN

Zachary Winslow watched as his targets fired the first of their shells at the estate. Grimacing, he realized that this was his cue to open fire, and he worked the trigger on his AUG. He had good cover, the trunk of a tree, and the 1.5 power Swarovski optic built into the rifle gave him a good clear view of the gunmen, framed by the exhaust smoke of their rocket launchers.

As per Bolan's instructions, Winslow put two rounds into one of the riflemen acting as the protection detail for the rocket teams. The gunner, a local Asian sort, jerked violently as Winslow's opening salvo took him in the center of mass, his rib cage churned up violently in the passage of two bullets decelerating from three times the speed of sound to a standstill. The hydrostatic shock inflicted by such loss of momentum transferred to the thug's internal organs, bursting his lungs and rupturing blood vessels like the trunk of a tree falling through soap bubbles.

Winslow quickly located the second rifleman. The gunner had seen the dull flicker of the American's rifle, but it was too late. The Secret Service agent pulled the trigger and erased the man's face with a third bullet.

Winslow saw that one of the rocket team's loaders was going for a fallen assault rifle. He shifted his aim and pulled the trigger all the way back to fire on full-auto. A volley of 5.56 mm rounds rocketed forward at three times the speed of sound, reaching maximum velocity thanks to the Steyr's full 18-inch barrel.

The stuttering burst ripped across the rocket loader's head and shoulders as he stooped for the rifle. Bones cracked under the sheer velocity, and deformed slugs spiraled like out-of-control circular-saw blades. Petals of copper peeled back from the leaden core slashed through fluid mass, slicing deep and causing far more tissue damage than they normally would have. Hydrostatic shock caused by the projectile's passage collapsed and ruptured cells, tearing muscle and dislodging blood vessels in the bullet's wake.

Winslow knew the deadly effects of these high-velocity bullets, the gory details of how a human could die with an object only fractions of a hundredth their body weight making contact with flesh. One hit caused horrendous trauma. Multiple impacts produced an unsurvivable injury. It was nothing to be proud of, and the brutal slash of blood and gore always popped up in his mind, imagination giving him the gruesome blow-by-blow details of rendered muscle and the end of human life.

He did wonder if anyone else entertained these images of anatomical apocalypse when they shot someone, or if he had found some new means of torturing himself mentally. He had gone from grieving, and then blaming himself for letting down his teammates, to now regretting every single shot he fired. Or was he regretting it?

The psychic slide show going on in the background was gory, informed by special effects from countless medical and forensic crime dramas. But it wasn't a distraction. Not as he was swiftly moving from target to target. He caught a second of the men, this one a guy who dropped his RPG and was clawing a handgun from its holster. Winslow cut him in two, putting him down in a brutal, final manner.

The last two hardmen seemed torn. One of them looked at the rocket launcher in his hands, then threw it down, turned tail and ran like hell. The loader lunged for the fallen RPG-7. Winslow dropped the hammer on him, finishing off the 30-round magazine as he peppered the would-be rocketeer with a dozen rounds.

It was grisly, butcher's work. He keyed his throat mike. "Erra?"

"Hang on!" Majid answered. She was curt, but there was no irritation in her voice. He could hear the crackle of her rifle, even through the throat mike. Winslow grimaced. He'd put down his opponents within moments. Majid still seemed to be busy with her squad.

The shooting stopped.

"Okay...I'm done, too," she told him.

"Sorry," Winslow said.

Majid clicked her tongue. "Don't worry about me. I take it you finished your group?"

"What now?" Winslow asked.

"We have to sit tight," Majid grumbled. She wanted to move in alongside McCormack in his battle inside the compound. The trouble was, they had no coordination with him. They had to control the perimeter, otherwise the commanders of this assault on Onn's home would escape. And if that happened, then this whole trip would have been for naught. The Malaysian local crime boss might have information as to who had begun the international operation, but Solyenko was the man who had been handpicked by the higher-ups, the ones who would know exactly what was going on in this assault on international economies.

"More than just sit tight," Winslow added. "We have to lock those gates. No one escapes."

Majid replied with a grunt of assent. She settled in, keeping her sights on the gate.

Winslow did likewise, sending a prayer of support to the man they knew as Agent Matt McCormack.

THE EXECUTIONER RACED down the road, his long legs eating up asphalt in loping, energy-conserving strides. His goal was to be upon the convoy bursting through the gates before they realized that he was even on the street. He'd considered using the rental car as a means of cover and transportation, but it was the only vehicle they had. If he wrecked it, then the others might not have a chance to retreat, especially since Bolan was going, once more, against overwhelming odds.

Solyenko and Goomabong had arranged the attack on Onn's compound as a means of tying off a loose end and to entice and bring down Bolan himself. Their plan had worked, but he'd bring them down.

The soldier leaped onto the rear of the last SUV in the convoy, gripping a roll bar and planting his feet firmly on the extended rear bumper. A gunman in the back of the 4x4 turned his head, spotting the big American, a bulky shadow in the predawn gloom, and realized that the man didn't belong. Bolan reached out with his free hand, MP7 dangling around his neck on its sling, and clamped his hand over the Asian's mouth. Bolan eased the weight off one arm and put it all on the head of his opponent.

The Asian couldn't make a sound as 220 pounds of

muscle and sinew, and a further forty pounds of combat gear, suddenly craned his neck to its limit. One hand was tight on his mouth, the other digging its fingers into his stretched throat. The hired gun's arms flew up, trying to pry off Bolan, but the Executioner's leverage was too much. Bones ground and grated against each other, tendons snapping like firecrackers, the sound blending with the autofire that the rest of the attack convoy and its counterpart were unloading on Onn's mansion. Even as Bolan smothered any reaction from the gunman, brass rained down onto the throttled mercenary, a MAG-58 general purpose machine gun firing, its operator oblivious to the deadly struggle at his feet.

With one final, violent twist, the mercenary's neck shattered, spine severed, windpipe crushed and jaw dislocated. Bolan's mass and strength had simply been a death sentence. It wasn't just the guns that made the Executioner so deadly. It was the knowledge, skill and willingness to kill that were the true weapons. Firearms were simply tools.

With a surge, Bolan slithered into the back of the vehicle. He pulled his Karambit fighting knife and rose, plunging it just under the machine gunner's navel, hooked talon point aimed upward. The concave cutting claw zipped open the shooter's belly in a swift movement before Bolan struck breastbone. The curved tip of the blade hooked under the ribs, tore through diaphragm muscle, then pierced the man's heart. A half second of motion and the machine gunner was suddenly limp, agonized by the brutal carving power of the Indonesian design. The fighting knife, forged and honed in America, had returned "home" for this battle, and it killed with deadly efficiency and speed.

The driver and the shotgun rider were still looking for enemies on the grounds, but the driver noticed that the MAG-58 on top of the technical was no longer firing.

"What—" the man began in Vietnamese.

Bolan was right there, driving the razor-sharp hook into his throat, just behind the jaw under his left ear. With a wicked tug, the taut skin and muscle under the driver's mandible turned into a yawning new mouth, exhaling ragged air and vomiting blood in a torrent. The mercenary sitting in the passenger seat whirled at the sudden action next to him, and he brought up his elbow hard, catching the Executioner in the side of his head with a jarring blow.

Bolan allowed himself to roll into the backseat, on top of his first victim in the technical, knowing that staying and fighting while wedged between the seat back and the roll bar was a good way to get his neck broken or his skull fractured. Even so, his brain was swimming from that first staggering hit. He did a quick inventory of his hands, flexing them, and realized that the elbow to his skull had forced him to drop the knife.

The shotgun rider struggled to bring his rifle around and shoot the Executioner in the backseat, but the dash and the raised windshield made maneuvering slow, difficult. The long barrel of his AK hung up for a moment, giving Bolan the reprieve and breath he needed to raise his booted foot and kick his adversary hard in the base of his skull. Bone imploded under the stamp of his waffle-treaded boot sole, vertebrae separated and neural tissue suffered massive, horrendous trauma. His neck broken, spine severed, brain lacerated by shattered skull fragments, the gunman in the passenger seat was done.

Four of Solyenko's thugs dead, and not a shot fired

yet. It was a good start, especially since the lack of gunfire was keeping Bolan off the radar. He shoved the eviscerated machine gunner's corpse aside, the body tumbling to the ground, intestines spilling out in a flood of rubbery tubes.

The MAG-58 was going to be the beginning gambit in this plan, and he intended to use it to the best of his ability. The general purpose machine gun was familiar to the Executioner. In the United States military, its designation was the M240, replacing the old, instantly recognizable M60. Bolan had gone on many missions with the Pig, as the M60 had been named, but the MAG-58 had also proved its worth to the soldier.

He swept the rest of the convoy. It was still rolling on, everyone's attention aimed into the compound, not at their backs. Solyenko had assumed that Bolan was already on the estate, which he was, technically, but the Russian had obviously thought that Bolan would be inside the mansion, not out here on the perimeter.

This was going to be a rude awakening and harsh surprise for the *mafiya* enforcer and his men.

Bolan lined up the sights on the lead truck, a pickup with a .50-caliber gun of some sort mounted on top of it. That was easily the most powerful weapon on the grounds, and this close, the technical that Bolan was in might as well have been made of paper plates for all the deadly punch of the heavy, half-inch slugs it spit. Bolan fired, drilling the gunner on the Fifty, 7.62 mm NATO rounds slicing through the man before Bolan whipped the band-saw stream of lead down and into the cab of the pickup. Sheet metal was not much resistance for the smaller 7.62 mm rounds that the MAG-58 punched out, and Bolan tore apart the driver and his passenger in a storm of sizzling lead.

With the initial burst and destruction of three people, the rest of the convoy was thrown into disarray. Only one of the assault group had the wits to look toward the back of their column of vehicles and see that a mysterious wraith in black was firing away with the light machine gun, and he seemed to be tearing into that truck. The enemy gunner wheeled his weapon around to hammer Bolan into the ground, but the Executioner cut him off at the pass, high-velocity slugs smashing through his ribs and mangling the mechanism of his gun.

Bolan lowered his aim and poured screaming thunder into the fuel tank of the dead gunner's vehicle, fuel splashing everywhere. Subsequent rounds in the Executioner's burst went to work on pounding the axle and drive train of the truck. No gas and busted mechanisms turned the damaged pickup into a poorly armored bunker for the two men in the cab, and they instantly realized that, throwing open their doors and fleeing.

More of the enemy was reacting to the sudden onslaught of death that had struck from their blindside. Bolan swept them, spraying lead in a wide arc. This was cover fire, not meant for any effect other than to delay Solyenko's hired guns from opening up in combat. This gave Bolan the breathing space he needed to drop down from the vehicle and disappear into the foliage alongside the driveway.

Even though he was a fast-moving wraith, making a quick dash to the shadows, there were those who still had the wherewithal to track his sprint. Gunfire opened up from the scattered, confused convoy of hired mercenaries, bullets chasing Bolan through the shrubs. He was under fire, but he kept his calm, zigging and zagging, varying off his original course into the flora of the estate. Solyenko's hired force made the assumption that their quarry would continue to run deeper into the protective, all-consuming shadows of the estate grounds.

Bolan shifted course and was making a beeline, hidden behind the trees, but rushing closer to the enemy force. By now, he was also certain that the attackers were radioing their second squad, informing them of the target that had appeared in their midst.

Bolan plucked an M-67 fragmentation grenade from his harness. He pulled the pin and hurled the bomb like a world-class baseball pitcher. The compact ball of doom reached about 85 miles an hour and sailed into the window of the truck he'd gutted with the MAG-58, the one whose gasoline was all over the ground. Machine gun fire wouldn't spark the fuel on the tarmac, but the detonation of the grenade within the cab would do the trick.

The fuse burned down, then the mini-bomb detonated. Spilled gasoline flared into flame as the grenade erupted, spraying shrapnel. Creating a wall, however temporary, of steel fragments and flame hampering pursuit.

The sudden flash of blazing fuel would also ruin the night vision of people who were looking for the Executioner. Bolan had shielded his eyes as a precaution, giving himself a greater advantage over the temporarily blinded enemy. He shouldered the MP7 in one smooth movement, sighted one of the gunners on another pickup and fired. Bolan shot the machine gunner down, 4.6 mm rounds slicing through whatever body armor the man wore, dumping him off the back of the vehicle.

Even as the dazed opposition was recovering, Bolan

moved on and took out the last two mercenaries manning the mounted machine guns on the technicals. Bodies spilled to the ground, the heaviest firepower on this side denied to the assault group. Firing from the shadows was not giving away his position, as he had a full-length suppressor on the end of the machine pistol, muzzle-blast swallowed by the foot-long can.

Bolan kept pushing at the enemy group. Three vehicles were out of commission, but there were still four more, and the crew of one of them had abandoned ship the moment their gunner was put out of commission. The Executioner had an advantage, the element of surprise, and he also had the shadows at his back. The enemy, though, had numbers and bigger guns. It was long odds, and the only way to cut them down before the forces against him doubled with the arrival of the second convoy of vehicles was to move aggressively.

Mack Bolan wasn't a man who was fearless. To be without fear was to not have a properly working brain. What Bolan did have, however, was a command of his reactions. The terror of facing down a superior enemy didn't result in scattered thoughts or fumbling fingers, but turned into adrenaline that fueled his muscles. Fear dilated his pupils, making his vision extra sharp, so he could pick up an incoming threat or an opportunity much more quickly. Bolan wasn't a man without fear, but he knew how to use his emotions as a benefit, and the fright of others as his edge.

The soldier had gone from a phantom shadow picking off exposed machine gunners to a nightmare, hurling explosive damnation into their midst. A silent assault had escalated from quiet death to a mounted machine gun shredding bodies to ultimately a truck becoming a blossoming curtain of flame and shrapnel. Gunmen ran from the line of vehicles, not looking back, and some of them dropped their firearms.

Those who remained were searching for Bolan in the darkness. The soldier rewarded their courage and stubborn drive to find him with a burst of 4.6 mm projectiles through their face or center mass. Brains and hearts were broken by the supersonic bullets; those who had stood their ground tumbled to it, blood pouring from gunshot wounds.

Bolan rushed toward one of the pickups, the one armed with the heaviest machine gun, and clamored into the bed of the vehicle.

The weapon was a Russian 12.7 mm DShK, the Soviet Union's answer to the United States' legendary M2 Browning. Bolan had encountered the DShK as both ally and enemy, and he had respect for the big 12.7 mm round. Now, it was going to have to carry him through his encounter with the other convoy. He wouldn't have much trigger time, especially if the other convoy rushed in, weapons hot, but the Executioner would make do with what he had.

He worked the bolt, ensuring a fresh cartridge in the chamber, then sighted down the line, seeing the glow of headlights growing around the corner. Standing in the pickup bed, he possessed a considerable amount of firepower, but he was a sitting target.

And right now, he heard the cracks of RPGs firing in the distance. It was from inside the compound. He had been monitoring the radio chatter between Majid and Winslow; they had taken down the groups outside.

Solyenko's men had to have had some RPGs with their convoy, and the warheads arced into the air, their bulbous, deadly points wobbling as gravity took hold of them, dragging them inexorably toward the row of abandoned vehicles that Bolan stood among.

In moments, he would be at ground zero to two high-powered explosions, not to mention secondary blasts from bursting fuel tanks and cooking ammunition.

CHAPTER TWELVE

The Executioner didn't have much time to react—instants for that matter. The RPG-7 rockets launched by the enemy were already coming to ground, steered by gravity in their parabolic course. Solyenko had trained his grenadiers well, allowing them to utilize the rocket launchers as indirect fire weapons. Bolan could have felt a twinge of admiration for the Russian as an instructor, but he was too busy vaulting out of the bed of the pickup, hitting the ground in a roll to get as much momentum as he possibly could.

He didn't slow down, even as he came out of his tumble, feet pushing against the ground. The shriek of the descending rockets grew in intensity, but he'd only managed to take a few steps before the shells landed, detonating on contact.

The pressure wave produced by the twin blasts buffeted Bolan, knocking him in a scramble to his knees. He threw his hands down, bracing himself, preventing a face plant into the concrete. Heat and force washed over his back, but the two warheads had to have landed short, in front of the line of trucks.

Their bulk had provided a wall, a firebreak that blocked shrapnel. Even so, Bolan's retreat left him tripping over a hedge at the side of the driveway. He allowed himself to lie in the grass, low and out of sight, listening to the sounds of crackling wreckage. The trick he'd used to cover his own approach had inadvertently worked once again, this time to his advantage, as well. His head rang from the overpressure of the detonations, and he felt the hair on the back of his neck curl from the heat.

This was still damned close, and he took a couple of refreshing breaths as he recovered. He'd taken knocks in the basement of the club, and now he'd taken a few more. As strong and healthy as he was, he was still human, and he was facing down a mechanized force with the intent, and more than enough firepower, to kill him. One thing he could count on was that Solyenko would want—no, *demand*—confirmation of "Matt McCormack's" corpse. Majid had told Bolan about the fear of him, and the preparation that had gone on in the name of the agent who had blown through South America.

The enemy was scared, and no one seemed to be moving too quickly to sift through the carnage to find his remains, which suited Bolan just fine. His war through South America had been physically taxing as he'd fought the elements, including a raging Orinoco River, a crocodile and a two-hundred-pound fish, in addition to sundry grenades, gunfire and hand-to-hand combat, which left him bruised and battered. That he'd been in peak operation form until the combined shock waves of two RPG-7 shells floored him was a testament to his considerable strength and resilience.

Even now, he was beginning to recover his breath and the might in his limbs. His head stopped ringing from the pressure unleashed by the twin detonations. All he needed to do was to get back up and unleash some hell. Sitting up, though, would have to wait as he unhooked two hand grenades from his battle harness.

Removing the pin from the first M-67 and lobbing

the bomb in a lazy arc over the heads of the remaining assault force was the opening volley. No one would notice it in the gray half-light of dawn, and even if they did, that falling fragger would call their attention away from the second smooth-skinned hand bomb as it sailed up and over, almost paralleling the course of its brother.

The first grenade popped in midair, shrapnel shooting out in a sphere of death. Bolan could hear the rattle of fragmented wire striking the skins of the pickups and technicals of the other half of Solyenko's death squad, swiftly followed by agonized screams. The second M-67 made it to the ground, bounced and detonated at waist height. Bolan had shifted the arc of that munition by about forty-five degrees, making certain that he got the most coverage that he could for the two hand grenades.

Now he surged to his feet, bounding back over the hedge, MP7 tracking and looking for targets. Gunmen were scrambling, either in fear and pain, or to reach cover in case more explosives were dropped into their lap. He could see a man with an RPG tube, looking bewildered, half of his face a bloody smear on his skull. The rocketeer was in a state of shock, his entire body slick and crimson from the damage he'd received from the air-bursting grenade.

Bolan gave the poor bastard a burst of 4.6 mm rounds through the face, destroying his brain and ending his confusion and suffering in this world. No one seemed to notice his approach. Bolan had flipped his grenades toward the back of the group, thus moving their focus from front back toward where they'd come.

Solyenko had to have really drummed it in that the Soldier was a terrifying force, especially if they imagined that he was capable of flanking them so quickly and silently, but then, they had fired their RPGs before they'd even seen him on the mounted heavy machine gun.

Suddenly more mayhem was added to this battle as a sizzling shell spiraled into a Jeep, turning it into a blossom of destruction. It had been fired from the far gate, meaning that one of his allies, or perhaps both, had opted to bring their force into this fight. Bolan hadn't asked for the assistance, but he could figure that the rolling thunder of grenades and warheads detonating had been a sign that things were deadly intense.

"That you, Zach?" Bolan asked over his throat mike. Even as he spoke, he took advantage of the Jeep's detonation to take down the crew of a pickup before they could realize that he was on top of them.

Bolan shot the driver through the windshield, 4.6 mm rounds easily punching through the safety glass, but deforming badly before they struck the fluid mass of the driver's torso. Further disrupted, the slender bullets became spiraling blossoms carving horrendous wound cavities through flesh.

"Yeah!" Winslow answered. "Majid is fairly certain you have that entrance bottled up, and she's with me."

As if in answer, to point out where she was, a gunman next to the pickup sprawled backward, violated by a burst of 5.56 mm NATO rounds from her AUG. Bolan smiled, even as he pressed the attack on the pickup.

The shotgun rider's attention snapped forward as Bolan used the front bumper to vault onto the hood. He shifted his aim and put more rounds into the guy in the passenger seat, zipping his head open like a melon. Brains burst out in a volcano of gray matter, ending the threat of this gunman before he could lift his weapon.

Bolan let the MP7 hang loose on its sling and leaped

onto the cab. A man at the machine gun was drawing a bead on the distant gate. The Executioner punched him in the kidney, dropping the gunner to his knees in paralyzing agony. There was another man in the pickup's bed with the gunner, a loader who also had a rifle for security work. This mercenary turned in reaction to the sudden violence done to his partner. Bolan snapped out a kick, jarring the rifle out of the crew member's hands. The disarmed rifleman paused for a moment, giving the Executioner an opening.

Bolan punched the man in the throat, knuckle caving in his larynx with a single shot. Gasping and sputtering, the choking mercenary tumbled backward out of the pickup, landing with a sickening crunch that he would never rise from. Bolan turned back to the agonized machine gunner and drove his knee hard into the point of his chin. The lower mandible acted as a guillotine, coming down with severing force on his windpipe. A second rising knee launched the bridge of his nose right into his brain, killing him instantly.

This machine gun was another light 7.62 mm weapon, not a vehicle-smashing Fifty like the one he'd had to abandon earlier. That didn't matter much, because against Jeeps and pickups, the 7.62 mm NATO rounds that erupted from the muzzle still had the punch and power to slash through the vehicles.

Bolan turned the light machine gun on the Jeep right next to him, held down the trigger, and turned the vehicle into a colander, leaking blood and torn shreds of human flesh. The roar of the LMG snapped the remaining forces out of their shock and surprise.

The grenades, the rockets, the rifle fire, had all overwhelmed them, hammering them with distraction, fear, even outrage. Now they heard the unmistakable bellow of one of their own guns working in among them, chopping them apart. Confusion, screams and explosions abounded, and Bolan swept the LMG like a scythe, reaping the straw man killers around him, always keeping his senses alert for a sign of either Solyenko or Goomabong. Unfortunately, neither man seemed to be present in this group of Asians. Solyenko and Goomabong were big, unmistakable hulks who would stand out in this crowd, even if they were operating inside the cab of a pickup.

Another RPG shell slammed hard into the last intact vehicle. This one split in two, the explosion rending metal and causing a tremor to shake its way up and through Bolan's legs.

"You're shooting dangerously close, Zack," Bolan warned over the throat mike.

"Sorry" came Winslow's reply.

"That's okay. Switch to rifle and come on in," Bolan returned. He let the LMG's controls go, switching back to his MP7, scanning the grounds.

"Did either of them show up?" Majid asked. She'd been already moving up, closing the distance between herself and Bolan. She held the AUG at a low ready, prepared to dish out a spray of high-velocity death against anyone daring to attack her. Fortunately the three of them had wrought so much damage among the enemy that no one was sticking around. Anyone who could even limp or crawl was making a beeline for freedom. Weapons were abandoned, as were bullet-riddled hulks and burning wreckage.

"No," Bolan answered.

Bolan hopped off the bed of the pickup he'd cleared out. "Let's go inside and see what Onn has to offer."

NIK ONN ALMOST didn't recognize Mila when she entered his office, blond-bleached hair and dressed in clothes that covered her body and shoes that didn't force her onto tip-toes. She had gone from his powdered little plaything to a very grim, determined-looking young woman. If her visage wasn't formidable enough, the rifle she carried, her bandolier of spare magazines and the pistol on her hip underlined and punctuated that she was now some-one who meant business.

She had been sent in first, with Bolan on her heels and Winslow bringing up the rear.

Makka stood beside the desk, having set down his pistol. The bodyguard didn't want to make a single mis-take, provoking the trio into further violence. The dis-play they had just seen, that they'd felt rock the Earth like a seismic event, had told them that these three were a force to be reckoned with.

Onn had his pistol in front of him on the desk. From the way Mila carried her rifle, he could tell that she was a professional, not a down-and-out Senoi girl.

"Your name isn't Mila," he said simply.

Her eyes narrowed, a frown bowing her lips. "Con-stable Erra Majid."

Onn tried to suppress his shudder, but it didn't quite work. He was shaken, and knew that while McCormack was here to make a deal, Majid was only barely contain-ing her anger.

"Listen, McCormack, or Soldier, or whatever I can call you—" Onn began.

Bolan cut him off. "It's all the same to me. All you have to know is that I'd normally be your judgment."

Onn shifted his gaze to the woman. He couldn't think

of her as a girl anymore. He also felt ill, sickly, his groin feeling as if it had been soaked in ice water, gone numb.

The woman had taken a lot of sexual abuse over the past months. Onn had never thought of her as having firearms skills, or even any ability to fight back, when he'd taken advantage of her on a daily basis, savoring not only her sexuality, but her humiliation with greedy, bottomless desire. He went over the word *Constable* again and again in his mind as he studied her. There was nothing of law enforcement about her. She was cloaked in trembling rage and dark thoughts of vengeance, a barely controlled animal straining at a leash that McCormack held.

"I surrender. I will go to jail. I will also tell you everything I possibly can about Solyenko and Goomabong," Onn said. He couldn't keep the quiver of fear from his lips.

Majid sneered. "Groveling before me, now?"

Onn looked down, shame threatening to smother him. He'd been caught, red-handed. What was worse, there was no way he could excuse what he'd done to her. The relationship he'd run was between master and slave. Consumer and slab of meat. The very conversation about what to do with her, disposing of her at Solyenko's cruel hands, was a livid scar of terror in his recent memory.

"McCormack—"

"I asked her not to kill you," Bolan said. Once more, he had cut him off.

Onn glanced at Makka. The bodyguard couldn't look at him now. The knowledge of what he'd done to her, and what he'd threatened to do, hung in the air like gasoline fumes, thick and heavy, waiting for one spark to turn the whole office into an inferno of retribution.

"But she can do anything else?" Winslow asked, sounding innocent and naive.

"Anything my heart desires," Majid grumbled.

Onn wanted to deflate, to shrink, to be sucked down a drain so he didn't have to withstand the all-consuming, chest-squeezing dread overhanging the office. No matter how much he wished, though, he had to sit and take it.

"Then let's get this over with," Onn answered. He turned to Bolan.

"Solyenko and Goomabong had gone to three different meetings with a local ethnic Thai pirate gang that was operating on the coast."

"Where are they based?" Bolan asked.

Onn thought for a moment. "They have a secluded little inlet about several miles to the south of Alor Setar in Kedah State."

"What makes you think that they've thrown in with them?" Bolan continued.

"Because Goomabong used to be one of them, and the minute Solyenko met with them, suddenly that Russian and Goomabong were tight. So, either they're sleeping together or…"

"Right," Bolan muttered. He didn't look too pleased at Onn's blatant homophobic accusations.

"No, those two are straight," Onn said, misinterpreting the Executioner's gruff response. "But Solyenko admitted that he was interested in disposing of Mila… Constable Majid."

Majid nodded in agreement. "And you looked like you were willing to go along with it, you sick bastard."

Onn took a deep breath. "I never claimed to be an angel. But we were worried about a possible leak."

"So you'd let me become hamburger on the end of Solyenko's—"

"Erra, calm down," Bolan interjected.

Onn noticed a small bit of affection between the two, though the way that the woman and the other American hovered closer, sharing surreptitious glances, showed that there was more, actual physical as well as emotional, attraction between the two.

Making any threats, any aspersions against Majid would inspire the two men to grim reprisals. Onn held his tongue. He sat in his desk chair, turning his anger inward, beating on himself for having lived a life that had slid him into this cesspool where torture and mutilation was a certainty, as well as a life in prison.

"Do you have an address?" Majid asked, fury seething behind her eyes. This was not merely a pretend game of "good cop, bad cop." These weren't cops, nor were they here in the performance of law-enforcement duties. The three of them had waded into Solyenko's assault team and gone for the kill, not arrests. Anyone wounded either had to crawl to freedom on his own, or had been put out of his suffering with a bullet to the head. The Senoi woman was genuinely furious, murderous in her intent.

And he remembered that McCormack had said that she had permission to do whatever she wanted, short of killing him.

Onn wrote down the address, including directions.

"So what are you going to do to me?" the gangster asked her.

She looked him over, sneering, the line of her mouth turned into a thin, trembling thread. Dark eyes blazed with cold rage. "I could castrate you."

Bolan looked surprised at that response, but didn't say

anything. Winslow seemed to exude satisfaction at her pronouncement. It'd be two against one if Majid pulled her knife and began carving off his genitals. And what could be done? Even Makka seemed to show shame in his boss. It was one thing to be a good employer to a security guard, but here he was, being confronted by one survivor of his sexual depravity and predation.

"Then go ahead," Onn said. There was no strength left in his voice. No life, no more joy. He had resigned, and the end was going to come. He could only hope that he could beg McCormack to shoot him through the head rather than administer first aid.

Majid leaned in closer. "You're not going to protest?"

Onn met her, eye to eye. "I've earned this fate. Why bother fighting it?"

Majid tilted her head, then leaned back.

"Come on. Get it over with. In fact, I release you from any deals that keep you from killing me," Onn added. "I've earned this fate. I'm a monster."

Makka even turned back, facing him.

"What about being alive, if only in jail?" Makka asked him.

Onn shook his head. "What's the use of being alive? To give me another shot at hurting someone?"

Majid frowned. "I'd say you're taking the fun out of this revenge, but pissed off as I am at you, I can't bring myself to be the same kind of bastard to you."

Onn looked at her.

"You're truly repentant?" Majid asked.

"I truly rue the path that dropped me into this crap," Onn answered.

With that, she stepped back, then swung around the butt of the AUG. The steel-reinforced stock of the polymer rifle knocked the man from the chair. Onn reached up to his face, feeling blood flowing from the injury.

His head hurt. The sting, though, felt like it was a relief, a cool drizzle after days of blistering heat.

"What about you, Makka?" Majid asked.

The bodyguard sighed. "I'm going to jail. But I sure as hell am not looking to get flogged for whatever he did."

Onn stood, his linen jacket now drenched red over one shoulder.

"Then surrender," Majid said. She looked back at Onn.

"Did that make things any better?" he asked her.

She shook her head. "Not a damned bit. But what you can do to atone is to help me."

Onn nodded. "Be your jailhouse snitch."

"Does that work for you?" Majid asked Bolan.

"If you can live with it, so can I," Bolan said. He looked out the window.

Police sirens were audible in the distance. He could also feel the thump of helicopter blades.

"We're not going to get after Solyenko and Goomabong today," Bolan said.

Winslow sighed. "No retreat?"

"Onn is going to be too valuable to leave alone," Bolan answered. "We'll sit on him until he's in jail. I'll also have to use my Justice Department connections to make sure Erra doesn't get flushed because of all of this carnage or the madness back at the club."

"Besides, you look as if you need a little rest," Winslow mentioned.

Bolan nodded. "That would be nice for a change."

The cauldron that Onn had felt his office had become cooled down. There was little rage left in the room. What there was, he directed at himself. He had much to atone for. The split on his face was a down payment for the rest of his life. The rest would come from keeping his ears peeled in a Malaysian prison until his dying days, which could become soon if he was found out.

Even if he took a sharpened fork handle between the ribs, it'd be a fair trade for the sins staining his soul.

CHAPTER THIRTEEN

The hunt for Solyenko, as Bolan had predicted, had been delayed for the length of a whole day, not because the Royal Malaysian Police were reluctant to believe Matt McCormack's and Zach Winslow's credentials, nor was it because they didn't believe the U.S. Justice Department and Homeland Security, who had phoned in immediately to inform them of the covert operation on their soil.

It all had to do with Bolan, Winslow and Erra Majid's debriefing, which had taken a while. Fortunately, in the time leading up to this conflict, Bolan had spent hours, less with Majid, going over what to tell the local authorities about what had occurred and what they had done. The Executioner was able to pass off the vast majority of the conflict and the damage that ensued on an internecine conflict between Solyenko and Onn. They also took the effort and energy to minimize Onn's compliance in the most violent of activities.

It was easy to backtrack their cover story, as it was Solyenko who had supplied Onn's nightclub security with the assault rifles. Their story was ninety percent true, and ensured that the gang boss was going to avoid a death sentence for treason or support of terrorism. For that, Onn was grateful, but he still maintained that he intended to do everything he could to inform on the Russian *mafiya* and its operations inside Malaysia, especially the Western Peninsula.

Bolan was exhausted, as were his partners, after hours of interviews. Fortunately the three of them had been well fed and given beverages to keep their strength up. Finally, however, it was time for them to clean up, and the soldier stepped under the hot spray of the shower-head. A hot shower was something that rejuvenated him in a way that few other things could. He recalled his dalliance with the bush pilot in Colombia—Magdelena—and thought that was another great means of rejuvenation. A hot shower, scrubbing the grime of exertion away, then sex, was about as fine an aftermath of a mission as he could conceive.

It was here, naked, shielded by a locked door, with steamy wisps of humidity rising around him, that Bolan allowed himself a flight of fancy. He stepped into the shower stall, and as he did physically, he mentally scoured away the dread and doubt, all of the bad that had built up between his ears. He willed himself to sublimate the images of violence and suffering, pushing himself deeper into a healing ritual. Without this meditation, this mind and body maintenance, the Executioner wouldn't have been able to continue so long.

Like a computer's hard drive that became cluttered with file fragments, the shower ritual helped him to put his thoughts in order and to shove the unwanted fragments aside, turned to trash after every bit of useful experience was drained from it. He allowed emotions to free themselves, let himself mourn lives lost, memories of friendly dead be buried. With the stream of droplets slashing down his face, he couldn't cry. Tears were not part of Bolan's arsenal of emotional responses.

But if he were a man who did cry, he could do it here, silently. He was in a locked fortress of solitude where he disposed of his sadness and his anger. He flushed his system.

Even with all of this release, all of this allowance of his body to discharge the negative energy he'd built up, there was still the grim reality of a stainless-steel, rust-proof Desert Eagle in .44 Magnum dangling off the towel rack in its nylon, rot-and-moisture-resistant holster—just a scant turn for him to pull the big cannon, in case of danger.

Nowhere in the world was there a true refuge for the Executioner. Even his home base, Stony Man Farm, had been assailed several times over the course of its existence, many times ending in pure tragedy. He couldn't forget the death of April Rose, ever. She had been one of the great loves of his life.

Soon, he'd have to say goodbye to Winslow and Majid. People who hung around too closely with Bolan eventually ended up either cut off from a normal life or dead. His friends and allies in Able Team and Phoenix Force were men who were constantly working, rarely having a chance to relax, feel free, or to spend time with families. The same went with the support crew at Stony Man, especially Hal Brognola, one of his oldest surviving friends, and Barbara Price, a woman who hadn't captured Bolan's heart the way that April had, though they still found comfort, solace, release in one another's arms.

Brognola and Price were constantly monitoring the world, looking for situations that would require the skills of Bolan or his allies, and in that deadly watch, they had seen the worst of humanity, studied the darkness of humankind at its cruelest.

The life that Bolan had chosen was lonely. He needed to protect Winslow and Majid, and part of him wanted to have the pair left behind, so he could slip away and go after Solyenko and his Thai pirate comrades. Winslow, however, had been dead set on bringing down the Russian once it had been confirmed that he was the one who had inspired the assault that had murdered most of his team members in Colombia.

Majid had suffered at the hands of Onn, but she had also vowed to bring down Goomabong, who she had called the "ape that wanted to twist my head off."

Denying the two of them closure would be as bad a psychic scar as the violence that had been done to them. Winslow and Majid needed to be in this, at least to the point of tracking Solyenko to the Thais' base.

Bolan got out of the shower. Its therapeutic, rejuvenative powers faded once he returned his thoughts to those who could die in his company. He toweled down, threw the belt with the Desert Eagle over one shoulder, and stepped into the tiny room where he had a cot and his gear bags. There was a note on the half-ajar door. He reached out, plucked the note off the door and shut it.

"Coastal pirate base surveiled. Place is empty. All boats pulled out."

It was from the Farm, via the communications at the Royal Malaysian Police barracks where Bolan called home base for now. He walked over to the cot. Solyenko had sent the attack force to burn Onn's estate to the ground, then grabbed everything that he could and did his best to disappear. Weariness washed over the Executioner. He was now back to square one.

He fought the urge to grimace, pulling the anger back into him, smothering it, turning it into fuel for future battle, but a sneer twisted his lips. Square one wasn't exactly what he had been reduced to. There was something

more out there. The Thai pirates with whom Solyenko
and Goomabong had sought haven had to call somewhere
else home, otherwise they wouldn't have been able to
evacuate so quickly, so completely.

He lay back on his cot. It was likely that the Thais
would be somewhere that they thought they'd be comfortable, untouchable. Given the peninsula and mighty
rivers allowing the inland city of Bangkok to have its
own seaport, there were countless places the pirates
could call home. The peninsula itself was between two
great bodies of water—the Gulf of Thailand and the
Andaman Sea. There were thoughts of carving a canal,
an undertaking akin to the canals in Panama or at Suez,
allowing for even more commerce to travel between the
two, rather than swinging around Malaysia.

Given the powerful criminal and political groups willing to resort to crime, it was no wonder that Solyenko
had enlisted Goomabong and his pirate allies to be his
muscle. They would be able to navigate not only the
waterways of the nation, but also the dark underbelly
of Thailand. Bolan and his brothers in arms had been
to Thailand several times over the years, dealing with
one menace or another, from Communist rebels to organized crime rings that employed children as slave labor
and prostitutes. Each battle in-country had been bloody
and nerve-racking.

Bolan knew that the Farm would be going through
those files and the information that the Thai government had on local pirates, scouring records for where
Goomabong would take Solyenko. Even so, he knew
that as he slept, he'd apply his subconscious to sifting
his own memories. The Gulf itself was a big place, but
it was unlikely that the Kuala Lumpur–adjacent pirates

would head there. It was more likely that they would be somewhere on the Andaman Sea.

They'd also be closer. He recalled the State Department's warning to its embassy personnel—even diplomats were prohibited from traveling to the far south of Thailand-Narathiwat, Pattani and Yala provinces without prior mission approval. That mission approval would come along with a security detail armed with submachine guns and assault rifles. Those three regions, in particular, were contested between Thailand and Malaysia, where ethnic clashes had sprung into terrorist car bombings and gun battles. The trouble was, those were on the other side of the peninsula, so he had to dismiss that area as their hiding place. Before sleep claimed him, Bolan remembered a young woman he'd met in Thailand. She would possibly know more.

He noted to contact her, then drifted off to sleep.

CHOI TRANH LISTENED to the soft tones of her cell phone ring her into wakefulness. Dark, almond eyes flickered open and she sat up, wondering who would be calling her and waking her. She flipped the phone up to look at its display screen, then felt a flare of tingles rush through her cheeks, memories flowing unbidden through her as she looked at the name "Belasko."

She hadn't seen him for a couple of years, but he'd stayed in contact with her ever since the day that he'd helped to pull her out of the dark, dismal life's end she could have faced in the belly of a ship that was part brothel, part casino and all hellhole. When she was young, she had been a prisoner, a young girl sold off. At first, she was just a little too young for sexual attention, so she'd been put to hard work in the fields, growing poppies. Then, when she'd developed, began to blossom, breasts forming, she'd been brought to the ship.

There, she was to have lived the rest of her life, to be used up and abused until she was either killed by a sex-hungry John, savoring the end of an adolescent's life, or she committed suicide. Neither of these came to pass. She had been saved. The name of the man, back then, had been Belasko. But she knew him by a first name, Mack, which she would never share with another human being, and by a nickname, Striker, one used often by his comrades in arms. It had been years, and now Tranh was a woman, an adult. And from those first, faltering steps, attached to the warrior who'd unleashed a reign of horror against a renegade general and heroin dealer, she'd worked hard.

Tranh was now in charge of a clinic. She hadn't gotten any medical skills, but she had been sponsored and endorsed by a lawyer, another contact of Striker's, called Singer. Tranh had breezed through law school and was utilizing her license, her knowledge and a bottomless desire to help others. She got kids away from the predators who harnessed them, leaving them to be fed upon by sexual scavengers who were too timid, too weak, to take an adult human woman. Tranh assembled a medical staff to treat their bodies, a psychological crew to attend to their spiritual wounds and even a small school through which she could help those kids, boys and girls, grow from urchins and victims into masters of their own destiny.

Life wasn't particularly simple for her. Through her journeys down the dark alleys of Bangkok's underworld, she'd made plenty of enemies, some of whom no longer walked the Earth. She also had plugged into the whisper stream, a current of gossip, rumor and news about criminals, catching threads of happenings from as far away as Malaysia or Vietnam. Tranh didn't deny that she was glad to have this insight into the rats' nest known as Bangkok's underground, if only because it made her a useful, often vital cog in Striker's worldwide war against what he'd called "Animal Man."

Belasko might not have been related by blood to her, but Tranh felt that he was the only father she could ever have, especially since her former male parent, a useless seed-planter, had sold her off to General Chang as slave fodder. She was loyal to Belasko, and he, being the man he was, would have remained loyal to her even if she'd never had another thing to do with criminal activity. Tranh had taken up the struggle to improve the world, feeling that this was the "family business."

She knew of others around the world who were in this elite little clan. One man, Johnny Gray, from California, often sent well wishes for her birthday, slipping her funds from Striker's war chest so that she could continue her battles. Johnny didn't come out and say it, but he was a true blood relation of Striker's, though his original name had been erased, his true identity submerged beneath ancient history to quarantine Belasko's loved ones. Uncle Johnny, as she'd considered him, had even arranged for Tranh to have the .45 pistol that she'd left resting on the nightstand by her head.

Its grip was small enough even for Tranh's slender, seemingly delicate fingers, but its message was potent. That Heckler & Koch .45 had done much to protect her over the years, but the gun was only a tool. It was Striker who'd told her what her truest weapon was—Tranh herself. Her intelligence. Her courage. Her stamina.

She hit the answer button, even as she pushed down the blossoming memories the name Belasko raised.

"Mack?" she asked.

She could *feel* his grin from the other side of the phone. "Tranh."

That voice was unmistakable. Strong, deep, capable of great menace or phenomenal warmth. "What do you need, sir?"

"I'm in Kuala Lumpur at the moment," Bolan told her. "I need to get some information from you, kiddo."

"You have but to ask," Tranh replied.

"Have you heard anything about a team of pirates operating between Thailand and Malaysia? Specifically in the Andaman Sea and its islands?" Bolan inquired.

Tranh wrote down the information. She also received the name and description of a giant by the name of Goomabong. While the Thai woman hadn't caught much in terms of any piracy on the Andaman Sea, she had heard of Goomabong.

"Goomabong. Yeah, he's an urban legend here in Bangkok," Tranh replied. "He's a man as wide as he is tall, with the strength to flip over a small van."

"Yeah. I've seen him personally. He looks the part," Bolan replied.

Tranh took a deep breath. "I'll see what I can get through my networks. What about your computer people back in America?"

"They're researching him through their connections, but sometimes HUMINT and RUMINT are a lot quicker to access than ELINT," Striker returned.

Tranh knew what the big American was talking about. HUMINT was Human Intelligence, while the others were Rumor and Electronics, respectively. Though Tranh had a computer and a smartphone, in the Bangkok underworld things were still done by lips to ear or by pieces of paper. No computer in the world could read a folded note tucked in a secret pocket of a courier's jeans.

"How fast will you need this?" Tranh asked.

"Give me about six hours," Bolan answered. "I'm still not in-country."

Tranh sighed. "I'll get to work, then. Hopefully, my little strands of spiderweb will pick up some clue about him."

"Thank you, Tranh," Bolan told her.

"It is only repayment for a life saved and raised," Tranh replied and flipped her phone closed.

Now what she had to do was get in touch with two men who were responsible for more dead bodies in Bangkok back alleys: Mick Hayes and Chuck Brewer.

If anyone could punch some information loose inside of six hours, it would be those two men.

Letting down Striker was never an option for Tranh.

ZACH WINSLOW WAS there first in the meeting room, if only because he had no one else to talk to. Erra Majid had her calls to make to the rest of her family to inform them of her safety and return to the land of the living. Bolan, in the meantime, was burning up his Combat CDA's batteries and Wi-Fi connections to contact Thailand and Virginia respectively. Since Winslow had been left in the soldier's care by Homeland Security, he didn't currently have a superior to report to, nor contacts to get in touch with. His family, what there was of it, hadn't spoken to him in years, none of them showing any like for a clansman of theirs being a member of "the damned revenuers."

That wasn't to imply that his "kin" were backwoods country folk; they were simply Americans who felt that federal income tax was unconstitutional, that the government should only get its revenue from sales tax and tariffs. As such, as an agent for the U.S. Treasury Department, Winslow had become an enemy of the people. That the Secret Service moved under the jurisdiction of Homeland Security mattered not one whit. It wasn't something that Winslow was proud of, or felt good being, but he had a duty, a calling.

The Secret Service wasn't an oppressive state entity. It protected the economy from forgers and counterfeiters, and it guarded the heads of that state, preventing anarchy to overrule the Constitution. Still, he didn't blame his family. They were afraid of a government grown more powerful and a nation that would feel less capable, a situation ripe for tyranny and social decay. Winslow wished that he could tell them what kind of real threats were out there, though; things that he'd fought against so that the public would have no inkling of danger.

He opened a case and looked inside. It was some of the gear that Bolan had brought in. Winslow's frown faded as he pulled out a pistol. It was a 9 mm SIG Sauer P226, the big brother of his duty-issue sidearm. There were two of them, as well as plenty of 15-round and 20-round magazines for both. Majid was Royal Malaysian Police, and the RMP utilized the P226 themselves as a service sidearm.

Winslow opened the case even more and saw that there was a second pistol for each. It was a copy of his Walther PPS, the slender little 9 mm pistol that had the same size as the classic PPK, but more power per shot. There were two of these, as well. He squinted.

"We're transitioning to the P99 by Walther," Majid revealed, startling the Secret Service agent. "I've got training on that design, so McCormack thought that I could benefit from having that as my backup."

Winslow nodded. "Cool. I just got it because it was skinny, but had a better grip than most others and not as high in demand as the Smith & Wesson slim 9."

Majid gave him a smile. "We're going to be taking the plunge deep on this one."

"Going into Thailand and fighting pirates?" Winslow asked. "I can't tell if a fight's going to be hairy, or it's going to be a cakewalk when I'm with McCormack."

"You haven't been with him long, have you?" Majid asked.

Winslow shook his head. He took a deep breath. "It's a long story."

Majid looked at the door. "I think we've got the time."

Winslow let her settle in and related the tale, finding himself meandering into his old nicotine addiction and his self-loathing for not being there when his friends were dying. He didn't realize it as he spoke, but each word was a weight off his heart. It was confession, self-purification.

And she listened, reacting. Finally she took his hand in both of hers.

"Listen, I don't know what we'll run into…" Majid said. She glanced again at the door.

Winslow felt his heart skip a beat. The two of them had been close for the past several days. They'd played enough at being a couple that he actually felt comfortable with her. The fact that she was intimating that she was looking for at least some human contact…

Winslow pulled her close and kissed her quickly before his nerves could derail this quiet moment. Majid answered with passion, winding her arms around him. Breathlessly, they broke the kiss, looking into one another's eyes.

"Is this going to make it weird for us?" Winslow asked her.

Majid shrugged. "I won't have time to worry about it when the bullets are flying overhead."

With that, the two submerged into another tight embrace, another deep, probing kiss. There might not be a tomorrow, so they gave in and lived the next hour to the fullest.

CHAPTER FOURTEEN

The Executioner had allowed Winslow and Majid their time together. He could sense the attraction the Secret Service agent had for the lady cop. Majid herself was betraying her own feelings and concerns. They had both been at his side instantly during the assault on Onn's estate, but it was telling that Winslow had swung around and joined up with Majid, or vice versa, and they'd made a unified attack.

They also had showed some great chemistry together as they were shopping for clothes and preparing for their infiltration of Onn's club. Bolan was glad that the two of them could share a positive, life-affirming sexual experience. Erra Majid needed the healing touch of a caring man, not an abuser like the Malay gangster had been. Zach Winslow had needed the touch of another person who cared about him.

Mack Bolan, however, was glad for the time alone to think. His sleep had been full of the usual Blood River dreams, the nightmares of loved ones, friends, even casual acquaintances and allies swept to their doom in his War Everlasting. Those dreams, however, had no effect on the deepness and rejuvenation of his sleep. He was rested, and he knew that it was just his subconscious reminding him of who he was fighting for and clearing out the emotions of guilt and loss, burning them up while he was safely asleep, when his body was paralyzed and unable to lash out.

His gathered notes were copious. Stony Man Farm had delivered plenty of information on operations that Goomabong's allies could have been a part of, from smuggling to hijacking. The Farm's computers had worked out a radius that would have made it feasible for such a quick evacuation from the Malaysian side of the border while providing plenty of opportunity for the Thai-based pirates along the Andaman Sea. The field of search had been narrowed down considerably, but Bolan still had the option of a dozen different islands and islets in the sea, or the coast itself and rivers stretching inland.

Either way, he was putting together the approach he was going to take. An island would have been preferable for an assault. There was less likely to be an entire perimeter watch, except on all but the smallest of atolls, so a stealth approach would be easier. Bolan had brought his allies along on a couple of potentially murderous missions, but he had no interest in a suicidal assault, or sacrificing either Majid or Winslow in a foolish operation. There were times when he wished that he could have simply phoned up his best friend and pilot Jack Grimaldi to swoop in with a fully loaded F/A-18 to blast the entirety of the enemy base to smithereens, but that wasn't his way. Bolan needed confirmed kills, but before that, he needed to find out exactly where Solyenko's orders were coming from.

The ex-Spetsnaz gangster was a dangerous and clever opponent, sending enough force against Bolan to nearly kill him twice, but he wasn't the kind of mastermind to set up a coordinated assault on international economies with printing presses and computer hacking. Solyenko was muscle. Skilled, dangerous and intelligent, but he was the hammer. Someone else was simply pointing out the nails.

That meant Bolan needed a face-to-face with the man. Or at least access to a corpse with still usable electronics on him, such as a personal data assistant or cell phone. Even a folded piece of paper would be a godsend. If not, then all this fighting, all this hammering away, a grinding journey around the globe, would have been for nothing.

The soldier heard movement from the trio's improvised conference room, the door opening. He saw Winslow, looking at once flushed and rejuvenated. There was a look of realization on his face, but Bolan merely gave him a warm, welcoming smile.

He entered, watching Majid go through her hair as she overlooked a tabletop with equipment spread out across its surface.

"Any word from your contacts in Thailand?" she asked.

Winslow looked relaxed, so, taking a cue from him, there was no purpose in her acting as if there were an elephant in the room. If anything, she looked better, too, freed of the weight of some traumatic memories.

Bolan shook his head. "They still have three hours, and I'm going to call them. My friend's in Bangkok, but our pirates aren't going to be that far north. Solyenko might be on the run, or he might hole up for a moment. Either way, the time it'll take to go to Bangkok and then fly back down south will likely give him more time to escape."

Winslow frowned. "I feel like we've wasted enough time recovering from all our bumps and bruises."

Bolan put a hand on his shoulder. "We needed the break. We've been going practically nonstop. When we haven't been fighting, we've been preparing. A few hours' sleep on a plane is no match for at least a cot and a hot meal."

Winslow glanced over at Majid, trying unsuccessfully to stifle a smile. "Made a meal out of me, and came back for more."

Majid turned to Bolan. "You're not…"

"This isn't high school, and frankly, you're both adults. Add to that fact, you are both adults who have, and will soon be, risking your lives," Bolan returned. "I wouldn't begrudge either of you some relief. It's a non-issue. No drama."

Majid took a deep breath and let it out, smiling. "All right."

She quickly turned toward Winslow. "I wasn't that bitey, was I?"

"A figurative meal," Winslow answered with a grin. "All right. Do you have a plan or two?"

"One thing I'm hoping to avoid is an approach up a river, and finding that we'll have our best luck with an island infiltration," Bolan told them. "I'm not going to be one who believes in luck or jinxes, but our pirates have been around for a while, especially since they've heard of Goomabong in Bangkok."

"So the odds are, they're going to be on an inlet," Majid said. "That means we have to swim ashore down a shooting gallery, right? A river emptying into the sea would likely have security outposts on both shores."

"Staggered so that they could annihilate any boats coming through," Bolan agreed.

Winslow rubbed his forehead. "So, we don't take a

water approach. If they're on the river, then it stands to reason that they're counting on impassable terrain to their backs. Forest or mountains."

Bolan squinted as he studied a relief map on his laptop screen. He clicked the zoom, looking for an appropriate spot. "If we do that, we can rappel into the forest and then walk through the brush."

"Wouldn't they hear a helicopter?" Majid asked.

"We'd have a few things on our side. One, we're a small group, so we won't need a heavy bird with a huge rotor diameter," Winslow countered. "Something like a Little Bird, right?"

Bolan nodded. "Plus, there are means of nullifying helicopter rotor blade noise. A combination of using the forest canopy, as well as a technology trick or two."

"Like the choppers your people used to take down Bin Laden?" Majid asked.

Bolan didn't answer, but his smile was answer enough.

"So, we know what to do for the worst, and we know the approach in the best possible case," Winslow muttered. "You've got a plan for just on the shore?"

Bolan nodded. "I had the time, and this isn't my first rodeo."

Winslow tilted his head.

"Trying to imagine me as a cowboy?" Bolan asked.

Winslow chuckled. "Can't imagine you *not* being a cowboy. In fact…you remind me of…"

"Do I want to hear it?" Bolan muttered.

"The Lone Ranger," Winslow finished.

Bolan let out a sigh of relief. "That works."

"That makes me Tonto," Winslow quipped.

"So, you have a plan for everything, and you're a loner

who just keeps picking up a small entourage," Majid said. "Sounds like someone else to me."

"This should be interesting," Bolan mused.

"Even in Kuala Lumpur, the littlest girl's heard of Batman. You even look a little like his alter ego."

Bolan raised an eyebrow, then smiled. He needed a few laughs, things had been tense and worrisome.

"What gave me away, the utility belt?"

Majid chuckled. "So, do you have something for our in-between option?"

"I've got that planned, as well," Bolan replied. "But there is one variable I really have reservations about. If the pirates have set up in a village, they'll have human shields. This is going to necessitate a much stealthier approach than even before. And if that is the case…"

"We'll be stuck on overwatch," Winslow concluded.

"I can move quietly," Majid interjected.

"I'm not doubting your capabilities," Bolan told her. "Either of you. But one moves much more easily than three."

Winslow didn't look happy about it, but he agreed. "He has a point."

Majid grimaced, but she could see the logic both men were talking about. "Let us hope that it won't come to that."

"Agreed. I could use the backup," Bolan said. "But once more, I can't go into the heart of the pirates' camp, and then control everyone leaving the grounds. Someone has to close the doors."

"Well, just as long as you're not being greedy about it," Majid conceded, her tone clear that she didn't think of Bolan as being a glory-hog.

"We'll go over the assault plan and the location as

soon as I get confirmation from my people in Thailand," he told them.

He smiled. "As you were."

Bolan ignored the glance Majid and Winslow shared even as he walked out of the meeting room.

BOLAN AND HIS allies were in the air again. No longer were they operating under the radar, though the helicopter that they rode in did fly the nap of the waves, moving along swiftly.

The chopper was an MH-6 Little Bird "borrowed" by the Sensitive Operations Group. It was flown by a pair of TF-160 expert pilots. The Little Bird itself was a black shadow against the night sky, zooming along at 150 miles per hour. Bolan was on one side of the ship, sitting on a bench designed for three men, while on the other, Majid and Winslow were both in place. Bolan helped balance the weight on his side with the crate for their assault supplies and heavy weaponry.

As Zach Winslow was frustrated by being sidelined while Bolan invaded the pirate base, the Executioner decided to allow his companion the opportunity to engage in some hardcore poetic justice. As such, Winslow was given a refresher course on the Carl Gustav. Technically, the gun was a recoilless rifle, but it was simply a shoulder-mounted rocket launcher. With larger warheads and better accuracy than the RPG-7, a two-man team could cause far more widespread destruction than a dozen men with their Russian-designed counterparts.

Winslow and Majid would be that two-person team. When the Executioner struck the pirate base, they would supply ground-shaking cover fire. The weapon had been a simple, everlasting concept, still in produc-

tion since 1948, as successful as its Warsaw Pact equivalent, changed only with weight-saving polymers and
alloys over the decades, delivering its deadly 84 mm
warheads with killer accuracy for well over half a century, at ranges out to 1000 meters. Few things would
be more cathartic than seven pounds of high explosives
detonating with tank-crushing force.

The Thai coast was dark this far south. They were approaching the frontier between Thailand and Malaysia,
though most of the ethnic friction and violence was on
the other side of the peninsula, in the Gulf of Thailand,
not here on the Andaman Sea. That didn't mean it was
unknown for criminal activity to occur here. The pirate
base was on the shore of an inlet, which was surrounded
by an expanse of jungle, reachable only by water traffic, no great shakes in terms of strangling off a village
from outside trade or supplies. However, the placement
of the village made it so that there were shanty houses
built, floating on the water, where the honest people lived
like refugees, living off the cast-asides from the pirates.
Goomabong and his brethren were the protection for the
Thai villagers against other forces in the area.

Bolan was loath to shear that layer of defense from
folks who were otherwise too poor to fend for themselves, but he'd spent a couple of hours coordinating
with Choi Tranh.

Before the villagers could fall too far, she and her resources would be on hand to catch them and keep them
afloat. It was simply an extension of the deeds that Tranh
had already done in defense of the children who had been
broken from the sex tourism slavery back in Bangkok
and the surrounding cities. Even as the helicopter was
flying along, the two men who worked as her muscle

and protection—"Dandy" Chuck Brewer and "Cowboy" Mick Hayes—were also on their way with a few friends from the roughhouse side of Bangkok. They wouldn't be here until later in the coming day, but when they showed up, they would both be on hand with enough firepower to hold off the most determined of raiders and bandits on the coast.

Hayes and Brewer had worked alongside the Executioner on a previous campaign in Thailand, Brewer having lost an arm, Hayes missing an ear from being caught in an aerial bombardment on Bolan's group. Hayes simply had grown his hair out to cover the mangled seam of scar tissue where the outer ear had been. Brewer adapted by adopting a prosthetic arm, which in turn only made his boxing skills all the more dangerous. They would be cover for the villagers until Tranh could maneuver Thai social work efforts to put the people of the inlet in a better position economically.

The Executioner was glad to have that kind of support present for a community that actually needed it. His tear through Colombia and into Venezuela had come with the support of Captain Villanueva, who could pick up the pieces, though Bolan's battle against the conspirators and money smugglers had been extremely focused, avoiding bringing harm to noncombatants, and often staying far from even the most run-down of shantytowns. This mission, however, had been pointed out by Tranh, who knew that she had the ability to help. Bolan wouldn't have gone in recklessly, guns blazing anyway, but now with a means of leaving people better off than they had been before, he felt as if he had a better handle on things.

Luckily, Winslow had showed that he was a fine shot with the Carl Gustav gun. No stray rounds would miss a building and soar into a floating shack bobbing on the inlet.

Bolan's own gear, his preferred AR and M203 rifle and grenade launcher combo, was something that the Executioner had deadly precision wielding. He held his fire when one of the 40 mm rounds could miss and strike innocents, though, the M16 upper on an M4 lower was as fine a scalpel that Bolan could ever wish for. He opted for the M16 barrel and upper receiver on a standard M4 lower for the purpose of having a collapsible stock on what would normally be a fixed-butt weapon. The original 20-inch barrel length squeezed every single bit of velocity, power and accuracy out of the 5.56 mm round, while the lower, made of carbon fiber with a six-position telescoping stock made the gun lighter and handier while maintaining a full-automatic option. The hybrid weapon was win-win, and even the Marines had a preference for the longer pipe, realizing that a 14.5-inch barrel didn't carry the same fight-stopping punch or "rifle" range of the shorter M4.

Bolan had the full-auto tuned to 800 rounds per minute, a rate that would allow him to leave the selector lever on full, while allowing him to tap out one or two shots at will, giving him match-grade accuracy with the assault rifle. All of that, coupled with heavy, precision-crafted hollowpoint rounds, and the hundreds of rounds in 30-shot magazines would give the soldier an answer for odds beyond ten to one. No matter how large the opposing force, Bolan was going to bring everything humanly possible to this battle. He also intended to be as humane to the bystanders on hand.

However, Bolan hadn't survived as long as he had without being fully aware that there were times when hostages became so enamored of their oppressors that they developed a Stockholm Syndrome–style allegiance, willing to fight and die for even the cruelest of masters. The Executioner would have to watch his back, though he grimly realized that he might be forced to kill some of the very people he'd worried so much about.

The ultimate goal of this mission, however, was going to be the capture and detention of Grev Solyenko. That man would have the answers he'd need to find who was so intent on developing a global economic crisis that they were willing to murder people on two continents and attack the two largest monetary superpowers in the world.

The Farm's cybernetics staff was digging deep into the programming, and the ploy was a twenty-first century update of a last gasp KGB operation to cripple the West. With the United States, and now the People's Republic of China both under assault, the ultimate goal was undoubtedly to put the limping former Soviet Union back on the world stage as a capable First World Nation. In the decades since the fall of the Berlin Wall, Russia had been laboring, engaged with struggles against former SSR states such as Kazakhstan, Georgia and Chechnya, as well as dealing with a workforce swiftly being marginalized by immigrants seeking jobs.

Russia was quickly growing a neo-Nazi movement, young street thugs being organized with the sole purpose of spreading terror and death among anyone who wasn't Russian, doubly violent if they happened to be non-whites. It was a historical irony that would have made the leaders of the Third Reich chuckle from their places in Perdition, but all Bolan and his allies at Stony Man Farm knew was that the racist agenda in Russia was

armed, trained and determined to kill to protect themselves and reestablish a pure country.

More than once, Bolan had gone head-to-head with
such agents of intolerance, and when all was said and
done, they were no less vehement or violent than any
of the other human savages he'd battled. Be it white,
black, Arab or Hutu supremacy, once the thugs went
from hurling insults to smashing skulls with rocks and
opening fire with automatic weapons and Molotov cock-
tails, such foes would find an eternal foe in the shape
of the Executioner.

Even now, sitting on the Little Bird's starboard bench,
Bolan was putting together an idea of what kind of muscle the bosses of this counterfeiting and banking cyber-
attack conspiracy would utilize. There were not only
neo-Nazi civilians at work in the cities of Russia, but
there were also units in the Russian army that would be
more than willing to turn back the clock a few decades,
returning to a tyrannical state run by the iron fist of a
government unafraid to run over citizens with tanks or
to make family members disappear in the middle of the
night. While it might not have been with the goal of producing a new Communist state or the rebirth of the Soviet Union, the effect would still be the same.

People would be brought to their knees by a group of
heavily armed, self-serving bullies. Those who resisted
would be murdered, homes and businesses destroyed.
Western Asia would once more be a dark bastion of op-
pression. Bolan had fought against hard-liners to prevent
such a rebirth of the old status quo, had lost the lives of
too many friends and allies to allow such a thing to happen. Whatever the goals and the ideology of the conspiracy, Bolan had one simple aim.

Complete destruction.

Scorched earth.

And as he approached his target at 160 miles an hour on a bird laden with enough firepower to wipe an armed camp off the face of the globe, Bolan was taking his first step in that direction.

CHAPTER FIFTEEN

Grev Solyenko held a straight razor in his hand, looking at the mirror polish on the blade, the long, keen edge that some had used in the past to slice open the throats of victims as well as for shaving. He thought about where he stood here, where he had ended up.

Right now, he was in a village, co-opted by Thai pirates, on the edge of a mangrove swamp. The building he stood in itself rode on stilts sunk deep into the silty, sandy bottom of the swamp. It was one of dozens sprawled around the base, but at least this one had been cleaned up. The previous owners were somewhere, at least their bones were, in the sandy bottom of the brackish waters below.

What technology that there was in this particular hut was running off a portable generator that snorted and belched, a once-clean red thing with a half-dozen plugs filled by cords in something that looked straight out of a fire department's manual on how *not* to use an outlet.

He could see his reflection in the polished flat blade, though it was warped, distorted by the bevel and spine of the thing. He could see the remnants of his shaving session, patches of leftover lather on his cheekbones or in his collar. The straight razor had done a good job of cleaning off his face, and for a moment, he wondered if he should have even bothered.

Solyenko had been involved in this operation since

the beginning, at least in terms of working on the security. His protection of the Kuala Lumpur computer center was the primary reason why he had been brought in. He'd been a burden on the *organasatya,* his destructive sexual tendencies usually attracting far more attention than even his skills with high explosives. This had been a shit detail, but as he'd proved his worth and skill here, his responsibilities had grown.

Solyenko actually felt as if he had a chance with the *mafiya* again. Then came the call to act against agents who had stumbled upon the counterfeiting. They'd turned to their number-one man, Solyenko, a ruthless genius at the art of explosive destruction. It had been his idea to slap the Chinese and the U.S. operatives with rocket-propelled grenades and anti-tank missiles. The use of more Western firepower, such as the SMAW-NE rockets, had proved to be a devastating bit of kit that, in any other circumstance, would have turned attention away from the Russians' involvement in this operation.

He simply hadn't counted on the foolishness of Alfa Molinov in attempting to kill the survivors of an identical attack in Colombia. Molinov had sent a death squad to take care of the two men who'd made it through the carnage, and in a display of the worst luck in the world, the attack had been cut off by the actions of a single, highly skilled man.

The Soldier had been identified by the name Matt McCormack, but Solyenko knew that it was just another cover name. He'd had other identities over the years, but only one thing was certain. The Soldier/McCormack was a force of nature. He had torn his way through South America, chasing leads and threads from Medellín to the Venezuelan frontier.

It was a pattern that had been observed by the *mafiya* over the years. The arrival of a lone operative and the subsequent destruction of the gang's schemes and the deaths of dozens of their members, culminating with the loss of an organization leader or leaders, all at the hands of this single warrior. The description of the man varied in facial details, but the overall stature—six foot two to four in height and 220 to 240 pounds of powerful build and strength, black hair and cold blue eyes—evidenced a commonality.

That was the description that had forced Solyenko to send off a strike team from Malaysia, a half-dozen handpicked killers, skilled with an arsenal of weapons, backed up by every bit of muscle that Molinov and his local allies could assemble. That force, nearly three hundred men, had been wiped out. Trillions of dollars in counterfeit bills for half a dozen countries had been destroyed, incinerated, the printing presses in Venezuela destroyed days earlier.

Even so, that had only been a part of the ultimate plan. Solyenko felt some satisfaction that he could do the job, but he hadn't counted on Molinov and his sloppiness and lack of operational security when it came to his smartphone. The fool had recorded his communications, and kept Solyenko's and Onn's numbers in his device's memory.

Because of that, the club had been compromised. What was worse was that when the Soldier showed up, he'd found even more than just a gang-run nightclub. He'd somehow detected the complex computer systems beneath, probably through the devices that Onn utilized to spy upon patrons, stealing information from their personal computers and cell phones. All of this had been well under control, but Solyenko had been betrayed by the overreach of others.

Because of them, Solyenko was damned.

He'd been called back home.

Solyenko stepped away from the straight razor. He looked at himself in his reflection on the computer monitor. His skull was clean to the scalp, scraped bare by the straight razor. He took a deep breath.

It had been the others who had failed, who had threatened operational security. The trouble was, he was alive and the others weren't, or at least Onn was in prison, holed away deeply to protect him.

The Malay gangster still didn't know who was truly in charge. They wouldn't get anything from him, other than Goomabong's association with the band of pirates he currently hid among. Solyenko looked out the window, the predawn gloom starting to lighten. Sleep was an elusive creature, ever beyond his grasp. It had been that way since the blowout in Tumaco, Colombia.

He was a hunted man. The Soldier had not only been a legend to the *mafiya* and their criminal underworld counterparts across the world, he had also been a menace that the Spetsnaz had trained to spot, recognize, and hoped to avoid. How many Russian or Soviet plots had been crushed by this man's interference? Enough that a group considered one of the most elite in the world feared him. If one man could cause the *organasatya* and the Spetsnaz to look over their shoulders for his presence, then it was no wonder that "McCormack" had burrowed so far, so deep, into the Kuala Lumpur part of the operation, destroying the banks of servers and computer records with which his masters hoped to take on the international market.

Solyenko had heard the rumors, the stories, first during his time in special operations, then when he'd "graduated" to the *mafiya*. For the longest time he'd wavered between belief and the thought that the Soldier was a mere myth, a motivation for soldiers to train harder and criminals to skulk more carefully.

Now, the truth was out, and Solyenko had called home. He'd told them that McCormack was on his trail, and that McCormack was the unstoppable Soldier.

That had to have been the greatest mistake Solyenko had ever made.

He'd called out. Hoped for an extraction. His masters had told him they would send a helicopter to pick him up.

Solyenko was dead certain that the helicopter would come, but it would arrive loaded to destroy the pirate base. It was what the ex-Spetsnaz trooper would have done, severing any connection between himself and a failure. As if he hadn't had enough to worry about with a one-man army hounding him, he was now acutely aware that he was going to be erased from the face of the Earth. There was no hope, no option, no way to escape.

And suddenly all those jangled nerves that had kept Solyenko awake over the past several days were calm.

Without a light at the end of the tunnel, he was free. He'd struck rock bottom, and this fall hadn't killed him yet. Survival was such a slim possibility that he appreciated every moment now. Solyenko knew that he was fated to die someday. And that would have to be this morning, either in the form of an aerial assault or with a bullet to the head straight from the gun of his assassin.

"Let them come," he muttered out loud. He picked up the phone, dialed Goomabong.

"What?" the bulky Thai pirate asked.

"I'm pretty certain that the Soldier is on his way here. And even if he isn't, I made a horrible error," Solyenko admitted.

"You called your bosses, and asked them for a ride out," Goomabong concluded.

"And now we're just a loose end that McCormack can follow to them," Solyenko replied.

"We?" Goomabong asked.

"I am. But you'll get caught in the collateral damage," Solyenko corrected.

Solyenko could feel the sneer on the other end of the line. "So, do you have a plan? Another case of running and leaving someone else to fight our battle?"

Solyenko sighed. "I don't think so. I'm just going to fight. But you can get out."

"Screw that," Goomabong replied. "Do you know what your bosses will throw at us?"

"I'm thinking a Hind gunship," the Russian answered. "Maybe more than one."

He could hear the Thai hum, musing over this news. "We've got some firepower that can knock a helicopter out of the air."

"And McCormack?" Solyenko asked.

"Hopefully we've got sufficient gun power to handle him, too, if it comes to that," Goomabong replied. "However, we didn't leave anything behind that could lead him to us here, or did you make a mistake there?"

"No," Solyenko said, holding off the snap in his voice. "But you don't think he'd let us get away. I'm sure he's got contacts who'd tell him where a group of pirates would be hanging out. Or maybe he's using aerial or satellite surveillance—"

"So, you have a gut feeling that he's on his way."

Goomabong cut him off. "Hell, you told me how he penetrated Venezuela. He found them, he'll nose his way around to us, too."

"Yeah," Solyenko answered. "What do you think?"

"I think I should have never turned my back on Nik," Goomabong muttered. "But the die is cast. What's your plan?"

"Fight until I can't," Solyenko told him.

Goomabong chuckled. "So we've got the same idea."

"Will your pirates be in on this?" Solyenko asked.

"They'll deal with anything that comes our way," Goomabong answered. "I'll rally the troops."

Solyenko smiled as he hung up. He regarded himself in the monitor screen. If he lived, he'd keep the bald look. If he didn't, at least he'd look good going out.

No more running, no more twisting out of traps.

He pulled his weapon off its spot on the wall. It was a folded-stock AKSU, the compact version of the old AK-74, itself an update on the AK-47. The AKSU was chambered in 5.45 mm, a mere .22-caliber round, but even out of the stubby barrel of the rifle, the bullets screamed along at 2400 feet per second. It wasn't an actual rifle, but as a close-quarters weapon, out to 100 yards, it was a full-auto room broom and carried much more punch than a pistol-caliber submachine gun. The AKSU was an old friend from his Spetsnaz days, and he felt good carrying it once more.

Let the Soldier come.

He'd lived in fear for long enough.

Now it was time to fight.

ERRA MAJID GRUNTED under the weight of the fourteen shells loaded into her backpack. Considering that each of them weighed a shade more than three kilos, the payload on her back was equal to her own body mass. Still, she soldiered on, thankful for the cushioned shoulder straps and waist belt that kept the pack from gouging her flesh and straining her back. The design spread all of that weight evenly, so she was more than capable of walking, as she'd been hiking for the past hour since the Little Bird had dropped them off.

Zachary Winslow carried only eight of the shells for his part, but that was because he was burdened with the tube launcher and its standing mount. He was also burdened with communications gear that would keep him in real-time contact with their ally Matt McCormack.

He also toted their long guns and the bandoliers for that ammunition. Since the two of them had already demonstrated great facility with the Steyr AUG, especially on single shot, McCormack had reoutfitted them with newer production rifles, but with different optics, match-grade triggers and 24-inch heavy barrels, and camouflage that would blend better with the forest to mangrove swamp where the pirates made their home.

In addition to the shells for the Carl Gustav gun, Winslow also carried a satchel of 40 mm grenades that would fit into the under-barrel launcher added to his AUG. Majid wondered just how much resistance McCormack expected, but then, she remembered the sheer manpower that Solyenko had arranged at Onn's home. If the Malay gangster hadn't sent his own troops away and made it a point to surrender to the three of them, Majid realized that the battle might not have gone as easily, though the bruising and battering that McCormack had received looked anything but easy.

Majid was surprised at how readily she'd lost her qualms of taking such a vehement offensive against the enemy. Here she was, climbing a trail to reach a cliff overlooking the pirate base and the mangrove swamp that it had been stuck alongside. She was going to be Winslow's loader, feeding 84 mm warheads into the recoilless rifle, launching shells that would take down the craft in the harbor.

There was no mistaking the pirate ships for anything used by the villagers. The marauders had the money to set up prefab buildings, bring in generators to run electronics, and they had a pair of hundred-foot-long power scows, big ships that could carry tons of fish or cargo. It was that kind of room that let them grab lots of loot, or carry contraband in exorbitant amounts. According to the satellite imagery, these men had loaded their scows with heavy machine guns and their own recoilless rifles so that they could hammer legitimate shipping into submission or blast pursuing law-enforcement vessels to pieces.

No, any qualms that Majid had were thrown out the window. Right now, she was in a fight for her life. Solyenko and Goomabong were keyed and ready to murder her, and as long as either of them existed, they were a threat to her. They were a threat to others, as well. She knew that Solyenko and Goomabong had been murdering long before she'd met them, and if they continued on their way, others would die, as well. The morality of taking the fight to them was clear.

Stand by and not help one man tackle vastly superior numbers and firepower, or join in and make certain that reigns of terror were ended, cut off in no way that they could continue their violence.

It was no contest. She would sleep calmly once this was over, no regrets, no guilt from overkill.

Winslow let out a groan up ahead. Majid was pulled from her reverie.

"We reach an impasse?" she asked.

"No. We're at our destination," Winslow replied. He set down the Carl Gustav and its mount, then turned to attend to her. The backpack was simply too heavy and too laden with explosives for her to be able to take it off by herself. Once Winslow put his strength into it, Majid realized how heavily burdened she'd been, undoing the belt and shoulder harness and slithering free. Despite the cool night breeze from over the Andaman Sea, she and Winslow were both drenched with sweat from the effort of hiking through the forest trails with all this battle gear.

Once she was freed, her muscles stretched. It felt so good, she smiled from ear to ear. The sensation of freedom, of release, it didn't feel nearly as good as the lovemaking she'd had with Winslow earlier, but it did inspire the need for personal contact. She wrapped her arms around Winslow's neck and let herself stretch her entire length along his body. Tendons popping, spine realigning, her weight hanging off his powerful frame giving her a chance to completely unkink. She felt like many a cat she had seen, pulling itself as slender as taffy in an effort to release tension.

Winslow smirked. "I can't use you the same way as you use me…"

Majid tugged him down closer, placing a kiss on his lips. "I don't think of you as ever using me."

Winslow smiled in response to that line. "I meant using me as your stretching post."

"Silly man. If I were tall enough, I'd let you do the same."

Winslow tugged her in tight for a kiss. "Thanks. I'll settle for help with my pack, though."

It took a few moments for the pair to disentangle themselves, and then undo Winslow's pack, heavily laden with ammunition for the Carl Gustav and their assault rifles. The two of them looked over the edge of the cliff the Executioner had directed them toward. Beneath them was a straight drop-off, hard-packed stone and earth that would be difficult to climb under normal circumstances, let alone having to claw up from a six-foot-deep mangrove swamp water delta. What land was below them consisted of hummocks where trees had once grown but were now cleared away, making room for huts for the villagers. The pirates had brought in Quonset-style prefabricated huts, the steel-corrugated ribbed hulls making the pirates' camp resemble nothing so much as a set of half-buried cans.

Majid was suddenly very happy for the heavy shells she'd carted up here, because she was certain that those steel-skinned buildings were certainly going to take a lot of punch to destroy. Two large ships were farther out in the water, at the end of a long pier. They were hundred-foot power scows, shallow-bellied boats that could maneuver in the relatively shallow waters of the deeper end of the mangrove swamp, but could carry tons of cargo and weaponry. There were also inflatable rubber boats with outboard motors tied off around the scows to give the pirates a means of interception.

Even at 500 yards, Majid could see camouflage netting covering machine gun emplacements all over the decks of the two boats. If anyone got to those, the half kilometer between the pirate vessels and their roost would be nothing to the heavy .30- and .50-caliber machine guns opening up in unison. At least if they were hit, they would die explosively, bodies splattered like burst melons under the onslaught of heavy, supersonic slugs that could cover almost half a mile with still enough energy to punch through body armor. Fortunately the pirate scows were well within the Carl Gustav's range, making it imperative that Winslow blow them to pieces before they turned on closer targets.

They would wait for McCormack to start the party. He had to infiltrate the floating city, and when he did, his actions would keep the pirates on hand from immediately turning their fire against the two at the top of the cliff. It was a risky gamble for both groups. The lip of the cliff could provide some cover, but lobbed, arced grenades could reach up the thirty-foot cliff face and blow Majid and Winslow away before they could get to safety.

As such, neither of them wanted to speak too loudly or move too swiftly to give away their position. They were utilizing passive night-vision goggles, not even daring to use illumination that would be akin to spotlights searing across the camp. As careful as they were, there was always the possibility that a stray sound would carry on a breeze to the ears of someone on guard duty in the camp.

Up here, stealth was their only cover.

But down below, the Executioner was alone and surrounded by the enemy.

If Winslow or Majid weren't careful, it was likely they could kill him themselves with a shot that fell short of its target. Making sure that they were on target while enduring fire from the pirate camp would be a two-pronged, deadly challenge.

They scanned below, hoping for a sight of their ally, the leader of this crusade into the heart of this lawless land. McCormack had carried them through this mayhem so far, but no man was indestructible.

The dawn was on its way. Already the sky was beginning to lighten from impenetrable black to something brighter, but still gray. The two of them looked at their watches.

The more light there came, the easier it would be for the pirates to shoot back at them.

"What's that sound?" Majid asked, straining her ears. There was something mixed in with the bugs, the distant surf of the Andaman Sea, the muffled running of portable generators.

Winslow had to strain to hear, but she could see his features go from concentration to concern. "A helicopter."

"Could it be the Little Bird?" she asked.

"Maybe, but…"

There was activity below now, cutting off Winslow's thoughts, focusing his attention like a laser. Lights were doused on the power scows and around the camp. At the same time, through their night vision, they could see several of the men coming out with long, pipelike weapons.

"Rocket launchers," Winslow stated. "That can't be the chopper that brought us in. TF-160 doesn't make mistakes like flying too close to an attack site. Certainly never loud enough to be heard for miles if they don't have to."

There was a moment of breathless silence, even the

insects going silent as the throb of helicopter blades increased its intensity in the predawn stillness.

Majid swung her night vision out over the water. It wasn't one helicopter. It was two.

And both of them bore the unmistakable profile of heavily armed gunships, bristling with underwing pods.

CHAPTER SIXTEEN

The mangrove swamp was hardly an ideal place to be swimming, but it was high tide and the saltwater around Mack Bolan was relatively warm. He was snorkeling through the swamp, laden enough with munitions and spare magazines for his firearms. His penetration of the pirate base wasn't going to necessitate deep diving, and the snorkel was light and could easily be spit aside on its tether to his goggles without fear of losing it, or of it interfering with him in any way.

The swim had been a long, slow crawl, skirting the masses of roots so he didn't snag his gear. Even so, he was in position before the others would be. Their cliff-climbing route gave them an overlook from the rain forest, ensuring that they would be well out of the center of danger, but not so far off as to be useless.

The pirate base had been laid out on hummocks of land that had been protected from erosion by curtains of mangrove roots, its floating huts reinforced with wooden walkways. The hummocks were small, but still sufficient to provide a base for the prefab huts the marauders had constructed. As such, the pirates lived in comfort, on dry floors, their needs attended to by air-conditioning units, satellite dishes and generators. It was as close to a thug paradise as possible. There was even one stretch of sandy beach that had been converted to a soccer field for the pirates.

These men had set up a nice slice of paradise for themselves, but Bolan would feel not a lick of guilt for having it turned into hell on Earth. He stayed in the water, moving between the hummocks and the mangrove roots, observing the guards on hand and noting that there was a lot of activity for this early in the morning. The troops had been roused, alerted to a threat. The Little Bird's flyby hadn't done that. Those TF-160 pilots were too skilled, too trained, and Bolan could confirm that the course they'd taken was well circumvented around the pirate base so that no sound of rotor slap would carry on the wind to paranoid ears.

Even here in the water, Bolan made sure not to break the surface any more than necessary, and only when he was in proximity to cover. The sentries were on full alert. Garbage was dumped into the water, and fish, most especially small, two-foot sharks, darted from the murky, silty depths to snatch up morsels and then disappear back into the shadows. The swamp bottom was a treacherous place, the perfect loose silt allowing a stingray to conceal itself with a shrug of its batlike wing fins.

Bolan's blacksuit had been made of fine, high-tech fibers and provided a modicum of ripstop and cutting protection, but a long, deadly barb could still penetrate the fabric. He couldn't help but think of how a famed naturalist had died when a startled stingray had reflexively lashed out, driving the barb through his heart. It was unlikely that he'd be impaled like that, but the venom in the sting would cause pain and impairment, and if he wasn't careful, he'd end up with a broken stinger jammed into a calf muscle. He avoided standing on the bottom for more than an instant.

He was able to locate Solyenko's hut, simply by the

extra guards on hand and the lack of trash being dumped as the pirates seemed to be busy clearing out the potential for fires, infection and shrapnel. Papers and trash were only going to make things more difficult, adding to airborne debris when an attack began. They seemed to be preparing for a lot of trouble because he spotted at least two men carrying the pipelike surface-to-air missile launchers necessary to fend off an aerial assault.

Bolan grimaced. Someone else was coming in, and he could tell from the activity in Solyenko's hut that it had to be the Russians. He swam around the back of the hummock, looking for a break in the roots and in the security, and was pleased to note that while there was still a snarl of mangrove roots, there were no guards at the back simply because there was no bridge anywhere but from the "front" of the islet. Bolan tested the strength of the mangrove roots, and felt that they were sturdy, at least as far as he could reach, enough for him to climb over and get on land.

With a powerful shrug, he slithered out of the water, doing his best to limit the knock and creak of the wooden tendrils seemingly exploding from the base of a nearby tree. Bolan allowed the water to slough off him. The blacksuit and his nylon harness didn't absorb and soak, so he wouldn't be dripping and giving away his position. He made certain, however, that he kept his tall frame tucked behind the trunk of the tree whose roots he'd climbed. They were thicker and stronger closer to the trunk, thus making them much better footing, allowing him to crouch.

He scanned the hummock and saw that there was sufficient shadow for him to remain concealed as he closed in on Solyenko. Bolan also scanned to ensure that if he was in sight of the guards at the front of the hut, there were enough branches hanging to keep him obscured.

He sized up the jump to the sand, tensed his muscles and launched himself. It was ten feet, and Bolan felt as if he had pulled his thigh on the takeoff, but he landed soundlessly in the soft sand of the hummock. He scurried on all fours, staying low and out of sight.

Against the back of the hut, he was able to hear the conversation. Voices had been raised, and he could make out Solyenko's irate Slavic tones even without utilizing any technology. The steel skin of the hut was a good conduit, and the Russian mentioned a name. It was in a lower voice, not the angry bellow that had perked his ears, though Bolan couldn't quite make it out. He got the start: a general.

Bolan reached into his gear, pulled out a small fiber-optic camera attachment for his Combat CDA and tucked it through an open seam in the wall. He was able to see that the wall he was up against was on an office tucked into the back of the elongated hut. It took a moment of contemplation and examination of the wall seam to realize that while it hadn't been put together tight, it was still solidly built, and tearing his way through would create more noise than he could hope to pass off.

Rather than force his way in, he looked at the windows, using the fiber-optic camera as a periscope. He could see that the office was more like an enclosed cubicle, with a door, but no ceiling, and frosted glass on the partition. The window would allow him entry, but he'd have to be careful. A quick bend on the fiber optic, and he saw that there were desks placed beneath each window, clutter on top of them.

Plenty of opportunity to make a racket sliding in from

the top. Bolan grimaced and took a folding knife to the bug screen, slitting it so that he could move through the opening. With a push, he eased halfway through the window, then scooped up objects from the desktop and passed them back to the outside, letting them drop to the sand. There was not going to be much time for silence and stealth, but he still needed the edge of a few minutes of quiet.

Even as he cleared the desk and slid the chair silently aside, he heard a grumbled name.

Karloff? Bolan ran through his mental roster of Russian generals that Kurtzman had been assembling. The list of possible suspects was long and varied. Russian politics were fractured, and there were elements willing to go in any direction, from a return to old-school KGB-backed communism to hardcore, racism-inspired fascism. The one good thing about Solyenko mentioning a general was that it narrowed the prospects of who was going to be the bad guy, but not by much. The Executioner was nothing if not studious. He had the lists memorized, and he was going through the ranks, figuring on either a current or retired general, but realized that he had to pick between the military and espionage.

He settled on the list that was between the two. A former member of the Glavnoye Razvedyvatel'noye Upraveleniye—the GRU. As the foreign military intelligence directorate for the armed forces of first the Soviet Union and later the armed forces of the Russian Federation, it made sense that Solyenko would be chosen by a member or former member of the GRU. The agency employed 25,000 Spetsnaz operators directly, as well as having six times as many undercover operatives in foreign countries. With the dissolving of the KGB into the Sluzhba

Vneshney Razvedki—SVR—the GRU had the biggest
operating network of international contacts. The new
Russian Federation had been glad to take the KGB apart,
if only because the power that the organization wielded
was one of cruel intimidation and memories of bad times.
If the Russians had ever wanted to escape the darkness
of their past, the serpentine force needed gutting.

On the other hand, the GRU had contacts, assets
and, most important, concealed operations still working around the world. The Kuala Lumpur computer center had to have been a slow but surely updated system
designed not only for international espionage, but as a
forward observation base. Bolan had encountered agents
of the GRU, and while many of them were just working
toward their nation's best interests, there were some who
were as dark and twisted as their KGB counterparts.

Bolan narrowed his mental search down to Constantin
Garlov, a retired general who had espoused the weakness
of the Russian Federation. While Garlov was hardly a
Communist Party star, he was still someone who longed
for a return to the bad old days when the Soviet military
was one of the most feared forces on the planet. Garlov
would most certainly have access to current and former
Spetsnaz operatives, as well as have friends and contacts
who could arrange for the force necessary to overthrow
the current Russian government.

Garlov matched the name Bolan thought he'd heard,
and he had the background, as well. The general had engaged in fighting the insurgency in Afghanistan back
in the eighties as a much younger man and, according
to the records, he still seemed to be in fine shape, kept
young and fit.

A dangerous opponent, especially since he was using multiple weapons at his disposal.

"…let's get the defenses set up and hardened. If Garlov gets here, he's going to soften us up first," Solyenko stated. His voice was much clearer now that Bolan had entered the building, slithering silently onto the desk, then to the floor. He let the window drop low and took a quick glance. The items from the desktop didn't stand out in the shadows of the prefab hut, mixed between sand and sea grass.

Bolan grimaced. Garlov was nothing if not thorough. Solyenko had to have sent out a distress call, and was now having second thoughts about it. This was exactly why Bolan had worked so hard, utilized his contacts and friends, to get to this pirate cove before Solyenko could disappear. The *mafiya* killer had made himself a target, and there was little chance that the general would allow this loose thread to lead to him back home.

He peered under the office door with his fiber-optic camera, and noted that Goomabong was present, along with a couple other men. They were donning combat vests laden with spare ammunition. Handguns and rifles were present, and Solyenko didn't let his weapon, an AKSU compact rifle, out of his grip.

Goomabong replied to Solyenko in Russian, for which Bolan was glad. His Thai was very rusty, and even then, it had been far from fluent. "The men are handing out 'blowpipes.'"

Bolan thought back to the pirates and their launchers. He now recognized the silhouettes as the older, cruder, seventies' version of the SAMs utilized by the British armed forces. The MANPADS—man portable air defense system surface-to-air missiles—were among the first generation of shoulder-launched antiaircraft weapons, and were soon replaced in inventory by the British Javelin. Even so, the MANPADS were more than fast enough at Mach 1.5 to catch up to a helicopter moving at a fraction of its speed. The five-pound explosive charge in the warhead would perform with devastating force against their targets, if the shooters were good enough. Because the guidance system was by joystick, the firer didn't need to worry about radar or infrared countermeasures. He brought in the weapon as if it were a video game.

It was a slower means of acquiring a target, but made it less dependent on sensors that could be scrambled or fooled by flares.

Bolan frowned. There was one major disadvantage to the system. The MANPADS had a magnesium flare in the tail and would leave a trail of light and fire behind. A quick enough gunner could take out the pirates on the ground before the missile completed its flight.

Even as the Executioner was analyzing who was coming, what was happening in the next office and the kind of firepower that Solyenko had on hand to repel the assault, he made a quick head count of the people in the room. One of the four, neither of whom was Solyenko or Goomabong, had left, obviously to relay orders to the rest of the pirates. He didn't have to be close to the table to feel the tension in the room as the former Spetsnaz trooper looked over the map on the table.

"There will be Russian naval vessels in the Indian Ocean, and they've been assigned to handle 'pirate problems,'" Solyenko said. "All Garlov has to do is point out our location to an admiral friend of his, and we will receive a visit in force."

Bolan pulled back the camera but kept listening intently. He quickly typed in a message to Stony Man Farm to see if there were any Russian navy vessels on pirate duty in the area of the Andaman Sea. It felt like an eternity, but within thirty seconds, Kurtzman was online, having gleaned the information from the NSA or perhaps the U.S. Navy's surveillance of the Russian fleet. There was a Udaloy-class destroyer on maneuvers, having come around to the Indian Ocean to watch out for pirates who would go after Russian Federation vessels that had passed through the Suez Canal. Bolan knew that an Udaloy generally had provisions for at least two Kamov Ka-29 antisubmarine helicopters, big craft that were capable of carrying two tons of cargo or up to sixteen troops on board.

Two Kamovs could bring in a company of Spetsnaz to cover up a lot of Garlov's sins. They'd hit the pirates hard and fast. Just in case nearly three dozen commandos wasn't enough, each of the Ka-29s had a GShG minigun, the Warsaw Pact variant of the American M134, a multibarreled 7.62 mm machine gun capable of 3000 rounds a minute of concentrated fire, more than enough punch to shred even a light armored vehicle. The GShG would be nose-mounted, and slaved to an optic targeting lens on the pilot's helmet. Backing that up on a flexible mount in the door would be a 30 mm 2A42 cannon. It resembled a miniature tank gun, and would spit out high-explosive rounds that could smash armor or go off with even more force than the 40 mm grenade launcher under the commando's rifle.

Bolan had also remembered that there were four wing stations for either missiles, rockets or torpedoes. The antisubmarine variant wouldn't have been applicable to the Udaloy-class destroyer's mission of fighting pirates and terrorists, so the navy would have opted for the assault version, something capable of pounding an enemy vessel, then dropping off a deck-clearing team to take command of the pirate ship. Bolan had seen the Russian navy hard at work on dealing with pirates, watching them systematically kill everyone on board who wasn't a hostage. Usually, Bolan would have been glad for such tactics to come in and sweep away a crew of murderous thugs, but he had questions that still needed answers.

Those inquiries would reach a dead end if Bolan didn't get a face-to-face with Solyenko.

He took a look at where Kurtzman had placed the Udaloy-class ship. It was only two hundred miles out from this little mangrove cove. Within two hours' flight for the Ka-29s, and plenty of round-trip range for the helicopters that could travel more than six hundred miles searching for a submarine.

"What's that sound?" Bolan heard Majid ask over his headset.

Winslow's voice was next. "A helicopter."

"Could it be the Little Bird?" she asked.

"Maybe, but…"

It was too late now. Any chance of tackling Solyenko and getting the answers from him was lost. He had to protect the man, and since he was in full-on combat mode, it was not going to be easy to subdue him.

"Rocket launchers," Winslow said over the radio, cutting through Bolan's immediate thoughts, his gauging of the situation and how to take Solyenko alive. "That can't be the chopper that brought us in. TF-160 doesn't make mistakes like flying too close to an attack site.

Certainly never loud enough to be heard for miles if they don't have to."

"Someone else is coming in," Bolan interjected over the hands-free mike, keeping his voice low. "Solyenko's bosses are going to cut this loose end before we get to him."

"They have two gunships," Majid added.

"Blow the pirate ships to hell. Rain thunder on the camp now," Bolan ordered.

"But…"

"I need Solyenko distracted!" Bolan stressed.

An instant later the soldier heard the pop of the Carl Gustav, almost instantly followed by the crash of a detonation out on the docks where the power scows had been moored.

That got their attention, Bolan noticed. Goomabong, Solyenko and the remaining pirate leader all snapped to full alert, but looked away from the back of the hut, staring in the direction of the exploding ship.

Bolan pulled his sound-suppressed Beretta and slid through the cubicle door as quietly as he could. Goomabong and Solyenko went to the window to see what was happening. Even as this was going on, the sound of "blowpipes" firing into the sky resounded. The defending pirates heard the slap of enemy rotors, and were shooting at the Russian navy helicopters. They had to have attributed the first shot to one of their own, which had been Bolan's plan. He was an old hand at distraction and human perception.

"What about the helicopters?" Winslow asked.

"Leave them alone," Bolan said out loud as he brought up the Beretta and punched a 3-round burst into the pirate who hadn't joined his boss at the window. A trio of rounds tore through his heart, destroying the muscle and ending the flow of blood in his body.

The pirate dropped to the floor, caught flat-footed. Beside the window, Goomabong and Solyenko heard Bolan's order to Winslow and turned. The soldier knew he needed to be quick, and he pivoted like a turret, tracking Goomabong. If either of the two leaders was expendable, it was the bulky Thai. But the man moved like lightning, charging the door and crashing through it, 9 mm rounds chasing him each step of the way. There was a grunt from the Thai titan, but it wasn't the sound of a fatal injury. Bolan had only winged him.

Solyenko, on the other hand, pushed off the wall and dived to the underside of the conference table. Bolan launched himself off the floor, tucking his legs up behind him as he rolled on the tabletop, scattering map pages and half-loaded magazines everywhere. Bolan's leap had been just in time as the AKSU chattered, spitting out high-velocity slugs at 700 rounds per minute. The little 5.45 mm slugs moving at twice the speed of sound sliced through the space his legs had been occupying only moments before, a cabinet behind him rattling violently as the supersonic bullets punched through sheet metal.

Rolling on the tabletop, Bolan knew that the moment the guns started blasting, things were going to be hard to de-escalate, but he needed to interrogate Solyenko. That meant he needed to get creative and quickly. Outside, he heard the powerful bangs of rockets launching and explosive cannon shells detonating. Even though he wished that the naval commandos and their heavily armed helicopters weren't here, he couldn't allow himself to wish them harm. They were good men, fighting cold-blooded marauders and murderers, thieves who stole from international shipping and commerce.

That was the reason for his admonition to Winslow to leave them alone. If there was one thing the Executioner could never allow, it was harm to come to a soldier on the same side. The men here to destroy these pirates had been sent to do the work of an evil man, but they were still fighting for justice. Bolan shoved that thought aside and let his ears open up, taking in all of the room at once.

Solyenko had dived under the table and had opened fire, but then, that was it. He'd gone silent and still. They had a thick piece of wood between them, so all they had to locate each other was their ears.

"Those choppers aren't with me," Bolan announced loudly, letting the curved roof of the hut cast echoes across the building. "But they're on their way to kill everything here."

"I know that, McCormack!" Solyenko snapped.

"Truce?" Bolan asked.

"I don't trust you at all," Solyenko replied.

"And you trusted Goomabong? He was out the door in a flash," Bolan said.

"I'm coming out," Solyenko answered.

Bolan grimaced. The Russian obviously knew that the Executioner needed answers from him, and because of that, he had temporary immunity. If Bolan pulled the trigger on him, answers would disappear. The murderous Garlov would disappear like smoke.

The trouble was that Bolan's continued existence was still going to lead to a bad end for Solyenko, either in jail, or summarily executed. Solyenko would only need him as far as it would take to keep himself alive. After that, there would be a bullet in the back of Bolan's head at the first opportunity.

"Do it slowly," Bolan told him.

This wasn't the first time the soldier had a scorpion riding his back while crossing a stream. He just had to be prepared for when the Russian reverted to his nature, or be stung in the back.

CHAPTER SEVENTEEN

Bolan checked the window as Solyenko stood across the table from him. He didn't trust the man, and here he was, giving a known killer and traitor an opportunity at a shot in his back. To the Russian's credit, no bullets struck the Executioner between his shoulder blades, but his ears were still keenly honed, waiting for the sudden rustle of motion as a gun was drawn and brought to bear. So far, he could see that the campground was ablaze with activity, and he watched as a pirate gunman was obliterated under the high-velocity spray of one of the Kamovs' miniguns. Bolan moved from the window and quickly rushed to Solyenko's side.

As soon as he vacated the front of the prefab hut, a rain of lead and copper jacketing slashed through corrugated steel, a blazing storm of flesh-shredding hell that would have turned Bolan into a misty cloud of gore. Even so, he could feel the rumble of bullets hammering the floor at his heels as he grabbed the Russian and hurled them both aside. The Russian naval pilots were doing their finest to blow apart any concentrated resistance, and from the sounds of things, other buildings were disappearing in flashes of fire and destruction.

Some of the fire was coming from Winslow and Majid, who were acting as an artillery team. They'd wrought havoc on the power scows, and now they were bringing in more heat on the pirate base itself. Bolan looked back and saw that the front of the hut was now a sagging sieve, solid metal turned to mesh that collapsed under its own weight. He took a deep breath, then looked at Solyenko.

"Out the back," Bolan told him.

The *mafiya* thug sneered, but knew the wisdom of the American soldier's orders. With a bound, he was back on his feet and racing for the rear office, clearing the desk and diving outside into the sand. Bolan wasn't more than two steps behind his quarry, slithering through the wreckage of the window that Solyenko had powered through. The big Russian was a bull, and he didn't have a fear of minor scratches from glass, not when there were aircraft pounding the base behind him with 7.62 mm and 30 mm rounds.

Bolan glanced toward the cliff and noted that his backup was firing at another building, blowing it apart with another seven-pound shell packed with high explosives. Even as Winslow and Majid cut loose with the Carl Gustav, 30 mm cannon fire chugged, fist-size bullets exploding on impact. From under the wings, the Ka-29s launched unguided rockets, sailing the artillery missiles into targets that neither of his Carl Gustav gunners had gotten to. The ground shook from the overwhelming force of a dozen explosions going off at once, a brief second between each wave of blasts as weapons cycled or were reloaded, then the world throbbed again with a sheet of explosive force.

Solyenko spotted a couple of men in an inflatable boat pushing into the mangrove swamp. They were the pirates, and one of them saw the two European men in the darkness, shadowy forms wielding assault rifles. One of the Thais brought up his AK-47 and triggered it.

Solyenko threw himself to the ground even as bullets cut through the night above his head.

Bolan sidestepped the initial burst from the pirate, bringing up his M16 and firing it from the hip. Bullets snapped across the distance between him and the fleeing marauders, 5.56 mm slugs stitching the rifleman and pitching him into the sediment-clouded brackish water of the swamp. The other one made an intentional leap into the water, realizing that his friend had been cut in two by expert marksmanship.

Bolan growled into his throat mike. "Nail the front of building 7 with a shell."

Winslow had to have had a loaded chamber, because in an instant, the prefab hut behind him shuddered under a thunderclap. Bolan felt himself bowled off his feet, but he recovered his footing and balance in a moment, glancing back and hearing screams and confusion behind him.

With a quick movement, he fed a 40 mm shell into the breech of his under-barrel M203 launcher. He took a moment to adjust his aim, then fired the grenade toward an intersection of the walkways that connected floating huts and hummocked huts. Wood splintered under the impact, a pair of pirates standing on the walkway hurled in several directions at once. Limbs had been severed by the ground-zero force of the explosion, and a leg cartwheeled along, out of sight.

Solyenko watched the sudden surge of destruction with widened eyes. He glanced back at Bolan, who ejected the empty casing and gave the grenade launcher a fresh shell. The Executioner's glare was locked on Solyenko.

"If you make a move, I'm good enough to take off

both of your legs, and leave enough of you to talk to," Bolan stated.

Solyenko grimaced.

"What do you need? Or do we wait until the mayhem's all over?" Solyenko asked.

"You stay alive, and you don't raise a hand against those men coming in here," Bolan returned.

"You're not going to fight them? Since when are you frightened of…"

Bolan surged forward and rapped the collapsing steel stock of his M16 against Solyenko's jaw. The Russian grunted in pain and toppled backward into the sand. Bolan kneeled over him and grabbed him from beneath each armpit. He lifted Solyenko's deadweight over the roots and dragged him through the water. With a hard shove, he got the stunned *organasatya* goon into an inflatable raft that had been vacated by both living and dead pirates. The water was high, and Bolan swam alongside the raft.

With a good shove, the soldier anchored the raft in a snarl of mangrove roots that were distant from the hummock and in the shade of the trees' canopies. Bolan climbed a root and looked through the raft, finding a tarpaulin he could use to cover Solyenko. His first priority, however, was to make sure the man didn't leave this parking space. He pulled out a set of cable-tie restraints and bound the man's wrists and ankles together.

Bolan used one more bit of kit, an injector with a Fentanyl dose, enough to keep Solyenko out cold for as long as necessary to clear the pirate camp. He could only hope to be back just before the dose wore off. Even as he gave Solyenko his injection, the man's muscles loosened, his breathing deepening. If the Russian had been faking unconsciousness before, he was out of the picture now.

The soldier turned and dived into the swamp again, putting some distance between himself and his prisoner.

If he was going to make some noise, he didn't want to draw enemy fire toward the prize he'd sought for the past day. He stroked across the swamp and grabbed the section of walkway that he'd damaged. The 40 mm grenade hadn't done anything to the base wood itself, the force rebounding off the surface and into the men who'd been standing there. It had also knocked off the orange plastic netting along the sides, allowing him to slither up onto it.

The battle was still going on. One of the Kamov Ka-29s had taken up a flying orbit around the pirate camp, naval infantry shooting from ramps and portals, the pilots cutting loose with the integral weapons to provide cover for the second craft to drop to a hummock and disgorge its troops. Bolan stayed low on one knee, scanning for where the troops would be disembarking, when he spotted a group fast-roping from the loading ramp. There were two riflemen providing cover for their partners, and as soon as the infantry teams touched sand, they broke off into pairs.

Like swim buddies, which cemented Bolan's assertion that they were the naval counterparts to Spetsnaz.

And if they were naval infantry special operations, then Bolan had to make damn sure he or his team didn't harm them. With a pivot, he scanned for threats that would be focused on the incoming Russians. At the same time, he got on the comm to Winslow and Majid.

"How are you on ammo?" Bolan asked.

"We've got about four shells left," Winslow said. "And you don't want us to engage the Russians."

"Stop shooting, leave the Carl Gustav, and withdraw to the extraction point," Bolan told them.

"What about Solyenko and Goomabong?" Majid asked.

"I've got Solyenko," Bolan replied. "If you get a shot at Goomabong, take it. He's all yours."

"Got it," Majid answered.

There was silence on the other end.

"But if you catch fire from the Russians, withdraw. I still want you at extraction in fifteen minutes," Bolan ordered.

"The recoilless?" Winslow asked.

"You have the disposal kit. Set it, but don't detonate before you get to safe distance," Bolan said.

The Executioner kept low and moving, watching for contacts with enemies and naval infantry. As soon as he came across a pirate, Bolan let him have two quick shots from the M16, 5.56 mm rounds scrambling internal organs in their deceleration from hypersonic speed. He did it to conserve ammunition and lower his profile in combat. Longer bursts would make him look like a pirate. Uncontrolled bursts were the norm for these killers, while the naval infantry were, like Bolan, shooting quick, precise bursts.

It wasn't much of a disguise or cover, but it was something that would make them pause if they noticed him. He was without a "swim buddy" so he would be recognized as being an outside agent. Bolan took his Combat CDA and hooked it to his hands-free unit. With a few taps, he was on the naval infantry's IFF marker to further give him some breathing room, enough to engage in communication with them.

Kurtzman had done a great job of keeping up with IFF—Identify Friend or Foe—codes for multiple foreign and domestic military squads over the years. With the advent of the Combat PDA, then CDA and its wireless capabilities, the soldier currently had a new option available to him should he inadvertently come across a potentially friendly force in the field.

The addition of the IFF signal, tied in to the encrypted frequencies the Russians were using, wouldn't increase Bolan's signature in combat. Only the Soviets would see him, and only if they had their optics tuned in. If not, well, no one else could hear the emanating radio pulse. Bolan spotted the second helicopter make another orbit around the camp.

Something felt wrong.

Even as his Combat CDA was broadcasting the IFF, it was also picking up on the comms from the Russian naval infantry elite troops.

"How do you have this code?" a voice asked in Russian.

Bolan glanced at the CDA for a moment. It registered no names. The Russians were quite good about OPSEC, operational security, but the fact the man addressed him told the soldier that he had gambled correctly.

Bolan replied in Russian. "I'm here tracking down Grev Solyenko, a Russian criminal."

There was a pause on the other end, either as the Russian commander was dealing with an incoming threat, or weighing Bolan's words. Perhaps both.

The Executioner, in addition to setting the CDA's IFF, kept himself alert for enemy action. In the brief pause, he noticed another squad of pirates about to blindside a Kamov, bringing up LMGs as improvised antiaircraft weapons. The Ka-29s were durable birds, but 7.62 mm NATO or 7.62 mm Russian rounds tended to do a lot of damage, even to armored aircraft. Bolan shot them, cutting loose with a half dozen short bursts, punching through the would-be killers with precision application of his M16.

Gunmen screamed and collapsed, hearts and heads blown apart as Bolan killed them.

"Spasiba." The Russian commander spoke up, watching the pirates fall to pieces.

"Needed some kind of proof I'm on your side," Bolan replied.

"Do you have a name, stranger?" the commander asked over the radio.

Bolan paused. "Just call me an American friend."

"Friend, yes," the Russian returned. "Call me Angrekal."

The helicopter above them looked down on the scene. Gunfire had died out. Between the efforts of the Executioner and Angrekal's men, the pirates had been obliterated. Bolan had gone through three magazines, and bodies bobbed in the brackish water, riddled with bullets.

"Where's the other Kamov?" Bolan inquired.

"I don't know," Angrekal replied.

Bolan didn't like the sudden surprise in that answer. Something was dangerously wrong.

LIEUTENANT KYRIL ANGREKAL of the Russian naval reconnaissance Spetsnaz was not happy to have the makeup of his company changed, but a week earlier he'd been saddled with a new platoon. These men were members of the GRU, Spetsnaz assigned to that espionage group, and the sudden change smelled fishy. It also didn't help that the platoon kept to itself, and even had its own crew for a Kamov Ka-29 that had been refitted as a dedicated gunship.

The recent change was a low point in this tour, an assignment that Angrekal had loved deeply, operating in the Indian Ocean, hunting down pirates who dared to attack the shipping of the Russian Federation. It was a good life for a man who chose the warrior's profession, a fight that was worth it, protecting innocent men and women and battling against irredeemable criminals. He had to admit that enduring actions during the various brushfire battles in troubles in the Federation states had given him a bad taste in his mouth, not so much those who took children captive and keyed them up to high explosives, but those who just wanted freedom and liberty.

Here, on the high seas, he had everything in black and white.

But things were getting murky once more.

Korylev—the only name the commander of the platoon had given—was taciturn. He was reluctant to engage in cross training with Angrekal's unit and fraternization had been at an absolute minimum. If the newcomers hadn't attended briefings before call-outs, he wouldn't even have known what half of them looked like. That kind of secrecy got under Angrekal's skin. They were intelligence weenies, and already untrustworthy.

They'd traveled two-hundred-plus miles by helicopter, segregated as usual to their own individual helicopters.

Korylev had received the call, and it was he who had roused the teams to action. There had been satellite photos, advanced reconnaissance.

"This is what we've been waiting for," Korylev had stated. "GRU command wanted my team here just in case of this."

Angrekal had looked at the mission map. "Pirates in Thailand? Why are they on military intelligence's radar?"

"They've been operating alongside another group that we believe has been making use of an old KGB installation in Malaysia," Korylev returned.

"KGB installation?" Angrekal asked.

"This isn't the first time we've needed to clean up old cold war shit piles," Korylev replied. "That's why we were pushed on you at the last minute."

Angrekal grumbled. "When did they discover this camp?"

"A few days ago," Korylev told him. "We've been spending the time attempting to consolidate our intel on the joint. Even so, it looks like we're going to be rolling in with light intel. This is all I have."

Angrekal looked at the camp layout. "What's the order?"

"We move in hard and heavy," Korylev replied. "I want to have our Kamovs open up and soften the joint. We throw enough lead, the rest should be easy."

"Easy to do what?" Angrekal asked.

"Wipe them out. Completely."

Angrekal frowned, looking at the map. According to aerial photography, there seemed to be more than a few civilians mixed in with the pirates, but mostly, they'd been kept ringed around the camp itself. A perimeter of human shields would give pause to any outside attack, and plenty of bodies to suck up bullets, buying the pirates time to rally and protect themselves.

"We have the buildings targeted. We hit them hard, then even if they do have people trying to escape on the boats, they can't outrace our birds," Korylev replied. "But if we waste time on the pirate ships, then we leave ourselves in the open, vulnerable to their fire, and they can grab bodies to use as shields."

Angrekal looked over Korylev's plan. It seemed solid. Clear-cut. The man even seemed to be in a precision mode that was enviable. He would have the gunners direct their fire with such skill and direction that the pirates wouldn't be able to take hostages. This didn't seem to fit in with Korylev's image as secretive GRU meat puppet with an agenda. But, could this just be another layer of subterfuge?

Angrekal didn't know. He just had a mission, and pirates needed to die.

Now, two hours later, Angrekal was introducing himself to an American who spoke Russian handily.

Angrekal could tell by the lack of gunners working from the gun ports and on the ramp that it was his platoon's transport. It was working overwatch, and Korylev's bird was nowhere to be seen.

"Leader to Hen, where's Korylev?" Angrekal asked over his hands-free mike.

"No clue. One moment they were here…then they're gone," his pilot returned.

"Eyes peeled, head on a swivel!" Angrekal spit. "Korylev's platoon might—"

There was a sudden roar of a minigun that broke through the relative silence of one hovering Ka-29. Angrekal looked up, the noise attracting his attention, but he already feared what would be up there as he looked. A stream of death perforated the cockpit of the Kamov, streams of 30 mm shells and the high-velocity, high volume of smaller 7.62 mm machine gun rounds struck his pilots…

His pilots.

The Ka-29 jerked violently, probably the last death spasm of Yuri, the twin-bladed helicopter tumbling sideways in the air, about to land in the wreckage of a rocket-blasted Quonset hut. The lifting surfaces struck the ground and bent, the counter-rotation of the two blades smashing bent blades against each other. The twin engine tore itself apart. In the meantime, the craft smashed hard into the burning wreckage of the prefab building, gravity collapsing its hull under its own weight. Yuri and Benny. Two good men, pilots he'd trusted for the whole of this tour.

Dead. Betrayed by that GRU-sent bastard.

"Korylev! You bastard!" Angrekal snapped.

The second of the Kamovs hovered into view, a seemingly invulnerable monstrosity lording over the carnage-filled pirate base.

His men on the ground were stunned by the sudden destruction of the first bird.

"Get to cover!" Bolan's voice bellowed over their headsets.

That warning spurred all of the men into action, even Angrekal felt the command as a boot to the pants, and he hurled himself toward the shadow of a war-shattered hut.

The Spetsnaz operative couldn't believe it, but the American stayed put, firing his M16 to call the Kamov's attention to himself.

CHAPTER EIGHTEEN

Mack Bolan didn't require years of experience in espionage and combat to realize that the disappearance of one enemy helicopter was a bad sign, and the sudden attack by one ship on the other was a blatant indicator of duplicity on the part of one segment of the Russians present. Angrekal let loose an agonized scream over the radio that merely cemented Bolan's assertions, and he burst into action.

"Get to cover!" Bolan ordered in his best Russian, extracting the depth and tone of a drill sergeant to snap the startled and betrayed naval infantry from the shock of watching their aircraft being attacked by what should have been one of their own.

Despite the vow he'd made to protect the Russians doing their duty, at least two were already dead.

The only bright spot here was that the Executioner now knew that he could open up on the surviving Kamov with impunity, knowing that the men in that aircraft were implicit in the conspiracy he'd come here to smash. The only trouble was that his M16 didn't have bullets of the right mass to punch through the skin or windshield of the Ka-29. Even so, he pivoted the muzzle of the rifle upward and emptied the whole magazine from his M16 into the cockpit, 5.56 mm soft-points disintegrating against the windshield, making dozens of chips and minor fractures of the surface layer.

It was a startle tactic. Bolan was taking the offensive, and he was running closer to the hovering helicopter. The crew seemed to be agog with the audacity of Bolan's move, something that the soldier had planned upon. Most people expected a display of violence to cow the crowd, and when faced with an aggressive response, they had to break the sudden shock of what had just happened. Safe inside the cockpit of the helicopter, the pilot and copilot had the room and opportunity to look on, astounded at Bolan, nothing urging them to take cover, to escape the insignificant rice kernels bouncing off their windshield.

That was good enough for the Executioner. They couldn't realize that he had his under-barrel M203 grenade launcher primed and ready to fire. There was an M441 in the breech, a high-explosive charge, but it was still beneath the amount of penetrative power that he would need to actually break through the safety glass or armor of the Kamov. However, it wasn't his place to bring down the helicopter. He just needed to take down the minigun or the cannon, or both, given a good hit. Bolan had fired the M203 on so many occasions that he instinctively was able to set up, post and aim in one fluid movement, even at a flying target.

A pull of the trigger and the rifle/launcher combo chugged violently, kicking against his thigh with the force of a shotgun's kick. An instant later the grenade sailed, spiraling through the air like a thrown football, traveling the minimum distance for the fuse to arm. The 40 mm shell tumbled into the undercarriage of the helicopter and struck, exploding with all the force of its six-ounce warhead. The aircraft shook violently, the pilots reacting to something with far more punch than the 5.56 mm bullets that Bolan had started this fight with.

The soldier knew that the crew would recover from the upset, and he took a hard run and leaped off one of the walkways, spearing into the brackish mangrove swamp, water sloshing around him to envelop him. The Ka-29 swung toward him, realizing that the operative who'd raged helplessly against it had something stiffer in his arsenal than tiny bullets.

Bolan could only hope that his accuracy had been fine enough to do damage to the mounted guns. If not, he at least had the physics in which high-velocity slugs upset in water much more easily, deflecting and deforming through the fluid. It wouldn't last forever, and if the 30 mm cannon hadn't been taken out, as shallow as the swamp was, he'd be peppered with explosions and shock waves.

Swimming, kicking along toward a snarl of roots, he could hear and feel the rotor slap striking the water, vibrations and sounds amplified in the thicker brackish swamp water, but no minigun fire was blasted at him. The grenade had done its work on the Russian buzz gun, but that would be nothing if they decided to cut loose with the bigger weapon.

Something struck the water to his right, and the crack of a detonating 30 mm shell sliced through the water and Bolan's skull sharply. He winced, but managed to keep his focus and underwater swimming course. All he needed was a few more yards and he'd be able to try again. The helicopter was fairly secure against ground fire, but Bolan could figure something out.

One of the first things that came to mind was that he'd had concerns about the steel skin of the corrugated-shelled Quonset huts. Bolan, as ever thinking ahead to what could happen, had his Desert Eagle set up and ready with a full magazine of .44 Magnum tungsten-cored, armor-piercing slugs, a live round in the pipe. There were another two magazines, and the big power-ful slugs would still have the kind of mass necessary to produce huge wounds in targets. Against the windshield of the Kamov, they *might* penetrate, but he had to be within range. He could also try another 40 mm grenade into the mast holding the twin counter-rotating blades of the helicopter.

Bolan broke the surface, and there was the sudden crackle of automatic gunfire. He reached up, snagged a mangrove root and hauled himself from the water. The rifle/grenade launcher swung on its sling, dropping out of the way, and he reached down for his Desert Eagle. The Kamov was still hovering, but its guns were silent. No one looked to be on board, so that explained where the Ka-29 had disappeared to. Somewhere along the way, it had dropped off its cargo of Spetsnaz commandos under the command of the officer Angrekal had called Korylev.

And with the distraction of the hostile helicopter, those same backbiters were moving into position to ambush Angrekal's men. Fortunately there was enough radio chatter for the secret to be blown the moment Angrekal cursed out the conspiracy's attack dog.

Bolan snapped the safety off the gun, scanning for targets to put down. He needed a quick means of differentiating between Korylev's men and the naval infantry. Once again, Bolan's observation of Angrekal's troops traveling in pairs as "swim buddies" gave him that insight. The naval Spetsnaz were still paired off. He could see that there were a couple of them who had grabbed their wounded partners and pulled them to cover, firing

one-handed. Others were holed up behind what concealment they could find.

On the contrary, Korylev's ground fighters were
moving in groups of four, providing overwhelming fire
power per encounter, and forcing Angrekal's fighters
back. The Executioner saw one of the groups, then put
the Desert Eagle away, securing it and bringing up his
M16/M203. A quick swap of magazines later and he
had the rifle shouldered, focused on the renegade Russians. Bolan shot the first of the quartet through his face,
5.56 mm rounds smashing his night-vision gear and
blowing the helmet off his head with the force of their
passage through his brain pan. The other three in that
fire squad reacted to the sudden decapitation of their
partner by scrambling and spreading out.

Bolan tracked one of them who had noted the dull
muzzle-flash of his rifle. The Russian gunman swung
his AK up to bear, but Bolan milked the trigger of the
M16 for a precision 4-shot burst. He realized that the
Spetsnaz would be wearing body armor and knew that
at least one of his bullets would be deflected. Unfortunately for the enemy commando, the first round struck
him in the upper arm, shattering it to splinters. The second round was brushed away by Kevlar, but the third
and fourth rounds went above the armor-clad intervening shoulder. The third was blunted by a collar of ballistic cloth, but the resultant blow struck with the force
of a heavyweight boxer's fist.

The Spetsnaz gunner's brain received an overload of
nerve impulses from the neck strike, but that was rendered moot as the last shot glanced off the man's helmet.
The bullet, moving at three times the speed of sound,
crushed through the Russian's temple and imploded his

face. Once again, the deforming skull unseated the ballistic helmet, and the would-be murderer toppled sideways.

Bolan swung back to the other pair, who had juked to the right. He was just in time to watch one of them take a chest full of rounds from two of the naval infantry Spetsnaz. Body armor would have been effective against one or two shots, but the swim buddies cut loose in unison, knowing what they had to deal with. Their 5.45 mm rounds had come en masse to overwhelm whatever protective qualities the body armor could provide. The traitor met his end with forty rounds shredding his gear, half of them ending up in his chest cavity.

The last of the group scrambled back the way he'd come. He reached for a grenade from his harness to throw it at Angrekal's group, but Bolan beat him to the punch. As soon as the guy got the cotter pin out, the Executioner chopped off his hands with a short burst from the M16. The live grenade dropped to the man's feet, crushed fingers falling with it. The handless man was too shocked by his sudden dismemberment to do more than take one step back.

The fuse ticked down and in an instant the Russian renegade was legless as well as handless. His body armor stopped the wave of shrapnel from perforating his torso, but the blast and fragments tore through his mangled lower limbs, ripping them out. Burst femoral arteries gushed out in a spray. The grenadier bled out in a heartbeat.

One squad down. Bolan hurled himself over the roots and onto the hummock that the trees surrounded. He scanned for more targets and was glad he had gotten behind the line of trees as a spray of lead came at him.

Bolan threw himself flat, ducking beneath bullets that had been deflected off course by the intervening trunk of the tree. The wood did little to stop the slugs from penetrating through it, but it did upset their trajectory violently.

Had Bolan made the rookie mistake of hugging the tree, the rounds would have punched right through the trunk and into him. Staying back, that bit of deflection was more than sufficient to buy him inches of safety.

The Executioner brought up the M16 again, looking for the gunners who'd tried to cut him in two.

This time, however, he was too late to stop the flying arc of a fragmentation grenade sailing through the branches of the mangrove above him. The round little ball of death plopped into the sand right next to Bolan.

GOOMABONG MIGHT HAVE been big, but he had enough of a layer of fat to make himself buoyant in the water. Underneath that, he had plenty of muscle, but Goomabong's round, heavy form was still built for swimming, and his powerful arms swept him along through the brackish swamp.

The sudden appearance of McCormack had been an utter shock, but Goomabong was fast and sharp enough to have escaped the Quonset hut before more gunfire chased after him. Unfortunately, out in the open, things were hardly better. The two helicopters had showed up and all hell had broken loose. He'd made it to the water with only a few strides, his thick legs also being long and powerful, hurling him into the briny swamp water. The only trouble with that was that when he went in, he was diving toward the center of the pirate base.

His bald head broke the surface, and he cast around,

noting that the helicopter gunners were concentrating their fire on the buildings and the sandy hummocks surrounded by trees. The big Thai felt some relief as even the sizzling shells being launched around were not going into the drink with him.

So, Goomabong wasn't going to catch any fire while swimming back to the perimeter of the camp. He was good and safe, at least until McCormack came out of the hut. The Thai giant got to swimming, despite the fact that he knew that the Soldier was going after Solyenko first. Goomabong didn't have anything in his knowledge that would put him on track to catching up with the masterminds of this conspiracy. Maybe in the crash and thunder of twin attacks intersecting at the pirate base, both sides would forget about his existence, or just be too wrapped up to care.

Either way, Goomabong swam with all of his might, threading between the islets, looking for a way out.

Grenades and commandos were added to the mix, the Malaysian-born Thai pirate noticing men descending from one of the helicopters on ropes. Volleys of 40 mm grenades sailed overhead, splitting open smaller buildings or landing amid groups of his fellow Andaman Sea thugs. Goomabong hit an about-face, kicking off a mass of roots and propelling himself back toward the hut he'd escaped. As he broke the surface and paused, sucking in a breath, he noticed that the hut had been peppered with machine-gun fire, perforated steel collapsing under its own weight, as if someone had stepped on a giant soda can. Goomabong was torn between a grimace and a smile.

Solyenko was likely cold meat now, the helicopters chewing apart the hut with no regard for survivors.

However, with the wave of gunfire already unleashed against the building, the helicopters wouldn't waste any more minigun or cannon ammunition on the seemingly deflated hut.

Swim time, and Goomabong pushed himself, paddling and kicking with all of his strength. His layer of fat kept him easily bobbing close to the surface, but thanks to the flashes of small fires and occasional muzzle-flares, his bulk was dark in the brackish water, mixing in with the murky swamp. He didn't intend to cross the ground out in the open; he knew that he was a big, tempting target. He would stick to the water as far as the edge of the swamp. Goomabong swung to the right, stroking beneath one of the wooden bridges connecting the hummocks, letting its wooden frame further hide him.

Goomabong took a rest, regaining his breath. He was fighting against the fear of gunfire and explosions ripping around him and the stress of swimming to safety. Fortunately he wasn't all flab. He was in good condition; he simply needed to suck down a few breaths and concentrate on his escape goals. Even as he treaded water, looking for a way out, he noticed a strange dark bulk in the flash of a machine gun's muzzle-blast. The shape was up against mangrove roots, meaning that it might have been a raft that had floated partially to freedom.

Its shape was still intact, suggesting that gunfire hadn't touched it. It was still water-worthy, and Goomabong could use the inflatable to navigate down a stream or river along the delta, moving farther inland. Travel by water would be easier than a hike across land, especially since the coastal swamps were a mix of sandy islands and plenty of waterways. Going on foot would be rough.

Goomabong also knew that trying to swim all the

way out would be bad. Officially, saltwater crocodiles were extinct in Thailand, but they were close enough to Malaysia and its sparse population that he didn't want to risk it. He also knew that these deltas would be a good hunting ground for bull sharks. An inflatable raft wouldn't be protection against the crushing jaws of those killing machines, but it would keep Goomabong's scent out of the water.

The Malay-Thai pirate swam for all he was worth, pushing along in the water. Midway to the raft, he heard the sudden roar of heavy guns firing, the tortured sounds of metal deforming. A glance back and he watched as one of the Russian helicopters dropped from the sky, landing on some prefab huts on the larger hummock. Steel screeched and rotor blades shattered on violent impact with the ground.

Someone had not to have wanted witnesses, which meant that even if Goomabong survived, he would be facing the vengeance of the Russian navy for the destruction of one of their birds.

"Shit," the big man growled. He pushed hard the rest of the way, ignoring any new mayhem rising from behind him, guns and grenades detonating, the battle renewed.

The pirates were all dead, and now the Russians were fighting against each other, or McCormack was cleaning house, fighting against Garlov's minions. It didn't matter. He grabbed the handholds on the inflatable raft, pulling it closer to him. With a surge, he kicked out of the water and was in the raft, bumping against another body. Goomabong felt a tarp and pulled it aside.

He was face-to-face with Solyenko, and the Russian goon was out cold. Goomabong gave him a slap on the cheek in an effort to rouse him. There was no response, and the man's breathing was deep and regular. He wasn't out cold from battery, nor was he sleeping. Solyenko was drugged.

Goomabong grimaced, looking at the helpless lump in the raft with him. He weighed what to do as the battle rose to a crescendo behind him. The Malay-Thai pirate grabbed the unconscious Russian and pushed him over the tube on the side, letting the bound and unconscious form splash into the swamp water next to the raft.

If the Russian drowned, then so what? Goomabong had sided with him for as long as things seemed tenable. What was the reward for that bullshit? Solyenko brought down the wrath of GRU-backed Spetsnaz and helicopter gunships in addition to the fury of the one-man army that they knew as McCormack. Goomabong pulled out his boat knife and severed the tether holding the raft in place. A moment of reaching around for an oar and he was ready to go. The long oar's shaft helped him push away from the snarl of mangrove roots where the raft had been moored.

He turned and looked for a way deeper inland. He knew there was access to a stream somewhere nearby.

Something splashed in the water close to him.

Had Solyenko regained consciousness?

No. Two bodies broke over the swamp's surface. A man was holding Solyenko's unconscious head above water, stopping him from drowning.

Goomabong weighed his options, then pulled the oar blade from the swamp. He'd use the flat surface as a means of crushing the rescuer's skull. He had to be careful not to knock himself out of the raft, but no problem there. The oar rose.

Something smacked into Goomabong's wide stomach—
a 9 mm bullet striking flesh and digging under the skin,
glancing off one of his lower ribs and staying just beneath
the surface. It was a minor wound, but the shock was enough
to make Goomabong release the oar, looking up. There was
a flash of a second shot, but this time the big pirate had
thrown himself down to the bottom of the raft, a bullet slicing the air over his head.

From the sound of the gunshots, it was a pistol. Goomabong dug for his own weapon, a Chinese-made SIG
Sauer knockoff, and sat up, looking for the shooter.

He saw a flash of bleached hair in the darkness, not
far. Ten yards. It was a small, slender figure holding the
gun, and it took only an instant for Goomabong to recognize the feminine form.

It was Mila, or whatever that little spy's name was.
He still remembered catching a face full of alcohol from
her, chasing her through the back streets of Kuala Lumpur, losing her in the market.

Karma had given him a chance to get back at her, and
Goomabong snapped it up. He pulled the trigger, punching 9 mm bullets in her direction. Even as he fired, the
raft jolted beneath him. It was the other man, the one
who'd rescued Solyenko. The Malay-Thai pirate growled
and lowered the muzzle of his pistol toward the face of
the man clutching at the raft.

"You're dead!" Goomabong snarled.

Something hot burned into Goomabong's shoulder.

Erra Majid had lined up the 9 mm P226 in her hands
and caught the bulky figure in the raft before he could
squeeze a shot into Zach Winslow's face. She had been
tempted to take Goomabong alive, or barely alive. Then

she could give him the kind of terror she'd experienced when she'd been caught in the corridor with him blocking the exit.

But Winslow was in danger, and something about being as cruel to Goomabong as he would have been to her made her stomach twist. Majid opened up, firing again and again, fighting to keep the grip of the pistol from shifting in her grasp. The roar of the 9 mm rounds bursting out of the barrel as fast as she could pull the trigger was echoed by her own scream. She'd had twelve shots left in the 20-round magazine, and after four seconds, the P226 was empty.

Goomabong was flopped over the edge of the inflatable raft, unmoving.

"He's down!" Winslow rasped over his throat mike. "He's down!"

Majid glanced toward Winslow, who was dragging the unconscious Solyenko back to shore, or at least the wreath of mangrove roots that she stood on. Majid holstered the pistol and reached down. Winslow pushed Solyenko into her grasp and the small Malaysian woman fought against the weight of the slumped Russian, trying to keep him from being sucked back into the swamp. They'd come too damned far to let this bastard drown.

Winslow scrambled onto the roots, then threw his own strength into hauling Solyenko up and out of the water. With the two of them working together, they got the Russian up and out.

Winslow looked down at the bound figure and saw that he wasn't breathing.

The Russian had set up the tactics that had murdered the agent's brothers, his comrades in arms. And now

he had drowned. There was no choice. Winslow tore
open Solyenko's shirt and set furiously to work, giving him CPR.

CHAPTER NINETEEN

The grenade thunked into the sand next to Mack Bolan as he lay prone and his instincts kicked into overdrive. With a hard push, he scrambled to his feet and exploded toward the water. He was in midleap over the mangrove roots when the fragger blew behind him. Concussion and shrapnel chased after the Executioner as he arced into the brackish swamp. The buffeting waves of force had torn the rifle from its sling around his shoulder. The weapon was lost, but Bolan hit the salty marsh and tumbled, letting the water cushion his fall.

As he floated, tumbling in the salty water, he closed his eyes and took a quick inventory. If he'd been cut by shrapnel, he'd feel the briny water burning in the wound. His skin was still intact, except for what he'd already felt from his prior battering. No new holes was always good news, so he unfolded himself and burst through the surface.

There was a figure standing on a bridge, another man at his back, firing an AK-101 into the distance. The stranger extended his hand over the water.

"Here!" Angrekal said, Bolan recognizing his voice immediately.

The soldier swam over to him, took the offered hand, and was pulled up onto the wooden walkway. Even as he rolled onto the planks, Bolan pulled the Desert Eagle from its holster, scanning in the blind spot of the naval infantryman who was Angrekal's swim buddy.

"Thanks," Bolan told him.

"Thanks for taking the heat off my men," Angrekal returned.

"What's the situation?" Bolan asked.

"Well, they lost one or two in the initial attack on my platoon. Then you came up and wiped out four by yourself."

"Your boys did some of that work," Bolan corrected him.

"Now, Korylev and the remaining commandos who can still walk or fight are pulling out," Angrekal stated.

"You going to let him get away?" Bolan asked.

"Not if I can help it," the Spetsnaz officer said.

"Where is he retreating to?"

Angrekal pointed in the distance. Bolan scanned, and while he heard gunfire coming from where he'd left Solyenko's drugged form, he could tell that Korylev had missed the Russian mobster. The mission had become secondary to escaping with his life.

"Would you mind if I tried to take the man alive?" Bolan asked.

"Go for it. He's got some questions to answer."

"Thanks," Bolan replied.

With that, he got to his feet and made his way along the bridges between the islets and buildings. He paused long enough to bend down and scoop up a weapon from a dead member of Korylev's group. As he retrieved it, he recognized it not as an AK-74, but a new AN-94. In design and firing mechanism, the two designs were similar, the AN-94 an evolution of the prior model, though certain mechanisms had been combined into one block, and there was a selector switch that had a setting for a 2-round burst. As the cyclic rate of the burst was 1800 rounds per minute, the twin bullets launched by that single pull of the trigger would fire long before the recoil even jolted the rifle off target. The AN-94 also had a side-folding carbon fiber and polymer stock that could keep it compact for vehicle transport.

It was a good piece of kit, and there were plenty of magazines for it as the AN-94 took the same ammunition and magazines as the older AK-74s that the pirates had on hand. Bolan looked back at Angrekal, then gave the Russian commander a gesture that he was going to flank the surviving traitors. Bolan emptied his pouches of the M16 magazines, replacing them with boxes for the AN-94. Set up with 240 rounds in eight magazines, he set off in a run, eating up the distance.

Korylev and his crew were putting up a sheet of fire and grenades against the naval Spetsnaz under Angrekal. They were good, quick, and they were keeping their heads down, but Angrekal was returning fire, keeping this crew of murderers busy and distracted. As they were fighting, Bolan could get a head count on them. In addition to Korylev, six men remained under his command, less than half the fighting force that had showed up. Angrekal had seven wounded, one dying according to the report that the soldier of the same side was getting.

The Spetsnaz commander groaned at the loss, and the Executioner sympathized with him. Losing your men was a hard thing. Bolan had to step it up to keep any more of the naval infantrymen from falling under Korylev's guns.

He had a good angle on the group and put the rifle to his shoulder, flicking the selector to 2-round burst mode. One pull, two pulls, three pulls of the trigger and the rifle cycled through its double-taps instantly, kicking out six rounds that hammered into two of the GRU-deployed gunmen. The 5.45 mm rounds sliced across the distance to Korylev's position, a stack of shattered cord wood that had once been a hut.

Bolan had taken out a pair of gunners, but he spotted two more in that group, wounded shooters who kept low, but had their eyes and guns trained on flanking positions. The conspirator team's assassins cut loose, and Bolan spun away, diving into the water as bullets chased after him.

The supersonic rounds skipped off the surface, skittering into the swamp, but the Executioner dived deeply, almost to the bottom. Something big rushed past him in the shallow waters, a long tail swishing back and forth. Bolan got a good look.

It was a bull shark, and fortunately for him, the creature had a mouthful of severed limb. The battle had been intense, and the pirates' body parts littered the swamp. Even for an aggressive predator such as a bull shark, the prospect of an easy, inert severed leg was much more appealing than a swimming mammal that was nearly two-thirds its overall length. Bolan kicked along, following in the shark's wake, reaching out and grabbing the short but stiff secondary dorsal fin just in front of the creature's tail.

The enormous strength of the 300-pound female bull shark nearly wrenched Bolan's arm from its socket as he was suddenly attached to a living torpedo. The shark was momentarily startled, befuddled by the contact, and it accelerated to full speed in an effort to dislodge its burden. Even as the two figures plunged through the brackish swamp, Bolan noted the sound of bullets striking the surface and punching into the water behind him seemed to fade. At an underwater velocity of twelve miles per hour, the ferocious meat-eater had outdistanced the renegade Russians' aim and brought Bolan closer to their position three times faster than he could have hoped to move just swimming on the surface, let alone out of sight.

Bolan released the dorsal fin, and the bull shark, still with a mouth full of torn leg, headed off into the predawn darkness of the swamp. There was more than enough blood in the water to have drawn at least one of the apex predators. The soldier hoped that he could get up and out before something else decided to take a taste of him. In the prior weeks, he'd drawn the attention of other meat-eaters—a crocodile and a massive catfish. Filling out a hat trick of submarine predators was not on Bolan's list of things to do.

He snatched a mangrove root for support, then braced the stock of the assault rifle between his elbow and his ribs. This wasn't going to be the most precise of gunfire, but at close quarters, Bolan was sure of the power of the weapon and the spread he could control. Shooting with only one hand wasn't the preferred manner of taking on an enemy, but Bolan needed the other hand to hoist himself up.

Muscles tensed, Bolan exploded from the water. As soon as the muzzle of the AN-94 was clear and swiveled at the enemy, the Executioner hammered off the initial burst from the rifle. He let loose with five rounds, the 5.45 mm slugs cutting across the torso of one of the gunners watching Korylev's back. Bullets cored deeply into body armor, one of them smashing the rifle and forearm of the defender.

Bolan kicked hard against a second root, using it as a ladder rung, pushing him farther up and into the attack. He twisted and shot the second of the gunmen facing him, a 4-round burst striking the man in the chest, then walking up and tearing through the hollow of his throat and shearing off his lower jaw. The Russian's head drooped and fell on stringy remnants of skin and sinew, windpipe, esophagus and spinal column blasted into ugly pulp.

With the two bursts in the space of a second, Korylev and his remaining commandos were already reacting. The first one to turn was Korylev, betraying reflexes akin to a cat's. Bolan didn't want this guy dead, not when he was an officer, perhaps even handpicked by General Garlov to go after Solyenko. Rather than shoot him, Bolan snapped up a kick, his waffle-treaded boot slamming into Korylev's stomach and hurling him onto his back as well more than 220 pounds of muscle and gear surged into him like a battering ram.

Bolan twisted the AN-94's muzzle toward one of the other GRU Spetsnaz troopers and fired. At a range of mere inches, the 5.45 mm rifle rounds exploded into the guts of the gunman, moving at full speed, carrying the totality of their energy through rupturing body armor. Intestines and the aorta beneath the armor exploded under massive hydrostatic shock, the gunman folding over violently and toppling away. The contact-range blast didn't instantly kill him, but the deadly disruptive force of bullets decelerating from nearly Mach 3 to zero knocked him clean out. He'd bleed out within seconds.

Another of the gunmen knew he couldn't swing his rifle around in time, so he lunged, using the buttstock as his primary attack. The reinforced fiberglass and polymer furniture came toward Bolan's face, but the soldier's left arm rose, batting the stock and deflecting a face-crushing blow. Even so, Bolan felt his left hand's fingers numb momentarily under the collision of flesh and blood against plastic and steel. The rifleman was off balance, his lunge turned aside, stumbling under his momentum toward the Executioner. Bolan snapped his left arm straight, bringing the rigid edge of his hand hard against the Russian's neck.

It was an old-school-style judo chop. There were newer, fancier moves in kung fu, but the judo chop was a classic strike that worked and worked well. As Bolan's hand came down, it focused hundreds of pounds of force on the nerves and blood vessels in the trunk of the Spetsnaz soldier's neck. The Russian's eyes bugged out from the impact, his head swaying and body following the insensate man out of the Executioner's way. Bolan wasn't certain if the ax-chop had been enough to kill his opponent, but he didn't have time to double-check. A third trooper leaped through the air and collided with him.

Bolan had more weight with him, thanks to his gear and sheer mass, and he'd been charging longer and faster. The Russian hadn't built up enough speed, so while the Executioner's rush slowed, he still kept going while his enemy was rocked backward. Bolan swung his left hand around, his fingers extended, spearing toward the man's face.

The next instant, Bolan's fingers were knuckles-deep in blood and viscous fluids. The Russian's orbital sockets were excavated by the force of his poke, and a wild, terrified scream burst from the commando's lips. Bolan grimaced at the crude, violent manner in which he'd had to respond, but there were still two more men trying to get at him.

The Executioner stabbed his AN-94 into the upper chest of one of these men, but the Spetsnaz fighter twisted, scissoring his forearms around the weapon. With superior leverage, the Russian twisted the rifle out of Bolan's fist. Now the soldier was unarmed in the face of two men, one of whom having pulled a revolver from a cross draw with the speed of a snake. Bolan wrenched himself free from his blinded foe and threw himself at the quick trooper who'd disarmed him.

Three .357 Magnum rounds exploded from the revolver, their muzzle-flashes lighting up the predawn. The sheer power of those bullets accelerating to 1400 feet per second was palpable, the pressure waves slapping at Bolan as they zipped close to him. The man who'd twisted the rifle from the Executioner's grasp turned back, reaching for a knife when he jerked, stunned by Magnum bullets striking his body armor. At this range, the Magnum rounds didn't quite penetrate the Kevlar and trauma plates, but it still stunned the Russian soldier enough to push him into Bolan.

Bolan grabbed the living shield and twisted, shoving the stunned man back toward the Magnum gunner, who cut loose with the last rounds in his cylinder. Bolan could see the impacts in the face of the wounded Russian, hammer blows that struck his back, racking him with agony before he slammed bodily into the Revolver Man. Bolan kept up his attack and charged in, stomping his boot into the guts of the injured man, making certain that the guy on the bottom was sandwiched against the ground. The back-blasted man's face was pale, twisted in agony, and when Bolan removed his foot, the poor guy rolled over and away.

There wasn't much fight in him. Revolver Man, on the other hand, tossed aside his empty weapon and tried to sit up. Bolan surged in and brought up his right forearm. The hard edge of Bolan's forearm struck the Russian's windpipe and smashed his head back into a tangle of mangrove roots with enough force to release a spray of blood. His scalp split on hard contact with wood. The Executioner felt a fist slam into his ribs, deflected from his kidney by a pouch full of first-aid supplies. The wind still shot from Bolan's lips, so he rammed the palm of his left hand under the pinned Russian's jaw. With the neck held still and the head braced against the roots, the only thing that could give on the Spetsnaz trooper was his jaw, and the mandible bone cracked loudly, bursting from its moorings.

The pain from that attack was nervous-system overload. The Russian was out cold in an instant.

Bolan leaned back, taking a breath, his energy having been exhausted in the brief explosion of violence against Korylev's last defenders. He'd almost let his guard down enough for the man he'd judo-chopped to get in a clear shot, but the rustle of movement, the grunt of exertion, warned the Executioner of an incoming attack. Bolan squatted, bending his knees and getting his head out of the way of a vicious swing. The flicker of a ribbon of silver informed the soldier that the stunned man had the presence of mind to make another attack, but this time with a knife.

Bolan straightened his legs, powering himself backward into his ambusher. He felt his back and shoulders collide with the Russian behind him, and in a moment, both men were on the sand, the Executioner rolling one way while the surprised Spetsnaz fighter scrambled to find his knife. Desperate fingers speared into the sand, touched the grip of the fighting blade and pulled it from the hummock.

Bolan knew at this range, being unarmed against a knife was almost suicide. His body block had worked because the Russian had missed, committed too much energy and momentum to the attack, and had been, if only for a moment, off balance. Now, the trained killer was going for the knife, and it would be instants before that point came seeking his flesh. The Executioner hurled himself farther back from the Spetsnaz soldier, wrenching his Desert Eagle from its holster. In the flash of a fast draw, Bolan punched a single .44 Magnum round through the assassin's breastbone. Kevlar and trauma plates were no match for high-velocity tungsten. The super-dense, ultrahard metal point of the armor-piercing bullet sliced through the vest, struck the man's breastbone, and blew it to splinters before ripping his heart in two.

The Knife Man was dead even as the point of his blade whistled within an inch of Bolan's throat.

Too close for comfort, the Executioner mused as he turned and looked for Korylev.

"Son of a bitch!" the blinded soldier snarled as he lashed out, wrapping both arms around Bolan's left leg. The attack was sudden enough to catch him flat-footed, and now with the weight of a human pinning his foot, Bolan caught a glimmer of movement, knowing full well that he had to stand his ground or be dragged to the sand. Korylev, on the other hand, was not so hindered by circumstances.

The GRU commander charged in, throwing an opening salvo of jabs and chops. It took everything in the Executioner's repertoire of martial arts and every ounce of speed he had to block or deflect the onslaught. Korylev danced away from the assault, grinning and confident. The man was sizing up Bolan. He knew he was a prize too precious to be taken out with a bullet.

The American, on the other hand, was a deadly threat, and one to be taken down quickly. Korylev charged in again, but he hadn't counted on the Executioner's willingness to use the handgun…

…as a club! The butt of the heavy three-pound pistol swung around and caught Korylev in the wrist, intercepting a punch that had the speed and force to collapse Bolan's windpipe. When metal met bone, bone cracked. Korylev's fist loosened, his fingers springing open at the shock of a shattered wrist. Korylev scowled, but continued to push. A looping hook slipped past Bolan's shoulder, bouncing off the back of the soldier's head just behind his ear. Stars flashed behind Bolan's eyes, but the warrior didn't give in to the pain. He hammered with his free hand under that brain-scrambling hook, punching the commander in the armpit.

The impact knocked fetid breath from his lungs, staggering Korylev into retreat. That bought Bolan enough time to bring his senses back together, to blink away the pain, and prepare for a renewed attack. Spetsnaz were dangerous men, and they spent much of their time honing their hand-to-hand combat skills, or fighting with unusual weapons. If there was one thing the Executioner was glad about, it was that Korylev didn't have a shovel or an entrenching tool. The Russian special operations men had developed a deadly fighting style based around the shovel, even using them as throwing axes.

A knife was one thing to ward off. The sharpened edge of a shovel blade, however, could slice through a man's arm as if it were a hunk of deli meat. Korylev kicked, hurling sand into the air and toward Bolan's face. The soldier blinked, then twisted hard, wrenching his leg loose from the grasp of the blind man. It wasn't going to be much, but now that the American warrior could move both feet, he could compensate for the temporary loss of vision from sandy grit in his eyes.

Korylev pressed his attack, his good fist jabbing and slashing. Bolan was able to block one in three blows, but only the fact that he'd broken the Russian's wrist, limiting him to one-handed attacks, had kept the Spetsnaz boss from turning the American's face to a pulp. Even so, Bolan grunted as one punch landed in the pit of his stomach.

The soldier folded under the impact, unconscious reflex putting his shoulder blades right in the path of a falling elbow that stabbed into his back. The one-two combination took Bolan's breath away, blood roaring in his ears from the deadly punishment. Another elbow-shot like that, and the Spetsnaz commando could induce some serious spinal damage. Rather than sit and take the beating, Bolan kicked forward, hurling his body into Korylev.

The collision of the two men lifted the Russian off of his feet, Bolan hurling them both against the trunk of a mangrove tree. Korylev's breath exploded from his lungs, his fingers now clawing at the Executioner's vest instead of fists and elbows falling on his neck and shoulders. Bolan eased off, then surged forward again, mashing Korylev between himself and the tree trunk. He could feel ribs shatter under the ram attack. The Spetsnaz boss held on to Bolan's vest with all he had, not wanting to free the Executioner for a third charge.

Rather than repeat the tactic, Bolan ripped the man off his feet, lifting him on one shoulder, then spinning him into the sand. Bringing down all of his weight on Korylev, Bolan was rewarded with a gurgling cry and the sudden limpness of those grasping hands. The soldier wiped his eyes, blinking the sand out of them.

The Russian thug didn't look as if he were in the best of health, but his eyes were still wide-open, anger still stretched across his gritted teeth. Bolan cut loose with another judo chop, aimed right at where Korylev's jaw met his neck. That slashing impact rendered the conspiracy assassin unconscious.

Breathing deeply, gasping for air, Bolan looked toward Angrekal's position. All of this had happened in the space of a minute, an ugly, brutal melee. The naval infantry special operatives were racing to his side, guns low, but eyes still scanning for threats on the perimeter of the wrecked pirate camp.

Angrekal helped Bolan back to his feet.

"He's alive?"

Bolan nodded. "Yeah. He'll live to stand trial. If you want."

"We'll see what's left when we're finished interrogating him," the friendly Russian lieutenant stated.

Angrekal looked from the unconscious traitor to Bolan. "Something tells me that when we get our answers from him, you're going after his boss."

Bolan nodded.

"And if that boss is in the sovereign nation of the Russian Federation?" Angrekal asked.

Bolan met his new ally's gaze, unblinking. "It wouldn't be the first, nor the last time I cleaned house on that land. I'd prefer to have some friends, but if not, nothing is going to keep me from General Constantin Garlov."

"Garlov," Angrekal repeated. "Oh, hell."

Finally, the pirate camp was silent, only the crackle of dying flames and the groans of the wounded to be heard.

CHAPTER TWENTY

Between the Little Bird helicopter and the remaining Kamov Ka-29, Bolan, Majid, Winslow and Angrekal's team were able to get back to the Wasp-class amphibious assault ship that had dispatched the TF-160 bird and crew. The Wasp carrier had agreed to pick up both birds under the pretense of helping the Russians with their damaged aircraft, which indeed the remaining Kamov had been.

Back at the pirate base, Bolan and Winslow had convinced the pilots of Korylev's airship to surrender themselves, Winslow with a near-miss shot from his Carl Gustav, and Bolan with a tungsten-cored .44 Magnum through the windshield. Preferring life over death, the crew had landed the Kamov.

It was then that Lieutenant Kyril Angrekal had pulled his sleek GSh-18 and put a 9 mm bullet through the face of the crewman who'd opened fire on the other Ka-29, a summary execution and a message to the other pilot.

As the gun was double action only, Angrekal didn't need to put on a safety or to decock the hammer. The firing pin was at rest, unable to be tripped by anything less than a deliberate pull of the trigger. As the magazine's reservoir was 18 rounds, with an extra one in the pipe, Angrekal didn't even have to reload.

"Your life is hanging by a thread," Angrekal had told the pilot. "I have people who can easily fly this aircraft back, but they're wounded by the betrayal of your commander."

Bolan had seen the rage in the Spetsnaz lieutenant's eyes, even though the rest of his face was emotionless. There was a slight tremor to his words, but other than that, he was under control.

Angrekal regarded Bolan.

"You won't raise a stink—"

"The man murdered your helicopter crew," Bolan said, cutting him off. "He earned the bullet to the brain. I'm just glad you didn't take the time to dismantle him slowly for that."

Angrekal's voice was still brittle, even though he attempted a joke. "I didn't have the life support to give him the proper send-off to hell."

With the arrival of the Little Bird to transport everyone back to the carrier, Angrekal had called his Udaloy-class destroyer, informing base that the assault team had taken casualties and damage in the attack on the pirates. Not long after, the American carrier informed the Russian navy that they had room to take in the nearly destroyed remaining helicopter for emergency repairs.

While that hadn't made the captain of the destroyer happy, there was little he could do. He was still a hundred miles past the carrier's range, and the Kamov had, at best, a nearly 550 mile range. Damage to the bird would have made the extra hundred miles deadly, especially since the destroyer only had two aircraft, and both had been used on the mission.

As the two helicopters hovered over the deck of the Wasp-class carrier, Angrekal had a question for his American ally.

"What is the plan?" Angrekal asked Bolan after they'd

disembarked and moved to the deck rail to watch the carrier crew assist the others.

The soldier filled him in on the overall mission.

"We throw in a few delays. Something that will take a couple of days to overcome," Bolan answered.

"'A couple of days,'" Angrekal repeated. "You don't want Garlov to figure out that you're onto him."

"Right," Bolan replied. "Do you think you can come up with a sufficient snow job?"

Angrekal frowned. "I'd like to speak with my admiral on this matter. But if I make contact with him...there's the possibility that he, or someone on his staff, might be working with the counterfeiting and financial hacking conspiracy for Garlov."

"You doubt your boss?" Bolan asked.

Angrekal chewed on his lower lip. "Personally, I think he'd be okay. But that won't give us a secure conversation with him."

Bolan took a look at his Combat CDA. The machine had taken a couple of knocks, but Hermann Schwarz knew full well the kind of roughhousing that the members of Stony Man's strike teams, and the Executioner himself, could put electronics through. He'd modified the shell with steel and reinforced polymers with rubber cushion pads along the back. Bolan had once mentioned that it looked like the sole of a combat boot, and Schwarz replied that it was supposed to.

"When was the last time you saw a boot crushed like a tin can?" Schwarz had quipped.

Bolan ran through the list that he'd sent to Stony Man Farm. Kurtzman had already received some data, specifically Garlov's name, and with the supporting observations from Angrekal, was starting on a full rundown on the retired general. "What's your man's name?"

"Admiral Caszimir Lypnyki," Angrekal answered.

Bolan entered it into the CDA and transmitted back to the Farm. "Give my people a few minutes. We'll see if anything shows up as a risk for our operational security."

"I take it that your people could also arrange a direct line to my man?" Angrekal asked.

Bolan nodded in response. He watched as wounded Russian operatives were taken off the Kamov. The severely wounded Spetsnaz from the fight in the pirate base had expired in flight. Angrekal showed signs of wear and tear emotionally. The soldier had felt the same way. Too many friends, too many allies, had fallen over the years for him to keep a heart hardened and armored against such pain. The only thing that he could hope for was to avenge them and to send prayers on to whatever plane of existence that was their destiny.

Angrekal kept his attention away from the helicopter where the dead were still on board. He concentrated on his wounded, kneeling and offering them support and compassion. Sometimes, that was the best way to deal with the pain of loss, to keep on with the living. It was easy to allow oneself to collapse into grief.

Finally, Korylev and Solyenko were brought off the copter. Solyenko had an oxygen mask, and was restricted to a gurney. In the effort to save the Russian thug's life, Winslow had broken the man's ribs giving him CPR chest compressions. Cardio pulmonary resuscitation was a last-ditch effort, and the breaking of ribs was a common occurrence. He wasn't going to be getting up and running around anytime soon. Even so, the *mafiya* gangster was back in restraints, wrists bound to the sides of the gurney.

Interrogation wasn't going to be on the list of things to do with him, either. Bolan could only hope that they could cajole answers through conventional questioning. As much as the soldier hated torture, and knew how the process was flawed, sometimes pain and intimidation could go a long way toward loosening a tongue. He hoped that a carrot would do as well as a stick.

Korylev, on the other hand, despite bruises and a broken wrist, was healthy enough to get rough treatment. Bolan kept himself between the traitorous prisoner and Angrekal, and the Russian commando did his best to ignore the man being led to the brig in handcuffs. U.S. Navy corpsmen were doing their best work on treating Angrekal's platoon, but the lieutenant still stayed close, hovering like a parent over men who had sacrificed themselves for their country's defense.

There were still three dead to deal with, men to mourn over.

But business came first.

Bolan turned to Winslow and Majid. "Good work at the camp."

"Nothing about us hanging around too long?" Majid asked.

Bolan regarded her, then gave her a warm smile, reaching out and patting Winslow on the shoulder. "I stuck with you two because you could think for yourselves. You did exactly what was needed, and exactly what I ordered you to do, which was to avoid contact with Angrekal's team."

Winslow nodded. "I had to save that bastard's life."

"Regrets?" Bolan asked him.

Winslow shrugged. "Well, he looks like he's been run over by a truck, and that was me who did that. And, I think I won a moral victory. If it had been reversed…"

"You did the right thing, and he would have killed you," Bolan concluded.

"I feel like a big damn winner," Winslow said with a grin. The expression of happiness didn't reach all the way to his eyes, not until Majid wrapped her arms around his waist. "If he makes it to a gulag, he'll get every ounce of karma coming to him."

"Erra?" Bolan asked the Malaysian cop.

"Goomabong is dead. I dropped him," Majid answered. "Right now, I feel drained. There's a little satisfaction, but it just doesn't feel like the weight released from my shoulders that I imagined it to be."

Winslow gave her a hug around her shoulders. She rested her cheek against his chest, and managed a smile.

"Still, I do have something to feel good about," she quickly added.

Bolan smiled. "Great work, you two."

Winslow and Majid stiffened. "Wait a minute, McCormack… You're not giving us the shove-off, are you?"

"Your personal involvement in this is over," Bolan told them. "And I want to give you two a chance to avoid what's coming next."

"Hunting down the big bad Russian general behind this?" Majid asked.

Winslow chuckled. "Can't be any worse than invading a Malaysian gangster's estate, or raiding pirates."

Bolan shook his head. "Garlov is someone who has support among active military, and spy masters, as well as Russian organized crime. I'll be going after him on his own turf. That will be dangerous."

"So, you're offering us a chance to sit out and survive," Winslow said.

Bolan nodded.

"Thanks for the offer," Majid said. "But we've come this far."

"Besides, I'm going to be down a few men from my platoon." A voice spoke from behind Bolan. It was Angrekal.

Bolan frowned. "How bad are they?"

"Hurt, but they'll recover," Angrekal said. "The corpsmen here are quite good."

Bolan nodded in agreement.

"Whether I get permission or not, my team and I are going to find Korylev's boss and drive a stake through his heart if we have to," Angrekal added. "If you'll allow us."

"I'd be honored to have you along for the ride," Bolan told him. "Think of ways we can get to him outside official channels."

"I've got a few former wayward youth in my crew," Angrekal stated. "I think something could be arranged."

"I'll see with a few of my own friends, too," Bolan responded.

"You've got people in Russia, too?" Winslow asked. He held up his hand before anyone could answer. "No. You've got friends in Thailand of all places. Of course you're going to know people in Russia."

Bolan nodded. His CDA vibrated—Kurtzman getting back to him with a text.

Admiral Lypnyki is clean as a whistle.

Bolan smiled, then showed Angrekal, who grinned.

"My people are thorough," Bolan told him. "They go

over stuff that could be considered circumstantial evidence, as well."

"Can we call him?" Angrekal asked.

Bolan typed a text back. In a few moments the phone in the Combat CDA was dialing. He handed the device over to the Russian lieutenant.

Angrekal held it to his ear.

"Hello?" came a bleary response.

"Admiral, it's Angrekal," he said.

Any sound of weariness disappeared from the older man's voice. "Nephew. What's the problem? And how did you get to this line?"

"The problem is ex-GRU, and I'm not sure who found this number for you," Angrekal responded.

"Ex-GRU?" Lypnyki asked.

"General Garlov," Angrekal answered. "He had a platoon of Spetsnaz inserted into my pirate-hunting endeavor. When we went after one camp, he turned on us. I lost three men and another four are going to be hospitalized."

"When did this happen?" Lypnyki asked.

"About an hour and a half ago," Angrekal responded.

"And where are you now?" Lypnyki queried.

Angrekal smiled sheepishly. "In the Andaman Sea, on an American ship. The destroyer is on its way to meet us."

"Garlov. Fuck me," Lypnyki muttered. "What did you do to get him on your ass?"

"I was incidental. He wanted someone in the area to deal with assets that had been in Malaysia," Angrekal responded. "I have a friend here with me who says he—"

"He was using a small computer center inside Kuala Lumpur." Lypnyki cut him off. "The GRU had sent a unit in about five years ago, before Garlov retired. They claimed that the KGB installation had been destroyed and picked clean. Nothing to recover."

"Apparently there was," Angrekal responded.

"And pirates were involved in it?" Lypnyki asked. "Of course they would be. Garlov would need muscle that was off the grid, but wouldn't be looked at twice if they were brimming with guns."

"Can you give me a smokescreen about our losses in the field?" Angrekal asked. "I don't want him to know that his sabotage had been derailed."

"Certainly," Lypnyki replied. "Your friend...is he there? Can I speak to him?"

Angrekal handed the CDA to Bolan.

"Hello, sir," Bolan said.

"Hello. My nephew said that he had a platoon attached to his. Do you have a name and description to go with the leader of that group?" Lypnyki inquired.

Bolan gave as concise a summary as he could, but Lypnyki cut him off, the details so well given that he recognized the operator. "Korylev is one of our bugs under the carpet."

"As in?"

"Something we wish we could get rid of, but can't pin down," Lypnyki responded. "He's got too many 'rabbis' over his head, one of them being Garlov, but he's got more."

"You think these 'rabbis' would join with Garlov in a scheme to take over the Russian Federation?" Bolan asked him.

"He might, but as we are now, if we returned to being a global superpower, we don't have the economic standing to throw much weight. It'd have to be all military," Lypnyki answered.

"Not necessarily," Bolan interjected.

"The Kuala Lumpur facility." Lypnyki groaned. "You confirmed your target?"

"Yes, sir," Bolan said. "He also had an operation in motion in South America. He was printing counterfeit notes of both United States and Chinese currency, as well as some smaller countries' denominations."

"Economic overload," Lypnyki muttered. "When China and America have their financial crises, Russia now has a bigger dick to swing in the arena."

"That is one way to put it," Bolan returned.

"Pardon an old man's vulgarity."

"Not at all," Bolan said.

"Have you begun working on Korylev?" Lypnyki asked.

"I'm trying to get a little more advanced knowledge," Bolan said. "People aren't so tight-lipped when you know things they thought were so secret."

"That's always been my observation," Lypnyki replied. "All right. Fire away. I'm at my desk. I'll see what I can look up."

Bolan rattled off the specifics. Lypnyki responded that he'd have answers inside an hour.

That was all that the Executioner could hope for.

KORYLEV HAD BEEN left alone, handcuffed to the chair in the otherwise featureless room. He could feel the slight motion of waves, and the riveted bulkheads informed him that he was being held captive in the bowels of a ship. The light was dim, so it had taken him five minutes to make out details along the walls.

Korylev corrected himself. He wasn't handcuffed. He was bound to the arms of the chair with nylon cable ties, loose enough not to cut off circulation to his fingers, but still tight enough to keep him from budging more than a few millimeters There were a dozen around each forearm that he could see. He didn't know about his legs, but one effort to move them told him that he was bound down there, as well. At least he had his clothing on, boots included.

He wondered where everyone was.

The last thing he remembered was being hammered by that big bastard, chopped in the neck, and left insensate. He had a blurry recollection of manhandling, getting stuffed into the back of a helicopter. He also recalled vomiting, though he didn't have a clue where that had been.

Footsteps approached on the other side of a closed hatch. Korylev tensed, muscles flexing. If he could slowly stretch the nylon cable ties…

The hatch opened with a thunderous boom and as Korylev looked up toward the door, he was greeted with the harsh blue flare of a flashlight. The effect was like being blasted in the eyes with a blowtorch. He clenched his eyes shut and whipped his head away from the glare. Despite shut lids, an omnipresent blue-tinted blob dominated his vision, and he'd turned his head so quickly, he felt the hot wash of a popped neck tendon. His head throbbed from the double assault, and his nausea was returning once more.

In the darkness, his senses had grown sharper, more acute than they normally would have been. The hammering thunder of the hatch should have been a clue.

Suddenly the unholy shriek of two air horns, one in

each ear, sliced through his brain. Korylev tried to shut his eyes tighter, and he felt blood flowing from where he'd bitten down hard on his tongue. His limbs were motionless, despite all the effort put into trying to tear himself loose from this damned trap. He was blind and deaf. Panic increased his heart rate. The logical part of the Russian's mind tried to calm himself, but autonomic reactions to pain, immobility and crippled senses ran wild.

He let out a bellow, trying to form a curse against his captors, but the words tripped clumsily over a rapidly swelling tongue. Korylev was reduced to a subhuman snarl.

"I'm not going to talk." Korylev finally spoke, adapting to his injured tongue.

The wild echoing ringing in his skull diffused any words being spoken to him. He strained to make out what was being said, but he learned that there were no actual words.

There was only laughter.

The interrogators were getting psychological on him now.

A hard slap across his cheek, and Korylev opened his eyes, his head swimming, faces obscured by the flash burn on his retinas. He could see the face of Kyril Angrekal hovering in front of him. The lights were now on in the interrogation room.

"All right. You told us about the general's home in Narodychi," Angrekal muttered.

"What?" Korylev asked. Bloody drool flowed over his lower lip. There was a second man in the room, tall, dark-haired, the only brightness in his black-clad appearance being two eyes as blue and cold as ice.

"You told us how Garlov kept an estate on the edge of

Narodychi," Bolan said. "In the Periodic Control Zone. It keeps people from poking too closely at his home, and affords him privacy. I'm surprised that he manages to get that much security on hand with all of that free-floating Cesium contamination."

Korylev pulled his lips shut in a tight, bloodless line. He scanned his memory, looking for when he could have spoken about such things. Before he could get his thoughts in order, Angrekal turned on the flashlight again. Pain seared through his eyes, stabbing straight into his brain. Confusion and fear coordinated to render his brain a scramble of thoughts and feelings. He wanted to break free of the chair, but there was nothing he could do. He didn't even have the concentration to go back to remembering what he'd said.

"Narodychi…" he repeated. What did he remember about that place?

Korylev *had* been there. The GRU colonel was one of Garlov's handpicked men, and even now, his ears ringing, his eyes seared by brilliant lights, he could remember the subtle splendor of the place. It was a sprawling estate, two acres, with only one real way to access the place—a road across the land that branched off a highway coming from the south and Zhytomyr. The access road was actually past Narodychi, turning north halfway down the route to Poliske, one of the major cities that had been abandoned, due to it being on the edge of the Permanent Control Zone. The estate itself was on the Periodic Control Zone, a relatively safe area most of the time.

Naturally, Garlov's estate was equipped with measures against radiation contamination, and one of the reasons why people didn't get ill there was a liberal dose of alcohol, protecting them from the higher than normal Cesium contamination. That, combined with atmospheric scrubbers, radiation badges and protective clothing made for a secure zone in an inhospitable zone. The land was spread across two acres, but the estate itself was high-walled, and the grounds kept clean and shielded from outside debris.

The next thing that Korylev knew, he was hearing that description being spoken. The conspirator's head jerked erect and he looked at Angrekal.

"You've told us quite a bit," Angrekal said. "Don't act surprised."

"How…?"

"Scopolamine," Bolan answered, his voice deep, full of timber, laden with menace. "You don't remember?"

"No, I don't," Korylev stated. "I don't remember anything of the sort."

"Well, how else could we know?"

"Solyenko," Korylev answered.

"He's barely alive." Bolan cut him off. A tablet computer screen showed an image of the Russian gangster strapped to a gurney, an NG tube in his nose, an oxygen mask over his face, IVs in his arm. It wasn't an altered image because it was a live video feed. "His Thai buddy tried to drown him. Nine ribs and his breastbone were fractured restarting his heart and lungs. You are our last hope."

Korylev blinked. He tried to get a clearer look. On the screen, the video feed of Solyenko was still playing.

What the GRU operative didn't know was that while Solyenko truly was getting that kind of medical attention, Bolan had already spoken to the gangster. Brought back from the edge of death, the mobster figured that a prison term in the United States was far better than a continued incarceration in Russia, or the cold oblivion of a bullet to the head. Solyenko spoke, giving up as many secrets as he could.

From there, it was extrapolation, supported by internet research and forensic accounting on the part of Stony Man Farm. They knew that Garlov owned property within the Chernobyl Exclusion Zone, an estate that was on the edge of one of the hotter areas, providing a nearly impenetrable barrier to intrusion on one side and a Russian police and military enforced perimeter for the whole area. Background radiation would also make radio surveillance all but impossible, static and interference wrecking any signal. Even satellite photography was left fuzzy looking down from orbit, at least when trying to utilize downward-pointing radar and infrared imagery.

What could be seen were the major structures, discernible in the visible spectrum camera. Unfortunately, due to the terrain, the infrared photography couldn't pick up individuals on the ground. Only orders for radiation safety gear could give a rough estimate of how much security Garlov had present. Even so, it was more than sufficient for Angrekal and Bolan to build upon. Every time they mentioned something that actually fit Korylev's recollections, they noticed the "hit" in the prisoner's reactions.

The effect made it seem as if they were either psychic, or they had actually heard the description from his lips. In reality, the two men were doing something that fraudulent "seers" had been practicing for centuries— cold reading. More modern variants also utilized the kind of instantaneous background research available to the more computer-savvy psychic, adding to the cold readings. Whichever the case, the apparent omniscience was unnerving to Korylev. It battered at his resistance to speak, to answer.

Each educated guess, each bit of foreknowledge passed off as mind-reading, loosened the man's tongue.

Soon, Korylev began to talk. It took another two hours of repetition, eerie prescience and intimidating certainty cracking the conspirator's shell further and further.

Thoroughly broken, Korylev was destined to spend the rest of his life in a Russian gulag.

The only prerequisite was that Bolan had to complete his attack on Garlov's compound.

And thanks to Korylev, navigating the radioactive wasteland would be just a shade easier.

CHAPTER TWENTY-ONE

Constantin Garlov knew that something was wrong the moment that Korylev didn't call in. He peered through the window of his office, looking over the snow-covered countryside beyond his estate's wall. The wind had been great today, and according to the radiation detectors, no Cesium-contaminated debris had made it inside the walls. It was cold out, just a shade over 30 degrees Fahrenheit, so his men were in relatively light jackets, further kept warm by armored load-bearing vests beneath the outer shells.

Being in the middle of the Periodic Control Zone, the actual dangers of lethal exposure to radiation had been significantly diminished. This estate had been put together in the late nineties, all of the Cesium contamination shoveled out and dumped far away, off-loaded into more radioactive land and packed under even more earth. It had been developed by Garlov personally as the ultimate getaway. There were few neighbors, only a few thousand stretched between Poliske and Narodychi, and even then, most of them were more to the north, in the least contaminated part of the Exclusion Zone.

If anyone stumbled too close, the guards didn't even need silenced weapons. A few bullets and the corpses were left for the wildlife to take care of.

The wildlife.

Garlov caught movement on the tree line. He brought

up his binoculars, and saw that it was simply a gray wolf. Their numbers had grown phenomenally in the decade and a half since humankind had fled Chernobyl. Not only had the wild canines thrived, but they seemed bigger, stronger. Elsewhere in the world, wolves generally were limited to a maximum upper limit of 120 pounds, but in the post-nuclear wasteland, Garlov had seen some truly monstrous beasts. The one at the tree line was a big bastard. Judging by its height in comparison to the tree it stood next to, the thing was 45 inches at the shoulder and closing in on 175 pounds. Such a creature hadn't been seen since the extinction of *Canis dirus,* the dire wolf.

Garlov looked at the thing, a shaggy beast, male as it lifted its leg to urinate against the trunk of a tree. The creature had no fear of the pale, hairless mammals who cowered behind the stone walls of the estate. Garlov wished that he'd kept a rifle rack here in his office rather than in his living room. This would have been the perfect perch from which to shoulder a rifle and put a bullet through the wolf's shoulder. After some decontamination, the monster's pelt would make a beautiful wall covering.

The retired general sighed. Maybe he'd go out later. After all, he had a helicopter on the premises, and from what he'd heard from friends who had been to Alaska, hunting wolves by air was thrilling and most diverting. With the additional challenge of a giant, highly intelligent and amazingly strong breed of the animals, it might even be more so.

That was all dependent, however, on how things were going. He had his men trying to garner further information from the navy. It appeared that one group of

Spetsnaz had been all but wiped out on hard enemy contact with the pirates of the Andaman Sea.

The only trouble with getting further information about who survived and who hadn't was that they were on board an American amphibious assault carrier because the remaining helicopter had been too damaged to return to its original ship, the Udaloy-class destroyer that had dispatched them. With injured men and a wrecked helicopter, it would take a long time to transfer from one ship to another, especially since there were hundreds of miles, allegedly, between the American and Russian craft.

It could have been a snow job, but Admiral Lypnyki was raising a fuss, unwilling to have one of his ships make a rendezvous far out of his way, especially with an American carrier of all things.

Lypnyki, Garlov mused. The general had never liked that pompous, self-important and entirely too righteous admiral.

For a while, Garlov had thought that Lypnyki might be a good addition to his plans for funding the conspiracy, paving the road to make a brand-new Russia, something that had finally severed all ties to the idiotic real politick of a faux communist tyranny and pushed forward to carve a true empire across the globe. Garlov had been privy to too much of the KGB, all of their egotism and bravado, and their lip service to a glorious cause when the ones in charge simply wanted a status quo that would keep the Communist Party off their backs.

No, the Russia he'd build up would be a military powerhouse, the rebirth of Moscow as the twenty-first century Sparta, where the strong became harder until they made the steel of Stalin seem soft and pliant. The world would tremble at the kind of authority that Garlov's New Russia would exert. No more would sneering Middle Easterners even blink wrong in Russia's direction. The Chinese would have been put in their place, as well, their wobbling new capitalist legs cut from beneath by the efforts of his hackers and the counterfeit currency. And America? The nation of slobs and addicts to bread and circuses would have sat in the corner like a drooling idiot, doing nothing until slapped and ordered.

Then the world would be on the right track.

Garlov looked at his desk. To pass the time, he thought he'd reread some Ayn Rand, his personal literary hero. She knew how the world had to be. The only way to be truly successful was to be true to oneself. Forget about compassion for the weak, there were few people in the world worth love. Damned few. All they could really be good for was to live as slave labor, as fodder. There were some of worth, and if Garlov was wrong, then a truly strong man would come along and topple him, derail his rule. Criticism, admonishment, poor polling, those were the limitations of the weak.

Solyenko had informed him of McCormack, the man who had come to be identified as the Soldier. For a legend, McCormack had lived up to his name, going on a rampage through South America and then the Thai-Malaysian peninsula. However, Garlov couldn't conceive that McCormack was actually strong. He seemed to have had a retinue of followers, assistants along the way, and he skulked, hiding from the authorities in all but the most extreme of circumstances. The Soldier was a coward, a weakling who used trickery.

Now, the man was off the grid.

It didn't matter. Garlov was armed, not with a hunting rifle that would have been perfect for taking a giant wolf at 300 yards, but he had his sidearm and a submachine gun close at hand. Garlov was ready to fight, and by the iron of his will, he would survive, unbroken, and ready to start another quest for the rule of Russia. He'd stumbled once. He'd succeed again.

The computer on his desk had a pop-up, an alert from the security system. Guards outside were suddenly in motion. Motion detectors and radar had picked up something coming.

Garlov grabbed up his tumbler, took a deep gulp of alcohol, girding himself for the radioactive waste, then retrieved his weapons.

"Come now, Soldier. It's time to face your master," Garlov grunted.

MACK BOLAN WAITED for the crack of the single shot to fade. This far from the estate, he didn't have to worry too much about security hearing the gun go off, not with a copse of woods providing a buffer. However, that pop from his unsuppressed Beretta was more than enough to set the herd of deer running.

And the deer, twenty strong, would generate plenty of vibration that would be picked up by motion detectors. In the near evening, they would definitely attract a lot of attention from security. In the meantime, Bolan and his allies would be riding snowmobiles, the Swedish Aktiv Grizzly, and charging the estate right along with the herd. The sleds were monsters of engineering, each of them weighing more than 700 pounds, and possessing 497 cc two-piston engines capable of blasting out 5700 rpm and 38 horsepower.

While this was a larger vehicle than Bolan was used

to, the snowmobile accelerated and cut across the countryside with confidence and power. The base of the vehicle was broad enough that it wouldn't accidentally tip over if faced with uneven ground, and that 38 horsepower was more than sufficient to get the snowmobiles moving at high speed.

Riding behind him because she was from a place that knew nothing of snow, let alone snowmobiles, was Erra Majid. Winslow was piggybacking on Angrekal's sled. There were three other snowmobiles in the formation; the remaining six healthy commandos from Angrekal's team. To make the most of the distraction of the running deer, all of the sleds were cutting through the wood at a leisurely 20 miles an hour.

A benefit of the more relaxed pace as opposed to a full-out 70 miles an hour was a lower noise signature, as well as the reduced risk of ramming into a tree with sufficient force to split a human body in two.

Bolan, Winslow and Majid kept their sidearms from their adventure in Thailand, Bolan with his .44 Magnum Desert Eagle and Beretta 93R, and Winslow and Majid with their SIG Sauer P226s with the slim, flat Walther PPSs tucked away as backup.

Angrekal and his team were rolling with GSh-18 autoloaders, the Russian answer to a safe, flat Glock without a safety catch to impede consistent and fast shots. None of the Spetsnaz seemed to have a concern about the punch of their pistols, especially since they had been designed to run with the extremely hot 7N21 variant of the 9 mm Parabellum, ammunition that they had shared with Bolan and his allies. The 7N21 was a steel-cored design meant to take the armor-piercing attributes of the smaller 5.7 mm and 4.6 mm cartridges of FN and

Heckler & Koch, but still possess all the surface contact area and mass of a handgun with proved fight-stopping power. The result was between a regular 9 mm and a .357 Magnum in kinetic energy, and the steel core provided more than sufficient stiffness to defeat all but the thickest of wearable body armor.

Bolan felt the muzzle-blast when he had discharged his Beretta into the air. The rounds were more powerful, but he preferred the Desert Eagle for when it came time to take out an armored target. Either way, the Executioner was glad for the gift.

To go with the handguns, the group went with close-quarters, house-clearing weapons. The Russian PP-19 Bizon was a 9 mm Parabellum submachine gun that was essentially a shortened AK-47 chambered for the cartridge. It was fed from an ingenious and reliable 53-round helical magazine that projected under the barrel and in front of the trigger guard, making the gun vaguely look as if it were equipped with a grenade launcher, not a drum of armor-shredding firepower.

Two of Angrekal's men were up-armed with something a little more than just close-quarters weapons. They had PKP Pecheneg light machine guns, 7.62 mm chambered weapons that had the same punch as an old American .30-06 and a similar range. While those were heavier, they would provide a lot of covering fire and reach much farther, punching into harder to reach areas than even the armor-piercing loaded Bizons.

Majid and Winslow, thanks to their performance back at Onn's estate, were also given RPG-7 grenade launchers. The American and the Malaysian law enforcers knew that this was to keep them on the perimeter of the action and out of the thick of battle.

Neither Majid nor Wilson showed any regrets at being relegated to heavy-hitter duty. Punching big holes into enemy forces with high-powered warheads had gotten them through two battles already, and they had both acquitted themselves admirably. One thing that they would have to do was disembark, then open the door into the walled estate. After that, the light machine gunners would set up inside the grounds, giving Majid and Winslow cover to link up and continue hammering out six-pound warheads at the enemy.

In the meantime Bolan, Angrekal and the other four commandos would advance, closing with Garlov's gunmen. It wasn't the most perfect of plans, but the group had little time. Any more delay, and the retired general would likely lose his nerve and make a run for it. Once the ex-GRU officer was in the wind, there would be little means of bringing him back down.

Garlov was a deadly enemy and a cold-blooded killer.

It was stop him here, stop him now, or more innocents would suffer in the future.

Over his shoulder, he heard Majid gasp in surprise. Bolan glanced sideways, wondering if someone had crashed, or if enemies had appeared in the woods next to them. Instead of a human cause for her sudden surprise, he saw a group of galloping quadrupeds. They were big, dark flashes of gray that loped toward the deer. It took a moment for him to figure out what they were in his peripheral vision.

Wolves, larger than anything he'd ever seen, were running after the herd of deer as they scattered through the woods toward Garlov's estate.

"I never knew they were that big," Majid whispered.

Bolan kept his eye on the road. "They usually aren't."

"Did...did the radiation make them grow like that?" she asked.

Bolan shook his head. "There haven't been humans around for the past quarter century. No hunters, plenty of game, plenty of protein to grow bones and muscle. It's good to be the apex predator."

"Sounds like something you're familiar with," Majid mentioned.

Bolan didn't often have reason to smile when en route to an assault, but this time he did. In a way, the well-fed, naturally powerful and wild wolves and he were kindred spirits. Both hunted in dangerous, hostile environments. The wolves hunted to feed their cubs. Bolan hunted to protect his fellow man. Wolves went after animals with natural weapons—sharp hooves, antlers, powerful legs—and risked their lives to do right by their pack. Bolan's foes often had assault rifles, rocket launchers, sometimes weapons that could destroy cities, but he still charged in. Wolves used tactics and intellect, because the mere power of their jaws, while awesome, was simply not enough to ensure a kill. Bolan's years of battle were only made possible by tactical experience and brilliant planning.

"Yeah. It's good to be the apex predator," Bolan answered.

The trees were starting to thin, and the deer burst out into the open, wolves continuing their chase as Bolan and his allies slowed. The wall of the estate and the top of the dacha behind it were visible. If they burst into the open too soon they would be targets. They needed the gunners on the walls, in the towers at the corners, to see the wild animals racing out of the woods, to have a momentary distraction after ramped-up concerns then the sudden relaxation of nerves at a false alarm.

It was an old psyche-out tactic, and Bolan knew that it would at least buy them the vital seconds it would take for Majid, Winslow and the LMG gunners to set up. The sudden off-balancing effect of rocket warheads slamming into the estate would give them the room to dash across the open ground to the gate of Garlov's compound. It was human nature, it was the simple tactic of surprise and audacity that had carried the warrior through countless battles, always steps ahead of enemy gunfire as he crashed their defenses. Sometimes, confusion was the best armor plating that a warrior could don.

Even now Bolan was watching the guards in the towers glancing down at the gates with a pair of binoculars. The tension. The anxiety had built up, and now the herd was rushing across the ground, passing by the estate, wolves on their heels. The Spetsnaz, Winslow and Majid trusted Bolan to give the command to commence the attack. They needed to wait for that moment, the instant when armed men regarded a sudden alarm as false. Depending on how sharp they were, that might take a while.

A rifleman with a scope was scanning the woods. Bolan and his allies were wearing winter camouflage, the snowmobiles also having been painted to blend in with the trees and snowy ground. Staying still, weapons and gear sprayed with camouflaging paint, they were as close to invisible as possible. The marksman swept through the woods, but Bolan could tell by his lack of reaction, lack of pause, that he hadn't noticed the obscured attack group. Even so, Bolan's shoulders were tense, his jaw clenched as he waited for the rifleman to relax.

There would be at least a minute of alertness, of unrelenting paranoia. Was it just a bunch of frightened animals? Or were they steered, herded as Bolan and the Spetsnaz had actually done? Those questions would be racing through the sentries' minds, and they would be on edge, waiting for something to happen.

Majid and Winslow were kneeling, as were Angrekal's machine gunners. Their weapons were ready, aimed, but they remained still. Any motion would betray their presence. They had to hold their ground.

The waiting was tough. They were all perched on the knife's edge. This was a contest of patience and awareness. Bolan admired the professionalism of the Russians, the Malaysian, his American ally. As a trained sniper, and across his lone war against the forces of Animal Man, Bolan had spent untold hours sitting, looking through a scope, waiting for targets to appear, enemies to make their move, for the perfect shot. Even then, that stillness had to balance against a readiness. Too much readiness and a sniper's jitters might make him betray his position or open up prematurely. Too much calm, and he might doze off or completely miss the subtlest of opportunities or threats.

He knew the challenge that faced every warrior on the cusp of combat.

But his allies were holding strong.

Just a few more moments.

Bolan counted the heartbeats, watching the doomsday numbers falling, trickling down to zero.

The machine gunners had the towers targeted. The Pechenegs with their full-powered rifle cartridges would easily cross the distance, delivering deadly hammer blows to the men on guard.

Majid rested her RPG-7 on her shoulder. She had the

gate in her sights. The 84 mm warhead loaded in was a thermobaric shell, which when it struck would release a cloud of combustible fuel. An instant later that flammable fog would be ignited by a secondary flash, creating a superheated event horizon, the brief burst of a miniature sun that burned at 3000 degrees Fahrenheit, eating up oxygen, then quickly followed by an implosion of onrushing air. The RPG shells had proved utterly deadly in clearing out caves and houses in combat. In the open, against a hardened structure, they'd still have more than enough energy to rip the gates from their moorings. Guards nearby would either be flash-fried or suffer internal injuries from the pressure waves given off as the implosion occurred.

Winslow had his weapon aimed, as well, waiting to sail it through the hole Majid created, detonating it inside the compound. His shell was a fragmentation warhead. Compared to a 40 mm grenade launcher, the RPG-7 warhead carried more shrapnel and more of an explosive charge to disperse it. Anyone beyond the gates would catch a wave of supersonic metal fragments that sliced through uniforms, some body armor and any body parts exposed.

The four-point punch only waited on Bolan's signal. Once he gave the word, he, Angrekal and the other three would throw their snowmobiles into gear and accelerate into the compound, path cleared by thunder and a rain of lead.

Counting down.

Moment by moment.

The riflemen in the towers began to laugh. Weapons were put aside. Laughter brightened their faces in the gray, wintry daylight.

"Now," Bolan whispered.

Machine guns and rocket launchers roared to life, and Garlov's fortress shook with violence.

CHAPTER TWENTY-TWO

Erra Majid didn't like the cold. Her skin crawled with phantom tingles as she imagined the Chernobyl area radiation attacked her cells one by one. There were wolves that were nearly twice her weight. And worst of all, there was the damned cold and the necessity for heavy clothing that weighed on her even more burdensome than eighty pounds of 84 mm Carl Gustav shells. There, in the hot mangrove swamp, her limbs were free, they could sweat, they could *move*. Here, the leggings, the heavy boots, the damned coat… Her fingers ached, knuckles throbbing from the cold. Taking a step in the three-inch crust of snow was far worse than wading through the mangrove swamp and its soft, sucking sand.

This place was as far from her comfort zone as humanly possible. But she'd see the mission through to the end.

When Bolan gave the word, she pulled the trigger on the RPG launcher. The percussion that kicked the shell from its tube was now familiar to her, the gunpowder charge kicking the missile out at 372 feet per second. After a mere tenth of a second, its rocket motor kicked in, doubling its velocity. The warhead was a 105 mm thermobaric charge, a piece of firepower that was much different from the anti-armor/anti-bunker rounds she'd used back in Kuala Lumpur. She had been told that it would make a hell of a blast.

As soon as the rocket took off, it was on target and, sure enough, it went off. There was an initial crack, and the next thing she knew, there was a 65-foot-wide fireball flaring at the gates. The flash of atmosphere burning was quickly snuffed and smothered, the blossom of fire collapsing in hard on itself, producing a secondary thunderclap. The gates themselves were gone, torn from their hinges, and the guards who were on sentry duty at the gate were gone, twisted masses of charred human wreckage strewed on the ground.

An instant after her shell struck, Winslow's fire cut through the gap she'd blown, and the shell sailed onto the grounds. That warhead went off behind the wall, creating its own thunderclap. This was a very narrow shell, instead of the bulbous-headed beast that she'd fired, a 40 mm javelin that, in effect, was meant to spread shrapnel. In a heartbeat, she heard dozens of screams before they were cut off by the roar of snowmobile engines and the Pecheneg machine guns.

Bolan tore out, and once more, Majid caught a faceful of that hated white snow, soaking her sore, cold, reddened cheeks. She turned that anger into energy, a warmth deep in her gut, helping her to fight off the chill and stuff another grenade into the launch tube. Up on the wall, she saw that the guard towers were lit up, the walls of the little crow's nests perforated, the men in them gone, wiped from existence by streams of medium-caliber bullets.

The RPG shell clicked into place and Majid aimed higher, toward the upper floors of the dacha. The RPG-7 boomed again, tossing its lethal payload into the air, sailing over the twelve-foot security wall on the estate and hitting a window twenty-five feet off the ground. As this was another thermobaric round, it punched through the glass, releasing its fuel mixture into the air. The sixty-six-foot-wide fireball that had blown the gate to pieces was compressed indoors, and suddenly every window facing her on that level burst outward, flashing bright white.

Winslow followed with a second shell, this one hitting the top level of the building, and once more, plumes of force kicked out windows. The Spetsnaz and their Pecheneg guns quickly followed suit on their assault against the main building, one of them walking fire across the fourth level while the other fired short bursts at men who were stationed on the roof of the dacha. Majid watched two of Garlov's defenders tumble from the roof, stitched by the light machine gun.

Majid clicked a third round into place, looking for more targets, scanning for someone who had withstood the fuel-air explosions on the top two floors. There was someone opening fire into the tree line from the roof. The Spetsnaz who had been hammering at the roof grunted, retreating as rifle fire crackled across the distance between themselves and the main house. The only thing that kept the naval infantry commando from taking a hit was the fact that at 300 yards, the shooter on the roof hadn't taken bullet-drop into account, his opening bursts hitting the snow ten feet in front of him.

The woman shouldered her launcher again, took aim at the rifleman's muzzle-flash, raised the elevation on her shot what she estimated to be ten feet, and pulled the trigger. Moments later the warhead detonated on the roof, the thermobaric fireball whiting out the gray wintry sky for an instant. She lowered the weapon and strained her eyes, looking for signs of the man taking shots at her allies.

For good measure, Winslow took a pot shot at the roof, arcing his rocket lower than where Majid's hit, but when his shell struck, the roof ruptured from below, splintering and then collapsing in on itself. If the gunman had survived her shell, then he had been dropped from the roof and onto the floor below by the ceiling dropping out beneath him.

The machine gunner was back on point, sweeping for targets.

No one seemed visible for any of the four to take a shot at.

They had to watch the perimeter, though. If their friends failed, it would be up to them to contain any escapees. But for now, it was going to be a close-quarters battle, with Bolan at the forefront.

THE EXECUTIONER HIT the throttle on the Grizzly and the 700-pound vehicle snarled to life, the bellow of its 490 cc engine swallowed and smothered by the salvo of opening fire against the estate. The other four snowmobiles were hot on his tailpipes, and Bolan accelerated, following in the wake of Winslow's RPG shot. Ahead, the thunderbolt of Majid's thermobaric warhead flared brightly, and he could feel the shock waves rolling off the massive burst. Winslow's shell landed instants later, and Bolan's snowmobile was tearing along at 60 miles an hour.

The fragmentation rocket landed twenty yards in, and when it went off, its radius of destruction, twenty-three feet from impact, had spread out into a forty-six-foot-wide blanket of flesh-shredding metal. Bolan's sled, now topping 65 miles an hour, roared through the remnants of the gates and he braked, powering into a sideways skid. The Grizzly was a broad, stable beast and when it decelerated, it kicked up earth and snow in equal amounts, creating a smoke screen for his allies to move through with relative safety.

Bolan looked to where the sled was skidding to a halt and noticed a defending gunman backing up, firing wildly. He looked hurt already by a slashing bit of shrapnel from Winslow's grenade, and in his injured, frightened state, his gunfire climbed under recoil, spraying over Bolan's head.

The snowmobile hit the poor guy, and he was sucked under the spinning treads of the decelerating vehicle. There was an ugly snagging noise, and the unmistakable shattering of leg bones and thrown treads resounded. The snowmobile snarled, and it took everything in Bolan's ability to kick himself out of the seat and out from under 700 pounds of tumbling machinery.

The Russian guard he'd run over, however, was not so lucky, his pulped form wound tightly around the fast-moving machine.

Bolan hit the ground and came up with the PP-19 Bizon. The others were through the gate, but the soldier, taking the lead, had drawn the lion's share of the attention. He shot one of the guards, stitching him with the high-impulse 7N21 9 mm ammunition, the steel-cored slugs traveling at 1500 feet per second having little trouble slashing through his body armor, let alone his vital organs and rib cage. Torn apart, the armed thug toppled backward, vomiting blood. The Executioner pivoted and leaped toward the toppled snowmobile, its engine still idling, and he vaulted over it, rifle fire chasing him, but unable to punch through 700 pounds of rough-neck winter transport.

As his heels struck the snowy ground, Bolan allowed himself to slip and drop onto his backside, gunfire snapping over his head and peppering the walls. The dacha shook in front of him, glass bursting from the third-floor windows as another thermobaric shell detonated. The concussive force hurled through the inside of the mansion had to have been horrendous. If no one was directly affected by the superheated area of igniting atmosphere, then the pressure waves would have batted them around violently.

A few seconds later the fourth floor rocked and even more glass rained down on the Executioner. Luckily, he was decked out for the cold weather, including a hood, which kept splinters of windows from slicing his scalp and face as they dropped around him.

Bolan rose, spotting a pair of gunmen who were trying to flank his Spetsnaz allies, and held down the trigger. Seven hundred rounds per minute ripped from the short barrel of the subgun, five rounds crashing into the lower back of one of Garlov's defenders, tossing him to the ground. Bolan shifted the stream of body-bursting firepower to the other man, and rounds tore into his shoulder, smashing the joint to ribbons before the high-velocity steel-cores speared deep into the man's lungs.

Gurgling, the gunman still stood, trying to hold on to life. Bolan put him out of his misery with a 2-shot burst to the face, the 7N21 penetrators exploding from the back of his skull, taking his brains with them.

Team Angrekal's operatives opened fire in Bolan's general direction, and he fought the urge to duck and return a salvo. Out of his peripheral vision, he spotted an *organasatya* thug catch a storm of SMG slugs, pushing him into some decorative shrubbery beneath one of the first-floor windows.

Bolan lifted a thumb, acknowledging the assistance, then popped the partially spent helical magazine from under the PP-19's barrel. He stuffed it into a vest pouch, then replaced it with another 53-round spiral tube of ammo. He racked the bolt and looked toward the entrance to the dacha. Garlov would likely be inside, and he wouldn't be the only one. More explosions rocked the roof of the expensive home, meaning that there were still hostiles up above, catching hell from Winslow and the others.

Bolan reached down to his harness, withdrew a fragmentation grenade, armed the bomb and lobbed it through the entrance. He backed out of the spray of shrapnel that would eventually come through the door and heard the fragger erupt.

A staggering shape, half alive, half bloody, screaming mess, stumbled through the doorway. The Executioner brought up the PP-19 and put a short burst through the suffering man's skull, and his agony ended swiftly.

The soldier lunged through the double doors and entered the dacha. The grenade had done a lot to clear a safe passage into the building, but Bolan wasn't going to stay in the open for too long. He ducked into a room off the foyer and shoulder-slammed into a defender who seemed to be recovering his senses from the thunderous grenade.

The Executioner was too close to shoot him, but he brought up his elbow and speared the guard in the throat with the joint. That powerful impact was enough for Bolan to feel the gunner's windpipe collapse under his elbow. With a sharp pivot, he slashed the barrel of the SMG up and across his jaw, breaking it. He tumbled, insensate to the ground, and Bolan made sure he stayed on the carpet with a quick burst to the back of his head.

Outside, Angrekal's fighters were dealing with gunmen who were coming in from what looked like a workshop and a barracks inside the grounds. Bolan's Spetsnaz allies fought back with grenades and SMG fire, and from the sounds of things, the enemy was more gangster than former military, cutting loose with long, sloppy bursts while Angrekal and his professionals were countering with short precision blasts.

Bolan swung out into the hall, then ducked back as a storm of automatic fire slashed toward him. He looked around the room off the foyer and grimaced as there was only one way out, and that was through a window. Still, it was better than fighting his way through streams of gunfire that would tear him to pieces. He paused and plucked the pins of two grenades, a fragger and a flashbang. He tossed them, one after another, rebounding them at an angle off the wall on the opposite side of the hallway.

As soon as the second minibomb was gone, he turned and hurled himself through the window, his bulk and strength making easy work of the panes and frame. He landed outside in a tumble and was on his feet in one fluid movement. The double blast behind him was more than enough to shake the dacha.

Bolan rushed along the wall toward where he figured the hallway to be. Once he reached the window he needed to enter to flank the enemy, he grabbed the sill and hauled himself up with one hand, bracing his feet against the wall under the window. He could see that two of the gunners were still up, staggered and confused by the sudden explosions, but they were swinging back into position to gun down anyone trying to storm the hall. Distracted, and not thinking outside the box, the two gunmen were cut down from behind.

Bolan ripped off four quick bursts, smashing the two *mafiya* gun thugs off their feet and into the hallway. He dropped back to the ground and ducked. His gunfire through the window was now being answered by killers across the hall. Compact weapons turned the window into a rain of glass, which Bolan sidestepped to avoid. He reached into his harness for another grenade, armed the bomb and tossed it through the window.

This was a flashbang, and so close on the heels of the previous stun grenade, it bought the Executioner a quick moment that he took to grab the windowsill with both hands to exit the dacha. Rather than lead the way with the PP-19, he pulled his Desert Eagle from its quick-draw holster and brought the weapon up. The front sight intersected one of Garlov's men as he staggered, blinded by the grenade. Bolan slammed two .44 Magnum slugs through him, the first shattering his breastbone, the second punching the Russian in the nose and leaving the back of his head with a gaping, dripping cavern.

The other man pulled the trigger on his weapon. Still seeing stars and flares in his vision, he was simply spraying lead wildly. Bolan dropped to the ground as bullets tore through the air at what would have been waist level. He pushed the Desert Eagle forward again, sighted on the dazed killer and shot the Russian through the heart. The big slug tore through the thick muscle after destroying a rib on the way in. The Executioner followed up with another shot that clipped the dying man's forehead, snapping his neck back even as he dropped lifeless to the floor.

Bolan scrambled back to his feet. He ejected the partially spent Desert Eagle magazine, giving it a fresh load. He then took the Bizon and fed the hungry chatterbox another tube of fifty-three armor-piercing rounds, tucking the still partly loaded prior tube into a pouch on his harness.

So far, he wasn't waiting for his guns to run dry, but this was his last helical drum of ammunition. Next, he would have to resort to a more conventional stick magazine, and he had six of those. It wouldn't have the same sublime balance and sheer firepower of the drums, but the PP-19 was good and reliable with whatever mechanism fed it.

Gunfire rattled outside, and the building shook as another rocket-propelled grenade struck home. The soldier scanned the area and found the main stairwell. No guards were posted close to the bottom, but he could sure as hell bet that the second floor was going to be teeming with resistance. He checked to see how many grenades he had left, and he counted two fragmentation and one flashbang.

"McCormack!" Angrekal said over the comm unit.

"Acknowledging," Bolan replied.

The Spetsnaz lieutenant sounded a bit out of breath. "We've got gunners on the second floor, side one. They're too well dug in and behind brick and mortar. They've got good angles on us."

"I'll take care of that. Have the support teams move up closer," Bolan said.

"Right," Angrekal replied.

Bolan tugged one of the fragmentation grenades

from its spot on his harness, plucked the pin and let the bomb cook for a moment. With a hard, looping underhanded throw, he arced the grenade up the stairs. There were shouts of surprise as the deadly object appeared and thunked on the floor. In the same instant, the grenade detonated, killing everything within fifteen feet of ground zero with overpressure and flying shrapnel.

Bolan swung around the bottom steps and vaulted the railing, pushing hard and fast on the bang. The Bizon lead the way, and he threw himself flat at the top of the steps, seeing a gunman at the end of the hall. The guy had been busy pouring fire at Angrekal and his men, and the grenade had interrupted his constant stream of bullets. Now, he was curled down, ducking beneath Spetsnaz retaliation, and was a sitting duck for Bolan facing him at floor level. A 4-round burst, and the gunman writhed, belly torn open, Parabellum bullets burrowing up from his abdomen into his rib cage.

No longer cowering, the man went limp, bleeding out on the floor.

A figure appeared in the doorway near the window at the end of the hall, an AN-94 rifle in his hands. He spotted his dead friend, then swung up his rifle, seeing only empty hallway, Bolan still low to the floor and lying on his back at the top of the stairs. The man saw no one standing and edged farther out into the hall, finally looking down through the railing surrounding the stairwell.

He spotted Bolan's face and the muzzle of the PP-19. A snarl of Bizon fire blazed between the struts for the railing and destroyed the features of the rifleman.

Bolan rolled and looked toward the back of the dacha's second floor. There was a racket being raised as men retreated. There had to have been another stairway, and doors were being thrown shut and locked to impede further pursuit. Bolan knew that it meant there was some way out of the building, maybe even the compound, that stretched under the outer security wall. There was probably even transportation at the other end, and little way to access that escape route from the outside.

He pushed himself up and charged to the end of the hall where two oaken doors seemed latched shut. The Executioner held off trying to kick them open and fired a short burst where they met. Seaming brass latches seemed to hold the doors locked, but with the Bizon's armor-piercing steel slugs, he found that the mechanisms were made of far more than brass and wood. The doors were steel-cored, as were the door latch plates.

Bolan was prepared for that. He reached into his pack and unfurled a breaching charge. It looked like a spiderweb of putty with bricks of butter set strategically along its length, all on a folding metal backing. He opened up the charge, slapped it against the door, then pulled the arming pin. The Executioner stepped back just in time to watch the compound explosive patch go off. Steel sandwiched between layers of oak and latched shut with bolts of inch-thick rebar buckled under the cutting power of the blast. A hole the size of a manhole cover had been blown through the barrier, and Bolan shoved one of the doors aside.

A doorway stood at the end of the hall and he spotted a shadow just behind the jamb. Bolan cut loose with the PP-19 again, sending steel-cored slugs through the opening. There was a grunt, then a chatter of return fire. The guy was hurt, but still in the fight.

Bolan slung the PP-19 and took out his Desert Eagle again. The lighter 9 mm steel-cored bullets hadn't

gone through the wall and the door jamb material, so it
was time to cut loose with the tungsten-cored, Teflon-
jacketed .44 Magnum rounds.

Bolan fired three times, each bullet tearing chunks
out of the door jamb. Another gunshot came chasing at
him. Bolan charged forward, throwing himself to the
left and getting a better angle against the defender. He
looked into the bloody face of a wounded man, struggling to hold up his handgun. He pulled the trigger, ending the hardman's existence and his suffering.

A quick glance down the stairwell he was defending
showed that Bolan's suspicions were correct. The stairs
looked as if they led to the basement.

Transitioning back to the Bizon, he went in pursuit
of Garlov.

Nothing was going to stop him now.

CHAPTER TWENTY-THREE

"Come in, McCormack!" Lieutenant Kyril Angrekal said into his throat mike, using the name Bolan had finally provided. The house had gone quiet after he and his team had cleared out the "hot" windows on the front. He'd heard the explosions inside the house, and knew that the soldier had been busy.

Two of the men had stopped shooting and had apparently disappeared. With the sniper fire abated by two guns, Angrekal was able to turn his attention on the rest of the entrenched shooters. Bullets flew and opposition fell. Unfortunately there seemed to be no response from inside.

"McCormack!" Angrekal repeated.

"Angrekal," Bolan returned. "Can you read me now?"

"What's going on?" the lieutenant asked.

"Get mounted up. Garlov's making his way out through an underground tunnel built into the basement of this dacha," Bolan told him. "I took a flight of stairs when I caught some static. This place is either too well shielded or the background radiation…"

"Or both," Angrekal replied. "I'll saddle up and look for where his getaway is."

"Not alone. Swim buddy system," Bolan ordered. "He's dangerous, and he still has men with him."

"What about the house?" Angrekal asked.

"Secure it, don't enter. Let someone else trip booby

traps—" Suddenly there was a grunt on Bolan's side of the radio communications. Then there was nothing but hazy static.

Angrekal was torn between entering the building or deploying to cut off the escaping Garlov.

Despite his misgivings, there was really only one choice. Angrekal snapped his fingers. "Yuri! On me! The rest of you, button down the compound! No one enters!"

With a twist of the throttle, Angrekal and Yuri took off, blazing out of the gate and swinging around the outside of the dacha.

He could only hope the big American was still in the fight.

FOR A BIG man, the Russian was sneaky and stealthy. Bolan hadn't noticed him in the shadows until he'd burst from his hiding space and crashed a powerful forearm along his jawline. Only battle-tested reflexes allowed the soldier to back up, to roll with the impact, so that Garlov's monster didn't shatter his jaw and knock him unconscious. Even so, Bolan was lifted off his feet by the blow's ferociousness, and he clawed out, grabbing that baseball bat of a forelimb to keep from spilling to the concrete floor. The big Russian wasn't taken off balance by the sudden addition of weight on him.

He stood, Bolan clutching the arm.

"You still have head on shoulders," the giant muttered in thickly accented English.

Bolan sneered and released the forearm. He addressed his opponent in Russian. "You going to talk me to death, or are we fighting?"

The guard was closing in on seven feet in height, and he had long, flowing blond hair, his face adorned with a similarly straw-colored beard, neatly trimmed. Blue eyes lit from within in delight. He was tall, with long, rangy limbs that belied the power of the muscles corded around them. In his proportions, a lean chest and equally sleek biceps looked normal, but those arms had to be at least twenty inches around, and his chest was a good forty-six inches.

Bolan didn't see any reaction from his large foe, then grabbed the PP-19 on the end of its sling, whipping it up. The next thing the Executioner knew, a fourteen-inch-long boot sole had slapped him in the chest, kicking him five yards down the hall. Bolan didn't know where the submachine gun had gone, and the sleeves of his parka had been torn with friction on the rough concrete floor. His cheek felt as if it had been gone over with a cheese grater, and it took him a moment before he could inhale. He glanced over and saw that his Bizon was three yards away, and the giant guard was advancing on legs that made stovepipes seem stubby.

Bolan didn't bother with the SMG, instead pushing off the ground and reaching for the Desert Eagle. He knew that the Tueller Drill stated an opponent could cross 21 feet in 1.5 seconds, less time than it took to pull a handgun and fire the first shot. That lesson was reinforced as the human freight train crashed into the soldier, lifting him up so that his head and shoulders actually bounced off the ceiling of the underground tunnel. Lights flashed and popped behind Bolan's eyes, and he swore that he heard laughter a moment before he was rammed into the ceiling a second time.

Bolan's vision was obscured by his hood scrunched over his eyes, but he didn't need to see to grab the Russian's arms, sinking his fingers into sleeves and skin-like claws. Bracing himself against those oak-tree strong limbs, Bolan snapped both of his knees up hard. There was a grunt that cut off the big man's laughter, and suddenly he felt himself slicing toward the floor. Bolan hung on with one hand, then reached for his foe's face with the other.

He could feel skin tearing as his thumbnail snagged and stabbed across his adversary's eyes. The Russian let out a growl, actually hurt as Bolan could feel the orb of his eyeball. Before he could force his thumb into the socket, a hammer blow knocked Bolan off the big thug.

The Executioner was able to see again, and he knew that he had to take down this beast of a man before he ran out of weapons or Garlov got away. He braced himself, then charged forward. His opponent was still grounded, so Bolan put all of his momentum and weight into chopping down on his foe. He got through the giant's crossed arms with a spearing punch that landed on the side of the Russian's neck. The man groaned.

Bolan pistoned his knee into his foe's ribs, feeling them move beneath his strike, even through the polycarbonate shell he wore beneath his pants. This caused the Russian to gurgle. Bolan swung back and brought his knee down hard again. This time, there was the ugly crack of breaking bones, and the Russian folded over, trying to roll away.

Bolan wasn't sure what kind of determination or recuperative powers his opponent had, so leaving a stunned foe at his back was not a good idea. He snaked his arm under the big man's chin, positioned his other arm for the best possible leverage, and then twisted. Vertebrae crunched and the Russian was no longer a powerful fighting force, just a limp, jerking slab of flesh that twitched on the floor.

Bolan sucked in a breath, disentangled from the dead man and scooped up his Desert Eagle.

That was all he had time for. Garlov was at the end of this tunnel, and time was ticking down.

Taking one step after another, he fought his body's protests and broke into a run.

GARLOV GRIMACED AS he raced for his life down the corridor. He would have preferred to stand and fight, but once the rocket launchers started destroying the dacha, it was over. A strong man could stand against others, but not when they cheated. Such was the way of the weaklings of the world, using whatever tricks they could find to bring down their proved superior.

He heard Yakov's final gun battle. It lasted only a few moments, but it had ultimately been punctuated with a flurry of booming blasts. The weaklings had to have brought a shotgun along with them. That had been the only way they could have hit what they were aiming at, to have brought down a brave and loyal soldier as Yakov.

Garlov vowed that they would all pay. He needed to get away, to regroup, and he had a place where he could rebuild his support, his forces, his plans to flush away the mindless drones sitting in Moscow. Garlov could see his men up ahead, younger and longer legs pushing them ahead of him. They said that they'd clear out the hangar, and once that was done, Garlov wouldn't have to stop.

They would just need to take off.

Josef, big, brave and loyal Josef, heard Yakov's demise and told Garlov to go on ahead. Josef was six feet nine inches and 350 pounds, all of it lean, sleek and deadly muscle. There had been no gunfire behind, which meant that Josef's pure might had been more than enough to carry the day, at least against one man. No telling how many he had to face.

Garlov kept running and he saw that two of his men were quickly pulling open the garage-style doors. There were a dozen snowmobiles present, and one of his troops tossed him a set of keys.

"Don't wait for us, sir!" the guard said.

Garlov grimaced. "No. I'm at least going to wait for Josef."

There was the snarl of engines outside and Garlov gripped his AKSU tightly. Those had to have been the same machines that had brought the raiders. "To arms!"

The ex-general aimed the carbine out the doors and opened fire as soon as he spotted movement. Two snowmobiles had burst into view, and the chatter of the AKSU ripped, echoing loudly in the enclosed garage. His guards also pulled their guns, one of the snowmobiles tumbling as its rider fell out of the saddle. The other one twisted, veering away from the deadly onslaught of bullets chasing after him.

Garlov charged to the entrance, reloading the AKSU on the run. The snowmobile was coming around for another pass, this time a submachine gun in one hand. Garlov opened fire, the compact rifle snarling his defiance. Rider and vehicle were separated by a loud crash, the snowmobile stopped by a thick pine tree trunk.

Behind him, the man who'd tossed him the set of keys for a snowmobile opened fire down the escape tunnel. Thunderbolts cracked in response and one more of Garlov's guards spun, clutching a ruined arm.

"Sir! Get going!" the man barked. He reached for his

weapon with his uninjured hand, but the moment he leaned out from behind cover, his head erupted, skull blasting to pieces as a .44 Magnum slug plowed through it.

Garlov growled, realizing that Josef, too, was dead or incapacitated, and went to the snowmobile that his man had indicated.

Key in ignition, firing up of the throttle, and suddenly Garlov was off, the Yamaha Phazer accelerating. He steered the machine toward a path through the woods, avoiding the two crashed Grizzly snowmobiles, zipping nimbly along the route toward the train tracks. Once there, he'd follow them to Slavutych, the home of the people displaced from Pripyat back in 1986, and the unofficial headquarters of recovery operations within the Exclusion Zone. The train tracks would take him through as far as he wanted, and once he reached the rail hub at Slavutych, he could pick any destination he wanted.

He revved the throttle, feeling the horsepower of the machine beneath him increase, pushing him farther from his enemies. Once he got a breath, he would return and rain hell upon them.

BOLAN TOOK CARE of one more hardman, then burst from the tunnel, firing the Desert Eagle into the remaining two gunmen in the garage, .44 Magnum slugs punching through their faces. He looked and saw that except for three corpses, the place was abandoned. The only sign that Garlov had been there was a lone missing snowmobile.

Outside, on the other hand, he heard the idling engine of a Grizzly snowmobile, and saw the staggering form of a wounded man. Bolan rushed outside and noticed that

Angrekal was limping toward a commando sprawled in the snow. Angrekal's arm hung limply, blood darkening his winter-camouflaged parka.

"Angrekal!" Bolan called out.

The lieutenant blinked, then turned blearily toward Bolan. "Yuri crashed into the tree. He isn't moving."

"You're bleeding," Bolan told him.

"I've called the others. Someone else can give me and Yuri first aid," Angrekal said, his voice harsh and raspy. "But you have to get moving. Garlov zipped out of here not thirty seconds ago."

Angrekal nodded in the direction their quarry had taken. "We tried to close this door, but the bastards opened fire before we could get to cover."

Bolan looked back. The machines in there had been imports, American designs. As such, while they didn't have the raw towing power of the Grizzlies, they were lighter and quite quick.

"I'm on it," Bolan told him, turning back and running to the Peg-Board full of keys.

Battered and bruised, Bolan could feel the aches building in him. Adrenaline could only do so much in the face of the abuse he'd gone through. He fought through the pain, fired up a Yamaha Phazer and accelerated out of the snowmobile garage. This was a completely different machine than the ones that he and the Spetsnaz had come in on, but the Grizzlies had been meant for carrying two people as well as a significant stockpile of weapons and ammunition.

The 500-pound machine he rode accelerated faster and responded to a much more finessed touch on the handlebars. The sled felt like a motorcycle, and as he powered up through the gears, he found himself approaching fifty miles an hour when he saw the rooster tail of snow spray coming off the back of Garlov's ride.

Bolan hit the throttle and withdrew his Desert Eagle from its holster. Letting Garlov go now was not in the cards. He would have to get much closer to have a chance of hitting the speeding enemy snowmobile as they bounced over the trail. In a way, he was glad that the path was so bumpy and uneven. These machines were capable of nearly 80 mph while on hardpack, and there was no doubt that Garlov had been taking it easy at 50 mph to avoid shaking his machine apart.

Bolan noticed the ex-general toss a glance over his shoulder. Now that he was noticed, Bolan didn't have much choice other than to fire his first shot. It was a quick one, the .44 Magnum slug easily outracing Garlov and his ride, but Bolan's round was nowhere near his target. Garlov swung his arm back and bullets crackled in the distance. The gunfire missed Bolan, showing how this was a simple case of letting each other know that they were armed.

The Executioner needed to get closer to end this fiasco. He fought to keep concerns over Angrekal and his men out of the forefront of his mind, but they were there. Garlov had run up quite a tab of debt over the course of this conspiracy. Good men ended up dying, slaughtered because of their interest in protecting the economies of their nations, enforcing laws against counterfeiting, and all because one retired general felt that he had a better clue as to how to make a more perfect Russia, the rest of the planet be damned.

Bolan slammed the throttle up, passing 65 miles an hour, and he cut the distance between himself and Garlov by half. The Russian conspirator tried to accelerate, but the soldier kept the hammer down. The tachometer was well into the red line, and there was no pulling back. Either the Phazer was going to burn out, or Garlov was going down. There was no way that Bolan's prey was going to gain another inch on him.

Snow struck Bolan's face, kicked up by Garlov's Yamaha, and the hurled flecks felt like hot needles striking his skin. He gritted his teeth, pushing past this new abuse reddening his cheeks to the point where they felt as if they were on fire, and swung closer toward Garlov.

The next thing Bolan knew, the former general swung into a hard turn to the right. The soldier steered after him, riding up onto the mounded ridge keeping train tracks above the surrounding terrain. A millisecond slower and Bolan would have hit a railroad tie or the rail itself, and become a spiraling, out-of-control rocket, likely landing beneath the 500-pound snowmobile and crushed into red paste.

Bolan steered off the gravel-covered mound and swung in behind Garlov. The road running parallel to the tracks was hard-packed snow, and the former GRU general hit the throttle. His vehicle started to inch away, but Bolan kept up the pressure.

Garlov was a dead man, one way or another. The Executioner stiff-armed the Desert Eagle again and fired, but missed the fleeing general. There was too much up and down movement, too many wobbles left and right, to line up a concise shot as the snowmobiles zipped across the countryside. Up ahead, there was a train on the tracks, moving at full steam. Bolan remembered the briefing about the area, and the closest city where Garlov could run to was Slavutych.

There, the madman could steal a car or legitimately hop on a train and disappear into the Russian Federation.

No-go with that.

The train roared next to them, drowning out even the engines of the snowmobiles as the chase advanced closer to Garlov's finish line. It would still be minutes before they got there, but Bolan didn't want this to turn into a rampage through a crowded city. He had two last options, a fragmentation grenade and the flashbang grenade.

He didn't have to be close to score with either of those weapons.

Bolan plucked the fragger off his harness, thumbed out the pin and whipped the bomb with all of his strength, aiming ahead of Garlov in the hope that the man would run into the blast. The former general hunched down, trying to squeeze a little more speed out of his machine. The grenade landed. A second passed and it detonated, going off twenty yards behind them both. Acceleration had taken them ahead of the blast, saving both men from the horrors of shrapnel and a crash.

Bolan grimaced. That only left the stun grenade.

Garlov swung back his AKSU once more and Bolan swerved, cutting to the opposite side as bullets ripped from the weapon. Garlov had hurled four or five bursts back over his shoulder, and this last burst came up short. It was three pops and the gun was locked empty. The ex-general twisted around and hurled the empty gun at Bolan.

The frame bounced off his shoulder, painfully, nearly knocking him off the sled and causing him to nearly steer his sled into a tree on the side of the hard-packed road.

Seven pounds of steel *hurt,* and Bolan knew that his shoulder had been dislocated by the impact. Now he only had one hand with which to hold on to the handlebars. His left arm hung at his side and he grimaced, trying to bend it, to pluck the flashbang grenade off his harness. His hand didn't want to move and he gritted his teeth against the pain, forcing himself to move. Fire seemed to burn in his shoulder, so Bolan knew he had only one real recourse.

He threw the throttle wide-open and swung the nose of his snowmobile right at the back of Garlov's.

One thousand pounds of machinery and four hundred pounds of man bounced off each other, the handlebars threatening to jerk out of Bolan's grip. He leaned into the turn, swaying back again and banging off the back of the sled.

"You fool!" Garlov spit.

"You're dead," Bolan growled.

Garlov clawed for the Makarov pistol in its holster. Bolan accelerated and sideswiped the ex-general hard. Bolan's dislocated shoulder struck Garlov's, sending a spike of flaming pain spearing through his heart. The agony seemed insurmountable, but the next thing he knew, Garlov's hand was empty. The pistol skittered finally to a halt behind them on the hardpack ice road.

Garlov punched out, striking Bolan in the biceps. The abuse almost caused him to pass out, but the Executioner knew that if he did, Garlov would get away and more innocents would die.

No matter how much it hurt, he had to stop the Russian.

Garlov wound up for another blow and Bolan punched out. The move was hindered by his agonized shoulder, but it made Garlov swerve to avoid the soldier's punch. Unfortunately for the Russian, he swerved too hard, overcorrected and tugged on the emergency brake to come up short from hitting the railroad tracks. Gravel and rocks flew as the treads tried to gain purchase, the skis at the front wobbling as Garlov tried to keep control with one hand, grabbing for the handlebars with his free limb.

Bolan leaned to the left and swerved up onto the mound with Garlov.

All it took was a bump.

The left front ski on the Yamaha snagged a railroad tie at 65 miles an hour.

One moment Bolan was charging parallel with the Russian general. The next, the sled was cartwheeling out of control, skidding off into the woods where it smashed into a pine tree, folding around it violently. Garlov himself landed on the tracks, bouncing once. Twice.

After the fifth bounce, the former general came to a stop, even as Bolan slowed his snowmobile. He turned, looping back toward the stunned, fallen form of the renegade Russian on the tracks.

Garlov groaned, pushing himself off the ground.

Somehow he had the strength to get up and kneel. He'd found a fighting knife on his belt and pulled it. Face dripping with blood, Garlov glared balefully at the Executioner.

"What business was this of yours?" Garlov asked. He was struggling to stand. He already had one foot beneath him, resting on his other knee to support himself. Blood drooled over his lips and a flap of forehead waved like a flag down over one eye.

Bolan glared at him. He couldn't move his left arm at all now. He snaked his hand around and grabbed for the Beretta's grip in his shoulder holster.

"Mankind is my business," Bolan grumbled. "Do you know how many people died because of your delusions of grandeur?"

"They were weak. Mankind doesn't deserve compassion," Garlov growled.

He was up on two feet now. One eye stared around the hanging chad of flesh partially obscuring it. The other eye was puffy, starting to swell shut. But he gripped the combat knife with certainty and strength.

Bolan aimed the Beretta 93R at his foe. "Enough of this…"

The knife suddenly produced a loud crack. From his position, Bolan hadn't recognized the Spring-blade, a Russian-designed ballistic knife with a powerful spring. One pull of a trigger on the handle and six inches of razor-sharp steel launched at 39 miles an hour. Bolan felt as if he'd been punched in the chest by that giant, and he toppled backward.

Bolan triggered the Beretta, but the weight and force of steel striking him in the chest had knocked his aim off. The soldier collapsed off the saddle of his snowmobile. His armored vest had stopped most of the blade's penetration, but there was still two inches of steel inside his pectoral muscle, having nicked his ribs.

Bolan grimaced. One arm was down, and the knife in his chest hurt so much that he barely had the strength to lift the Beretta to eye level.

He'd gotten within five yards of the man, and Garlov had knocked him down with one of the most unusual weapons in Russian war craft. The former general chuckled.

"Weakling," Garlov muttered. He took a step forward, then looked back.

"The train is coming," Garlov informed him. "Too bad if you were planning to have it take me out. Well, in a way it will. I'll jump onto a cargo car and be on my way out of here."

Bolan sat up. The knife moved against his chest. He could feel skin and muscle tearing on the point.

Garlov tilted his head.

"You actually are trying to keep going, aren't you?" he asked.

Bolan started to get up, then seemed to slip. Rocks flew from beneath his boot and suddenly the Executioner was rolling down the mound. He bit back grunts of pain as he bounced to the hard snow road.

He landed facedown, both arms folded beneath him.

Garlov laughed. He wiped the blood from his mouth and took a couple more steps down. "I thought you were a skulking coward. It doesn't help that you're a simpering fool, McCormack. That you think those who can't fend for themselves deserve protection, deserve love..."

Bolan pushed himself up on one hand, his right arm supporting him, left arm folded against his chest.

"What's wrong with your arm?" Garlov asked. He was looking around for something.

Bolan knew it was the ballistic knife blade. The same piece of steel he had clenched in his left hand. The stumble down the slope had been a torment, but the rolling had pried the blade loose from his armored vest, and the landing was enough to pop the shoulder back into the joint. "You separated my shoulder when you threw your gun at me."

Garlov chuckled. "Yeah. I can see where that might slow you down."

Bolan struggled to sit up. He leaned on his right arm.

His left shoulder still burned, still ached, still felt as if someone had pulled it like taffy then dipped it in boiling oil. But with it no longer dislocated, he had a strong grasp on the ballistic knife's shank, and he felt some strength in his arm.

"You lose your blade, Constantin?" Bolan asked him.

Garlov, in his cockiness, was now only five feet away. He looked down and saw the ballistic knifepoint clutched in Bolan's hand. The amusement drained from the Russian's features.

"Have it back," Bolan growled, exploding off the snow, kicking with every ounce of strength he had. The Executioner gripped the blade's shank tightly, bringing it down like an ice pick.

Garlov threw up his hands to ward off the panther-quick attack, but Bolan had a longer reach, and he had 220 pounds coming along with the knifepoint.

As the shank was only a rectangle of steel, Bolan's fingers slipped to the bottom of the blade, slicing open the pads, but the majority of the length of steel ended up in Garlov's right eye. The Executioner rode the screaming, half-blinded man to the ground. When the snow stopped Garlov's collapse, the knife plunged farther through his eye socket, smashing the bone at the back of the orbit and spearing into the brain behind.

One ugly crunch and the conspirator was no more.

Bleeding and battered, Bolan rose to his feet.

"Angrekal?" he muttered into his throat mike.

"We're on our way," Angrekal answered. "Garlov?"

"Executed," Bolan returned. "What about Yuri?"

"He's too thickheaded to have been hurt by a crash into a tree," Angrekal answered. "He'll live."

Bolan smiled. "Good news."

He looked down at the bloody mess on his chest. Nothing a few stitches and a little R&R couldn't fix.

Bolan walked toward the sound of snarling snowmobiles following the path of his chase, glad that all the debts of the past few weeks were paid in full.

* * * * *